Sexy
INK!

BOOK FOUR

THE Secrets & Stilettos SERIES

JAMIE
COLLINS

SEXY INK!

Cover Design & Interior Format by The Killion Group
www.thekilliongroupinc.com

For my forever friend, Christy B.
This one's for you!

~ Jamie

PROLOGUE

NEWPORT BEACH, CA
SUMMER 2014

L A COSTA LINGERED OVER THINGS like a good cup of coffee, a cool breeze, or a fine painting like it was the quintessential link between her soul and the universe. At the moment, something was beckoning from a small scrape on the beach, just at the base of the whitewashed stairs and edge boards visible through the pristine white baluster railing. She had been sitting in her favorite teakwood writing chair next to the open French doors, working on a chapter, when she spotted a quick movement in the sand. It was an agitated Snowy Plover, who was nesting her chicks beneath a strip of overturned beach drift not fifteen yards from the house. The bird was running off a zealous hound who was sniffing around too close for her liking, harassing the mutt with a series of dodges and pecks, punctuated with trilling *purrts* and whistling *tur-tweets.*

La Costa watched, mesmerized by the simple beauty of the moment. A speedboat whirred in the distance, and shouts of laughter from a troop of tourists paddle boarding nearby, chiming in with the upswell symphony of wind and surf, blended melodically with the shrill cry from a languid seagull drifting on the salty wind. A tiny sparrow chirped from the deck post. To an unaccustomed ear, it could all sound like nothing special, but to her, it was sweet music. And the magic of it all filled her with joy. She was lost in the soothing sounds of the Pacific as she let it all wash over her with the summer breeze. There was so much elation in simply being alive. God had given her a second chance in life. That was the good news of the sparrow's song. She would never doubt Him, or herself, ever again.

CHAPTER ONE

WEST MEMPHIS, AR
SUMMER 1987

BORN MAYELLA JACKSON IN WEST Memphis, Arkansas, on September twenty-eighth, 1971, La Costa had to fight for everything she ever had, starting with her very birth, which she managed to pull off on her own. Her mother, Tallulah, paid little attention to her own needs, let alone those of her new baby daughter. An alcoholic and addict from the time she left her poverty-stricken home in West Virginia at age twelve to shack up with a pusher and no-good reptile named Crete Jackson, Tallulah was a veteran card-carrying prostitute and junkie by the time she was fifteen. In fact, Tallulah did not even know that she was pregnant until the miraculous event occurred. She had been waiting in line for her monthly check down at County, when a sudden rush of water burst between her legs, causing her to hurry to the toilet, doubled over in pain.

The mysterious and powerful cramping pushed forth a small, malnourished fetus, which slid from her body onto the cold linoleum floor. The infant literally dropped out of Tallulah's womb—unassisted. A bystander emerged from a nearby stall, shocked to find the thin, gaunt woman mopping the bloody fetus, still tethered to her body, with toilet paper.

An ambulance arrived and took mother and child to the hospital, where the infant was medically evaluated and her official birth time, recorded. The baby was treated for jaundice and a host of complications resulting from her mother's imposing use of narcotics and alcohol throughout the pregnancy.

Tallulah, in shock and abhorrence, had high-tailed it, unnoticed, through the hospital doors, not to return until three days later.

Unbelievably, the hospital handed over Tallulah Jackson's baby to her when she came back to finally claim her. Tallulah had been informed by a relative that having the child in her care would ensure additional government benefits and a larger monthly check, so the child was taken home.

Tallulah was clearly still using, but temporarily sober when she showed up to, as she put it, "sign her daughter out." A social worker was aptly appointed to the case. Although the authorities had the baby's best interests at heart, they had no choice but to release the infant to her natural mother. A nurse was assigned to perform daily visits, in which she administered special medications to wean the baby from the drugs she had been subjected to. Slowly, her tiny body healed from the toxic effects of the damaging poisons that Tallulah had transferred into her fragile system.

Years passed, and Mayella survived despite neglect and hardship. Crete Jackson, the baby's biological father, left Tallulah when Mayella was barely two, leaving nothing behind but her name, which he had bequeathed to her from his dear departed grandmother.

They stayed poor and hungry in a two-bedroom flat on the south side of town in a series of tenements near the interstate. There were cockroaches, cold water pipes, and users dealing dope in the courtyard; there were gunshots and robberies most every night, and for most of the residents of the community, the only way *out* was to die.

Social services monitored the tenements for children, and when a non-reported minor was found, the city police would return with a warrant from the state to either place the child in school or remove the child into juvenile custody. As early as four, Mayella could remember climbing down into a shallow hole in the floor, rotted out from rodents and decay, waiting for her mother to give her permission to come out.

"Those po-lice men's what will take you away if'n they's catch you livin' here. You hide yo-self good, and stay till I say's to get on out . . . else you's be goin' wit them to the jail."

It was a terrifying torture to go down into the hole, but Mayella feared the shackles of a prison more than the temporary inflictions of the bugs and rats that descended upon her instantly.

Eventually, the authorities took Mayella at the tender age of six. Tallulah had left her alone, as she often did, and a kitchen fire erupted when little Mayella tried to fry an egg on the stove. A dishrag had caught fire, and she had pulled it, along with the skillet, off the burner and onto the floor, splattering grease onto her leg and hands and igniting the linoleum.

A neighbor later noticed Mayella's burns and called the authorities. She was removed from Tallulah's care immediately, but not before Tallulah added a few fresh cuts and bruises to the mix. The landlord had evicted them as a result of the grease fire, which, aside from making Tallulah angry and led to Mayella's whoopin', also forced them to live with Tallulah's junkie friend, Dixie.

Several years and twelve foster families later, as a young teen, Mayella was reunited with Tallulah in another run-down dirt lot in West Memphis, this time, finding that Tallulah's mother had joined them to save money. Tallulah was supposedly "clean," due to her finding Jesus—once again, self-proclaiming herself as being "twice-born *again*." She was working as a housekeeper for a big shot chain-store owner in the city's downtown district.

Mayella had arrived home to learn that she had two brothers, Eli, who was nine, and Rufus, five. Each sibling had a different father, although Tallulah never once had been married, not even to Crete Jackson. Mayella was fifteen years old, angry and obstinate, and had been more trouble than any of several church-going foster families could handle. She did not attend school regularly, preferring instead to run the streets. She did as she pleased. A spotty attendance record showed that she only completed eight full years of elementary school, and was deficient in attendance hours in high school her freshman year. She had decided that she would drop out once she reached sixteen—if she could make it that far, as life held little promise for her ever succeeding at anything.

She did, however, love to read books, and had taught herself everything she needed to know from the liberation of a stolen library card and books lifted from thrift stores when no one was looking. In the worlds of John Steinbeck, F. Scott Fitzgerald, and Tennessee Williams, Mayella found her refuge. Of course, her very favorite novel was *To Kill a Mockingbird*, as she saw her own self in the tragic persona of Mayella Ewell, who had also endured victimization by an abusive and poverty-stricken home life. In her heart, Mayella believed that she *was* Mayella Ewell, and much like her, could never dare to hope for better days. Reading was the only escape that Mayella could afford, living her childhood in the charity of white people's homes, where she was the token "example" of society's ails, and the product of their apple-polishing Christian generosity. She would stay only until she was done using them, and when she was ready to move on, she would simply cause enough trouble that her current foster family would be forced to ship her out to the next family.

She read every book she had two or three times each, just to take in the fantastic stories that were a far cry from the dismal life she was forced to endure, moving from one temporary home to the next. Junior high was a blur. Mayella was sullen and spiteful, and often not worth the other kids' hate or harassment for being so different. Mostly, they just ignored her. And that suited her just fine. She had no friends and simply hid in her books when transferring from school to school, making herself as invisible as possible, struggling to squeak by unnoticed. Only when she was placed with a black family did she feel more able to be herself. But even then, there was always the threat of not measuring up, and so it became easier to withdraw than to fight the insurmountable demands that pressed upon her unceasingly.

Once again, it was books that rescued her. Within them, Mayella felt safe, and most importantly, not judged. It did not matter to the story writer if she was black, white, red, or purple. It didn't matter if she was rich or poor. For the price of her undivided interest, she could open a book and leap into its pages, letting the words take her far away.

When she turned fifteen, there were no available foster homes left to take her, so Mayella finally went home. She showed up, much to Tallulah's surprise, with a backpack of contraband library books and a chip on her shoulder. Tallulah wasted no time reacquainting Mayella with all the reasons why she had been shipped away in the first place. Tallulah had, remarkably, quit the drugs and was clean, but she smoked three packs a day and was in deep denial about her daily need for the sauce—anything, didn't matter what. Gin, vodka, cough syrup, or paint thinner, if that was all there was. She was helpless to the addiction. Drinking was her only reason for living, and the way that Tallulah Clark had it figured, the world had screwed her over so badly that it was her solid right to try to soften the edges.

Eli and Rufus had already learned to fend for themselves, although the living conditions were far better than the atrocities that Mayella once had to bear. It was evident that their grandmother was failing in health, and soon Tallulah would be minus one regular check from the state to count on. For Mayella, staying there provided a permanent address, a patch of grass out front, a barely operating portable TV, and other kids in the trailer park, dirt poor just like them.

The boys got on a yellow school bus each day and were taken into town to attend school, although the other children from the district would have little to anything to do with the TPTs—Trailer Park Trash—as they were called. *Just like the Ewells* . . . Mayella would contend. She took a cot, which was set up in the living room, and stashed her personal belongings behind a dilapidated recliner.

Tallulah was gone a lot, presumably with her latest boyfriend, Rodney. That was, when she was not working cleaning someone's toilets or scrubbing their floors. *Nigger-*

work, she would call it. And it made Tallulah tired and mean. Mostly, she was hell on wheels—sober or not. A reality that made living all together under one roof a battle zone. Tallulah was not at all pleased that Mayella had returned. The last thing she needed was another mouth to feed. "I is in a good place rit' now. Yo' grammy, me, and the boys, we is all going good. Don't expect one more is what we needs, but if'n you can pull yo' weight . . ." Tallulah Clark was an unfit mother before, and so still remained. As far as she was concerned, Mayella was far enough along to strike out on her own. Didn't matter either way to her, where Mayella would go. It was of no concern.

Tallulah and Mayella fought incessantly, constantly at odds with one another. If Mayella hated her mother for bringing her into the world in the first place, having pumped her with vile drugs and cheap beer from the start, and robbing her of a home and loving family, she *really* despised her now. Tallulah was the pathetic drunk who allowed men like Rodney to beat her and to take what money she made cleaning houses in order to fund his own vile drug habits, while her own children lived on a constant repeat of cornbread and beans.

"You pretty smart . . . why don'tcha work, girl?" Rodney had asked one summer day as he eyed Mayella contemptuously from across the room. She was lost in a book at the time. It was Jane Austin's *Pride & Prejudice*, and it was her fourth time reading it. She sniffed, ignoring his question, retreating from his gaze. It was not in her best interest to ignore him. But she did not care. She despised him. He was, in her estimation, a degenerate prick. She needed glasses she, of course, did not have, and was squinting to read the page when his hand came down hard upon her shoulder, and with what seemed like an unnatural force, he shook her like a hunting dog rattles a pheasant in his jaws, hurling her across the room, where she hit the paneled wall with a thud, collapsing onto a lamp that shattered beneath her.

"You goddamn look at me when I talk to you, *bitch*! Ya hear?"

She cowered, and he lunged for her, striking her face as she squealed. Then he punched her hard in the stomach as she tried to get up, overturning a chair and just barely missing her head on the coffee table on her way down. It was nearly over. But not before his boot delivered a sharp blow to her chest, cracking two of her ribs.

Several neighbors responded to the commotion, appearing at the screen door with threats of calling the police. But he didn't care; he just kept beating her.

By the time an ambulance arrived, Mayella was unconscious and Rodney was long gone.

CHAPTER TWO

MAYELLA WAS NOT A BIT surprised that Tallulah blamed *her* for running Rodney off.

"He would have stay't if'n you didn't come and change up ever-thing. Ain't barely enough room for two woman's in this house. An' you damn sure one too many!"

It wasn't long before her mother found a replacement deadbeat, and the whole nightmare replayed again and again with every drunk, druggie, degenerate boyfriend that Tallulah brought home after that. When they didn't rob them, they free-loaded; some were just passing through on their way to jail or God knows where, others stayed until all hell broke loose and left Mayella and her little brothers to suffer the fall-out.

By autumn, Mayella had dealt with it enough. The filth and depravity were a slow death sentence. Having lived on the outside in foster homes that once made charity feel like prison, now she would have traded her soul for three square meals and a firm bed. What was she waiting for? she wondered. No one was going to deliver her from the destiny that Tallulah had perpetuated. No one. Except for *herself.*

The nightmare continued. Every day she dreamt of just

how she would do it. How she would find a way to leave for good and never look back.

The turning point came when boyfriend number five moved in. He called himself Reverend Dan, but there was nothing holy about the bastard. He had sired ten children by six different wives, although he boasted of being God-fearing and righteous. He was a con with a keen perversion for girls—young ones.

He got Tallulah to quit the booze, remarkably, and to follow the Word for a time. On Saturday nights he would dress up like a preacher and preside at a revival tent off of Broadway near Highway Seventy.

Right from the start, he took to fondling Mayella at night, while she slept. At least, she would pretend that she was asleep to ensure that it would go quickly. Reverend Dan was big and powerful. She had witnessed his mean streak with Tallulah and the boys. She knew what he was capable of. Her pleas for him to stop would be useless. Most of the time, he just slipped onto the cot beside her, covered her mouth so as not to be heard, and pleasured himself. She always knew when it was close to being over because his breathing would quicken, and he would groan as he vigorously rubbed himself against her until he exploded.

Sometimes she would awaken in a patch of dried semen, where he had ejaculated near her buttocks or thigh the night before. She played dumb and endured it, every repulsive second. This went on for months.

One night, in the heat of August, he stumbled in after eleven p.m., uncharacteristically drunk and disoriented. He clumsily climbed onto the cot beside her, just down the trailer from where Tallulah was in her bed, in the back, where she shared a full mattress with her mother, both snoring. The boys were spread out on futons.

This time, however, was very different. He would not be satisfied with the usual practice. She startled as he moved in closely, tearing at her panties, yanking them down around her knees and clamping his cold, snake-like fingers of one hand around her neck, spreading her painfully with the other. He stirred at the quickening of her gasps, which quickly turned to terror as he tightened his grip about her throat and moaned with his sour, whiskey-tinged breath into her ear.

"Ohhh, baby! That's how's you like to fuck now, ain't it? Yeah, I remember, suga!"

He forcefully plunged his member deep into her rectum, pumping hard against her buttocks, squeezing bruises into her flesh with his filthy fingers and panting wildly until, all at once, he came in a release of sputtering convulsions, and then collapsed with a whimper of sick pleasure.

He crawled off of her and instantly passed out. Mayella lay there quietly in the dark, trembling.

The night moon bathed the tiny trailer with yellow half-light that fell on the clock on the wall. It cast two momentary revelations at the turning of the hour, and she needed only a glance at the bastard's gnarly face that she had only seen once in a faded Polaroid stashed in her mother's photo album beneath her birth certificate. First, that it was officially her sixteenth birthday. And the second, that the monster next to her was not Reverend Dan at all—it was her *father*, Crete Jackson.

CHAPTER THREE

THE BUS SMELLED DISTINCTLY OF sweat and urine. The stench was ineffectively covered up by an industrial cleaner that made it even worse. It was the efflux of diesel fuel, chemical toilets, and cheap perfume. It was the smell of freedom.

The passengers were primarily vagabonds, ramblers, drifters, outlaws, and runaways, like her. Only, where was she running to? It didn't matter. As far as one hundred eighty-five dollars could take her. One thing was for certain, it would have to be better than the place she was running from.

She had taken one hundred fifty dollars from the coffee can above the stove, knowing full well that stealing the rent money would set her mother, grandmother, and her brothers behind with the trailer park rental on their lot, again. Maybe Reverend Dan would take care of it. She could not let herself think about it. None of it. Not about her father's "unannounced return" and the horrific thing he had done to her in the dark. Not about Reverend Dan's perverted transgressions, Tallulah's apathy toward it all, and her punishing resentment toward her, which made Mayella feel oddly responsible for her mother's descent back into the bottle as of late. Maybe they would blame *her* for the missing money. Say that she blew it on cheap gin.

Sorry, Mama . . . The words formed in her mind, but she couldn't feel their meaning. She would never have the will to actually say them. Tallulah wasn't deserving of her apology. Just her pity. Eli and Rufus, now that was another story.

She pressed her cheek against the gritty plastic window and set her thoughts straight back in the direction of West Memphis as the Greyhound lumbered due west, onto the interstate ramp, and silently, in a broken prayer, begged God to forgive her.

Mayella awoke on a bench in Clinton, Oklahoma. It was the last town her meager funds could afford to take her. She gathered her belongings: a duffel bag, a denim jacket, and a shopping bag filled with books. They were heavy and cumbersome, but they were her favorites. She would make it with little to her name, but the books were precious treasures she would gladly carry strapped on her back across the country if need be.

She found a drug store and purchased some beef jerky, a small carton of milk, and a sleeve of cheese-filled crackers. She stood patiently on the gravel embankment of the highway and turned her back to the sun, stuck out her thumb, and waited. Finally, forty minutes and three hundred passing cars later, a Ford pickup stopped and offered her a ride.

Two and a half weeks later she arrived in California, compliments of her thumb and the kindness of strangers heading west. She had gotten quite lucky around Amarillo and was picked up by a trucker, who took her all the way to Arizona. The final leg was a Wagoneer shared with a former schoolteacher, turned songwriter, named Lloyd Wooly. He was a divorcee and was on his way to Fresno to visit his son, whom he had not seen since he was six months old.

"The ex-wife has had a change of heart," Lloyd confided. "Though I don't blame her much for keeping a thousand miles between us." He gripped the wheel and actually choked on his words. "Let's just say, I used to be a no-good dick-headed son-of-a-bitch and leave it at that."

Mayella wished he would, but regretfully, she was forced to hear Lloyd's heartfelt ruminations all the way from Phoenix to Los Angeles. She simply listened and let him do the talking. She was a captive audience, and the price for passage into the Promised Land was a patient and ready ear. She kindly obliged as he rambled on about his sinful transgressions against Penelope, his childhood sweetheart. "The best goddamn woman who ever burnt toast!" She was, Mayella learned, a lousy cook, but had a heart of pure gold.

Darrol was Lloyd's son, and was about to turn seven the following Sunday.

"I'm gonna get him something real special for when I see him," Lloyd said. "Like a new bike or somethin' like that. You know, I never did have one of my own growin' up."

"Let's listen to some music," Mayella offered. Anything to silence the aimless litany about his past. He was so severely skinny that he reminded her of a sort of gangly scarecrow with tufts of hay sprouting from his head in all directions beneath his hunting cap. An unkempt mustache completed the look. His hands were dirty, and he smelled like he had bathed in gin—a week ago. She decided to grin and bear it. After all, he would take her all the way to

California, and for that, she was grateful. Maybe there was no Penelope and no Darrol waiting in Fresno. Who knew?

Lloyd was a West Virginia native about to be extremely out of his element in the posh suburban west coastal town he was heading to, but what about her? Mayella had never been more than fifty miles either way out of Arkansas—ever. Now, here she was, heading herself into the vast unknown. In a kind of twisted way, she and Lloyd Wooly had more in common than she would have liked to admit.

"I like to write songs 'bout how I see things. You know, little ditties I dream up. Someday, I hope I'm gonna sell them songs to Nashville. I even got a *gui*-tar back there in the back seat. Never know, maybe someday ole Willy Nelson would like to buy one of my songs. Yeah, ya never know!"

He popped a cassette into the stereo console and handed her a soda from a cooler stashed behind his seat. Soon the sounds of a slide guitar were streaming through the muffled speakers. She didn't know much about vintage country music, except what songs Elvis had made. It was all pretty depressing, if you asked her. She smiled and nodded, trying to seem interested. Truth being, she could barely think at all. Her mind was like a television screen with no signal. Just fuzzy white snow.

Lloyd continued to talk nonstop for hours. She watched the road brush turn from brown to green outside the open window, and the back of Lloyd's left forearm turn red from the sun to match his ginger beard. *White folk*, she thought amusedly. They weren't built for the sunshine. They drove that way for the three hundred seventy-five miles, with nothing in common and everything between them.

They pulled off the road several hours later into a gas station not far from downtown LA, and said farewell. It was a good thing. Lloyd had talked himself out and was starting to ask her questions about her own family, which she eluded skillfully. He was seemingly even more nervous about the prospect of seeing his son for the second time ever.

"You'll do fine," Mayella encouraged. "In a few more hours, you two will be sharing a hug. You're his daddy. He has to love you." Then she touched his arm awkwardly and said, "Thanks for the ride."

He offered her a smile and grinned. "Keep an ear out for one of my ditties on the radio, now!" he called out, waving.

She stood and watched the taillights disappear on down the interstate.

She figured that she was about five miles from the city. A budget hotel and the windows of a restaurant glowed in the distance. She was starving and could smell grilled onions wafting from the lively little diner, but didn't have the money to spare, so she began walking in the direction of the city and settled for a hard bus bench near a public park and a half-eaten box of Milk Duds, trying to decide what to do next.

Hours later she felt a shove. "Move it along, Miss! You can't sleep here!"

A police radio squawked, and a flashlight assessed her head to toe. "Let's go, I said! Move it along!"

Two white officers were peering down at her, sizing her up. *Runaway, no doubt.*

"What's your name, girl?" the first one asked gruffly.

"I ain't got one," Mayella retorted. "Is that a crime?" If she was going to be tough, she was going to have to act the part.

The fat one chuckled and snapped his gum. "Not last

time I checked, it ain't, but you'd better take your little *black* no-name ass on outta here, see? Or else we're going to find a reason to give you one—for the night—as in *lock-up*. Got it?"

A dispatcher called code across their radios, and the two scrambled back into the squad car, the first one calling from behind, "Don't want to see you here again. There's a shelter on Grand Avenue." They sped off, lights and sirens blaring, in the direction of the city lights.

Mayella picked up her bags, exhausted, unclean, and hungry, and started walking in the direction the cop had pointed.

CHAPTER FOUR

SUMMER 2014

*N*O *SECRETS,* LA COSTA REED'S soon-to-be released *eleventh* best-seller, indicated by preorders alone, would take its place of prominence on the north wall of her den, along with the other gold-framed book covers displaying an impressive body of work in the genre of mainstream commercial fiction. This book, however, would be the one that would foster another turning point in her already illustrious career. It was not the next installment to her beloved romance series. Instead, it was *her* story. A brutally honest memoir that would send readers fleeing for their tissue boxes and begging to know more about this much-loved romance author's provocative past. It was to be no less a jewel in the reigning Queen of Contemporary Romance's stunning crown. Private movie studios were already pitching loudly for film rights to *No Secrets,* competing with new developments in cable programming that was vying for their own controversial tell-all account of this celebrated author's life, which would only prove to sweeten the stakes.

La Costa had laid bare her unquenchable spirit in sharing her poignant life story. Once a lost and drifting soul, used and disregarded like yesterday's news. Now she was a supremely accomplished and beloved star—a successful writer, humanitarian, and mother.

Little Mayella Jackson was long gone. Dead, in fact, unto herself and to the rest of the world, never to surface again. Until some twenty-seven years later, when La Costa found the strength to forgive her transgressors and herself, to unlock the ugly secrets from the past and write about her abominable and jaded childhood.

Not only was she a gifted writer, but a *survivor*, and soon to become a modern-day icon, a living tribute to the miraculous victories capable of the human soul. An honor La Costa would take wholly to heart, thanking God each and every day for the good fortune she had gleaned, no longer locked in the web of hidden and unspeakable truths of exactly how she had so arrived at such a place. That had previously been a story of a very different color. One she vowed would never come to light—until now. The concept of breaking free and embracing the truth both frightened and empowered her.

No Secrets was about to celebrate its release into the world. It was the story about Mayella Jackson, not the breathless heroines that floated from the pages of her other novels, solving all of life's mysteries and winning the prince all in a tidy sum of three hundred some-odd pages.

"I want to do this, Tess," she had told her agent when she first contemplated writing it. "It's time. I'm ready now to tell *my* story." The question being, was the real world ready to hear it?

CHAPTER FIVE

NEWPORT BEACH, CA
SUMMER 2014

"TELL ME ABOUT YOUR EXPERIENCE as a stripper. I mean, how did all that get started?" the strikingly attractive reporter asked, balancing a fresh leather-bound notepad on her knee and pressing *play* on the small recording device that was set between them in the center of the coffee table.

La Costa had laid out a full pitcher of sweet tea and a plate of scrumptious bakery cookies, as was her practice with all personal interviews conducted at her home. This one, however, being the first time that she had agreed to do the interview at her Newport Beach residence. Previously, her personal haven had been off limits to press of any kind. Until now. It was the second visit from Felicia Hayden, senior staff reporter for *High Style* magazine, who had won the coveted opportunity to write what would be a candid four-page spread featuring La Costa's story in a gripping exposé for the magazine in concert with the official launch of the tell-all memoir, *No Secrets*. The private interviews were to be conducted in two three-hour sessions, and La

Costa had agreed to give the magazine exclusive rights to all the details behind her provocative life story in her own words, just as she had laid bare in her controversial and poignant biography.

It was day two of the interviews, and La Costa had begun to feel comfortable with having Felicia in her home, walking her around the various rooms and stopping to point out the many photographs, artifacts, and quotes that La Costa had in frames, lining the walls with milestones and memories that were dear to her. All was on display in the modest-size beach home that was a sanctuary of sorts for the calm-natured, resilient author who had an irrepressible spirit, and who, it seemed, lived every day with gratitude.

"I worked at a small club for nearly six months. It had become a necessary survival skill I had to quickly learn in order to make ends meet back in 1987, when I had first arrived in LA—when I was still Mayella Jackson."

Felicia nodded and jotted away on the notepad, not taking her eyes off of La Costa, whose melodic voice was as easy and smooth as if she were relaying a cherished Southern recipe for peach pie.

"I spotted an ad just seven days after I had arrived in LA. They were looking to hire exotic dancers and cocktail waitresses. I had been bouncing from train stations and all-night theaters for temporary shelter up until that point, so I decided to check it out. I was desperate to find work. The decision, as it turned out, changed my life forever."

Felicia captured every compelling word of La Costa's engrossing and hard-bought story. She was completely riveted and knew all too well that the readers of *High Style* would be too. Hopefully, they would be fascinated enough to grab up the first-run copies of the magazine exposé weeks before the official memoir would be released. Such candidness and valor created buzz and sold magazines.

"I was forced to share stairwells and public rest rooms with junkies and runaway juveniles who were always scamming unsuspecting travelers or passersby for their money. They used and abused themselves—and anyone else, really. It didn't matter. Out there, there were no rules. I ate my first hot meal in days at a homeless shelter in East Hollywood and was able to get a hot shower at another nearby mission after learning to ask around for such things."

La Costa explained how she soon found that the world of the homeless was an insane, horrific journey, far worse, perhaps, than the one she had left behind. If she was not watching her back, and belongings, she was fleeing from any number of low-life degenerates, who tried to rob, rape, recruit, save, sell, solicit, push, or pimp her.

"I was no stranger to the concealed habits and survival tactics of the depraved, but was finding myself sinking deeper into a pit that was growing darker by the minute. I was broke, hungry, and desperate for a job—any real paying job that would sustain me one more day. As it turned out, help was just a compromise away. The first of many tough trade-offs I would have to make in order to raise myself out of the dreadful abyss."

Felicia flipped the page in her notebook and nodded. Her short-cropped silver hair, coal-rimmed eyes, and chic, body-slimming trousers belied her true age, which La Costa guessed at being sixty or sixty-one. The woman could have been an actress or older model with her glamorous, striking looks and willowy frame. "Go on," Felicia said, pausing from her writing pad and offering La Costa her full attention.

"It was in a window of an establishment called the Hen House, a dive on Highway Ten, that I saw a handwritten sign saying, GIRLS NEEDED. It was a simple, no-frills strip club with theater-style bench seating, severely watered-down drinks and cheap jug wine. That was the extent of it. Five shows nightly, 'All Nude ... All the Time.' I had intended to work solely as a waitress, but was forced into performing once the owner, Günter, a burly, chain-smoking Swede, cut my hours down to two nights a week without warning. I was on the verge of getting a cashier position at the Quick Stop near the shelter during the day and was certain that between the two jobs, I could soon save enough to afford a cheap studio apartment in town."

Stripping seemed easy enough, once you got past the fact that it was demoralizing and dirty, La Costa would later write in her memoir—the unabashed account of her less-than-humble beginnings. *And, of course, it was every bit—all that.*

Felicia would later expound that Mayella Jackson knew this like she knew her own name, which was why she promptly changed it. From that point on, she was known as *La Costa*, a name taken from a story she had once read about a rich and noble Spanish princess. A far cry from being a poor black girl from the tough dirt lots of West Memphis.

"At the time, I felt a hundred years old, yet I was barely eighteen," La Costa said, staring out at the afternoon sun high over the Pacific.

Felicia paused and offered a gentle, non-judgmental smile.

The exposé would later reveal that La Costa soon learned to adopt the same blank stare that the other girls had while they danced. One by one, they would parade topless along a wood plank runway, pungent with fresh red acrylic paint, lined with inexpensive chase light runners around the perimeters, under the hot stage fill lights. A yank of a bikini string would reveal the rest, and each would gyrate for a full two to three minutes to a deafening stream of rock or heavy metal music blaring from large stereo speakers suspended from the ceiling by crude chains, wearing nothing but high heels, with vacant expressions that begged for so much more than life had served up.

The job paid more than schlepping cheap beer and watered-down cocktails, but the concept simply changed in the form of a trade-off. Now, what she was selling was sex—her body was on display for one dollar at a time. The first time she removed her garments completely in the smoky bar light in front of nameless strangers, she knew she had lost an irredeemable part of her very soul, or what was left of it.

Eventually, as time passed and the money came in, La Costa would later write in her memoir, *it became easier to view the Hen House as nothing more than a means to an end. Night after night, the patrons trickled in, and the girls danced whether there was an entire club filled with paying customers, or merely one pathetic soul looming in the dark, nursing a scotch and soda in the dark, and fantasy fucking the Honey Dejour tantalizing him from the stage.*

On a good night, she would explain, she could make up to seventy-five dollars in tips just from what the patrons would sometimes tuck in the garter she wore high and tight around her thigh. Mostly, she went out on stage in the same outfit—four-inch heels, a strand of fake pearl beads dangling between her voluptuous breasts, and tiny G-string panties purchased from the lingerie shop with her first twenty-five dollars earned.

It was important to have the right tools of the trade, La Costa would go on to explain in her book. *I wore an old pair of high-heeled cloth pumps that a previous stripper had left behind. Günter said that I could have them. They were badly scuffed, and the heels were wobbly, but they had to do. He also fronted me forty-five extra dollars for a can of shoe polish, glitter, and some glue. With the change, I purchased some dime-store makeup and a cheap wig. And that was it. I was ready to go to work.*

"Can you describe the workspace that you had?" Felicia asked.

"There were some inexpensive toiletries provided—mouthwash, razors, and feminine products, kept in a back dressing room, which was really a storage closet converted for the girls to use. It featured a few nude posters and a single stand-up mirror. There were no lockers or hooks, just empty shelf space here and there between the canned olives and pearl onions.

"The girls came, and they went. I never allowed myself to get close to anyone. Most of them were teen runaways like me, who lied about their age to get the job, although looking nothing like fourteen- or sixteen-year-olds. Instead, they looked every bit their fraudulent ages. Tired, worn faces from too much partying or too much heartache and neglect, either self-inflicted or from jaded childhoods or some such abuse at the hand of husbands, boyfriends, or johns. It did not matter much what brought them there. It was a secret sorority of silence that each one maintained. Friendships were not a part of the deal. Rivalry reigned in a competition for hours, prime stage time, and 'preferred' patrons, who tipped lavishly for special attentions. The girls knew who the high tippers were, and the customers knew the girls who were willing to give them more than an eyeful for a dollar."

Felicia shifted, unwinding her crossed legs, now letting the leather binder lay squarely across her lap, and referenced her notes. "Long before losing your cashier job that you also had at the Quick Stop, you write in your account that you were: *'forced to resort to turning tricks to make the rent.'* Is that correct?"

"Yes, it was a relentless cycle of use or be used in order to survive. Eviction was constantly looming, and the struggle to make my own way in the world—that world—was a challenge that far outweighed the shame and personal cost of what it took to do it. I was convinced of simply this: If I could make it through one more day, and then one more night, there in that place, then I could do anything."

La Costa's memoir would poignantly explain, *I did not think of my job as anything more than performing. I had told myself time and time again as I knelt in the darkness of doorways and parked cars with my head bent over a stranger's lap, that it was better than any atrocity done unto me against my will.*

Felicia raised a perfectly arched gray eyebrow. "Would you care to elaborate on what you mean by that? *Against your will?*"

La Costa shook her head and reached for her glass of iced tea.

A long, slow sip was enough of a cue for Felicia to understand. Some topics would be off limits, and this was one of them.

La Costa waited a beat, and then continued. "When I missed my period for the third month in a row and feared that I was pregnant, I freaked out. Günter got wind of it and subsequently fired me."

"Desperate and shaken," Felicia confirmed, checking her notepad, "you attempted to end the pregnancy with an overdose of diet pills and gin, correct? A thwarted stunt that landed you in Los Angeles County Hospital, when your landlord discovered you passed out on your bed after you did not report to work at the Quick Stop for three days straight."

"That's correct. He called an ambulance, and then promptly evicted me. Not one of my better days!" La Costa recalled solemnly. "Although there was little chance at that point that things could have gotten any worse. I had nowhere to come home to when I was released from the hospital. And I was still with child."

"So, now desolate and scared," Felicia said, "you faced yet another impossible hurdle and was once again back on the streets."

La Costa nodded. "The situation was either to be a death sentence, or a steppingstone for me. I chose to make it the latter."

"That's remarkable," the pensive reporter said. "What did you do? Where did you go next?"

La Costa refreshed both tea glasses and then continued. "To another shelter. St. Augustine's provided a folding cot in an open room with scores of filthy, diseased bodies hacking and moaning and babbling incoherently. All forms of humanity—men, women, children, teens, gays, straights, freaks and felons, druggies, indigents, the insane, and the walking dead—you name it, I saw it. One hot meal a day was served from the good mercies of the sisters of the church in a basement soup kitchen."

La Costa explained how she quickly learned from some savvy street residents where the daily handouts and best garbage scraps could be found. "The day I ate a half-eaten Chinese take-out from a dumpster, where a harried legal secretary-type had deposited it, was the lowest moment of my life. Ironically, somehow seeming to be lower even than prostituting myself for the price of a full course meal."

"And then, as if that were not enough, something else happened," Felicia prompted, again referencing her notes.

"The weeks passed, and my stomach began to swell. I started smoking cigarette butts wherever I could scavenge one, picking them out of public ashtrays or off the pavement to curb the constant hunger pangs and the incessant nausea. No one wanted sex from a pregnant black girl who was street-weary and dirty, who lived among the degenerate drifters beneath the freeway, in gangways and service tunnels. I figured that the baby had died when the stirring in my belly stopped and my feet went numb from the swelling."

At nearly twenty-one weeks, the reporter would later write, *she delivered the stillborn fetus in an abandoned building, alone.*

The words of La Costa's heart-wrenching memoir said all that was left to relay, and Felicia would use it verbatim: *I wrapped it in newspapers like a shank of meat and carried the blood-soaked bundle to the beach, where I set it adrift along the rocky ravine. Then I erected a makeshift cross in the sand, carving out a recess with my bare hands, not fifty yards from the shore. I was emotionless the entire time, attending only to the task and thinking nothing more. I had taught myself by then to detach from all that was far too fantastic to bear; to numb myself sufficiently from the unthinkable. Then I drained the contents of a discarded bottle of bourbon I had found. One full swallow was all it delivered. The liquid stung like fire as it ripped down my throat. I'll never forget the taste.*

I just sat there for a long while, sitting with my feet in the wet sand, watching the waves take my baby boy away.

CHAPTER SIX

LOS ANGELES
DECEMBER 1988

"WHY DON'T YOU TELL ME why it is that you want to work for us here at Sophisticate?"

"I could be useful in many ways. I am a fast learner. I have good ideas, and I have a knack for writing. I could maybe proofread ad copy, or such," La Costa said, averting her eyes. "I could even model maybe a little myself. I see there are a lot of black girls with your agency who are, well, *light-skinned*. I think that I am more representative of the ancestral heritage."

La Costa's heart was pounding. How stupid! What on earth was she saying? The Caucasian woman seated behind the gigantic desk stopped scribbling on the yellow legal pad in front of her.

"I assume that you have a headshot, dear?"

"No, ma'am."

"I see. You will be getting one soon, I trust?"

"Yes, ma'am."

She plucked her glasses off of her nose and looked squarely at La Costa, who was barely seventeen and had obviously lied on the application on more than one account. "You know, Miss Jackson, our girls must be at least eighteen to model for the agency in any capacity. Without any valid identification, I am afraid . . ."

La Costa nodded. She only wanted out. A way to earn a respectable living that didn't involve being ogled and groped for the bargain price of a dollar a dance.

The harried-looking woman sighed. She was a bundle of nerves herself, trapped behind a desk of contracts, composites, and unreturned phone messages. Stacks of magazines towered on shelves too weak to hold them, threatening to collapse at any moment. More loomed on windowsills and were piled on the floor. She had been without a receptionist for four weeks, and things were not getting any easier. She was short-staffed as it was, and backlogged with clients clamoring for models for their fall campaigns. There just were not enough hours in the day. Her former girl, Carla, was on maternity leave, and Lord knows, she needed the help, right now. She had certainly been pleased when the women's shelter called with the referral. The possibility of finding someone mid-summer was close to impossible, and she would have to take what she could get. But could the girl be trusted? That was the question.

"I have a receptionist position open. I'm in need of someone temporarily." She eyed La Costa hopefully. "Can you type?"

La Costa shook her head.

"I see . . . how about filing, then?"

La Costa fidgeted.

"Can you answer phones, dear? Can you do *that*?"

La Costa nodded.

"Bingo!" the woman brightened. "I'll try you out, and we'll go from there."

La Costa surveyed the office. It was beautiful. Messy, but beautiful. She knew that she could clean it up and make it more functional. A glint flickered in her eye. She had been managing chaos of her own for years. "Thank you, ma'am," La Costa said, smiling. It would be a *real* job!

"Call me Constance, dear," the woman said, sealing the deal with a handshake. Then she began rifling through a file drawer for a blank application.

One week later, La Costa met one of the agency's most striking models, Panther St. James. Everything about her was the real deal, except for her name. *Panther* was a nickname that she traded in place of her given name, Phyllis Jean St. James, which she had inherited from her dear Southern memaw from Independence, Missouri. The first time La Costa laid eyes on her, she thought that Panther was the most beautiful creature she had ever seen.

Two years her senior, Panther was nineteen, but looked as alluring and sophisticated as any twenty-something model. She had exotic good looks, delicate bone structure, a pert nose, and dazzling white teeth that positively sparkled against her light brown skin. It was her remarkable feline eyes that seemed to radiate with golden light that labeled her from childhood with the nickname, *Panther*. "Cat's eyes!" her grandfather would say prophetically about his granddaughter's remarkable feline features. "Along with the temper of a lion!" he would add unapologetically. Eventually, the moniker just stuck, planting in the then-six-year-old girl's soul the notion that she was indeed, something of a novelty.

It was a great advantage, especially in the business, to possess the benefit of a youthful body and grownup looks. But Panther only moonlighted for Constance's modeling agency to support her lavish shopping and cocaine habits. Panther primarily made money working as a stripper at an elite gentlemen's club downtown. She was a "Kitten," as the girls were called at Lucy DuMont's famed Mink Kitty nightclub. There certainly was no place at The Mink Kitty for crow's feet or wrinkled skin. All of Lucy's girls had to have the bona fide goods, and Panther delivered. The Kittens were Lucy DuMont's biggest draw, and the former West Harlem Madame knew a thing or two about drawing bees to honey. Nobody knew the skin business better than Lucy DuMont.

The first time La Costa met Panther, she was like most all the other models, dressed down in a faded T-shirt and well-worn designer jeans, sporting a long, silken ponytail wrapped like a sable mane into a twist on top of her head. Her killer thoroughbred legs made her something to be reckoned with. They appeared to go on for miles up to her neck, cinching her runway-model status with the blessing of a towering height of five feet, eleven inches. She weighed in at a sinewy one hundred twenty pounds. Her flawless mocha skin glowed radiantly, and her signature amber eyes were rimmed in charcoal points around the edges—proof positive that she lived up to her name.

Panther had been with Sophisticate Models for the past year and a half and was one of their most requested for product shoots and convention appearances. She mostly turned them down, however, preferring instead to dance two to three nights a week at the Mink Kitty, where she made more money in one weekend than in two whole months of passing out flyers at car shows and boat expositions.

At Lucy's club, Panther was a headline draw. One of only a few Showcase Kittens who stripped twice nightly at designated showtimes. She worked a total of forty minutes a night and went home four to five hundred dollars richer. Panther had a million-dollar body that just wouldn't quit, and she loved to strut and shimmy in G-strings and teddies on the main stage dance pole.

She was the sleekest and sexiest stripper I had ever seen, La Costa would later relay in her memoir. *The first time that I had ever seen her perform, I was mesmerized.*

The two had become fast friends during Panther's many visits to the agency. They quickly bonded when Panther revealed details about her "night job," and came to learn about La Costa's stint as a dancer at the Hen House off Highway Ten on the amateur circuit. She was the only soul La Costa had told about her past. "It was far from glamorous," La Costa confided.

"You should come on by and see one of *our* shows," Panther offered, tossing a pink business card onto La Costa's desk on her way to a go-see. "I can even arrange for you to meet Lucy, if you'd like. Pays a lot better than this temp gig, and you GOT the goods, *gurl!*"

The offer stood for two months before La Costa took her up on it. The stint with Sophisticate was good, but it was temporary, and the pay was only minimum wage. Rumor had it that Carla was returning and wanted her position back at the reception desk. La Costa knew that it was only a matter of time before she would be let go. She was also desperate to get out of her crappy skid-row-esque apartment. Working at the Mink Kitty sounded like her ticket to much better days, for certain.

Currently, she was living in one-room war zone efficiency, where roaches and drug pushers were her only neighbors. Door locks and window bars did little to discourage break-ins weekly, or to shut out the sirens and gang-capades as she referred to it that exploded nightly in the city streets behind her complex.

Empty tenement units and stairwells served as convenient hiding places for crack runners—mostly children, some as young as seven or eight, who hung out outside her door. They had no guardians in sight, and were schooled not in a classroom or playgroup, but on the gritty pavements and combat courtyards of the projects.

Most lived two-to-four families to a single unit. The level of stench and squalor was unspeakable. La Costa had only been living there for a couple of months and was beginning to imagine that life at the shelter would be better than the rat hole in Central City off of East Seventh Street. But the grim reality remained. Without a real address, La Costa would not have been able to get a job, and so, she agreed when the shelter arranged to have her share the run-down government subsidized apartment with a blind woman named Dottie.

The shelter had made the arrangements. In exchange for low rent and a monthly bus pass, La Costa would see to it that Dottie was looked after, which was easy enough, because fortunately for La Costa, at age eighty-nine, the old woman was too senile and slow to do much else than sit in her recliner near the window and listen to squirrels scratch at the screen with a three-legged cat named Marigold folded in her lap.

When Dottie wasn't rocking in her chair and stroking Marigold's ears, sheared and ragged from one too many brawls, she was praying fervently for the Lord to take her "home." Sometimes she did this for hours on end, calling on Jesus Almighty to claim for himself, her weary soul.

L A COSTA IMAGINED THAT DOTTIE was somebody's grandmother, tossed aside and left fatefully alone. It made her think of her own grandmother, June—Tallulah's mother, back at the trailer park, sick, old, and mean as a wet hen most days. As for her paternal grandmother, she had never known her mother to speak of her, or Crete's father. They were no more than ghosts in the wind to her. La Costa never knew a grandparent's love, let alone the love of her own mother and father, without it coming with a price. Crete was the sickest bastard she had ever known. He could be dead for all she cared. Even if she didn't know of a loving grandparent, she would not have wished on any of them, a fate as horrible as dying in a ghetto flat with cockroaches and filthy walls and garbage heaps for gardens. Luckily for Dottie, she could not see her surroundings.

La Costa had indeed come such a long way herself, yet was barely able to make the climb out of the poverty-stricken ghettos that constantly held her down. The offer to work at The Mink Kitty would change all of that. Then, La Costa would have a way to claw her way out of the grim darkness into the light, never to look back from where she had come. No, a destiny like Dottie's was not in the cards for La Costa.

Just two days before La Costa was about to give her notice at Sophisticate, she was informed that her temp job was about to be terminated. Remarkably, the very next day, Dottie had passed peacefully in her sleep. It was divine timing, as far as La Costa was concerned. Fate had sealed the deal. She would leave the apartment complex and pursue her next life adventure—taking Panther up on her offer for a futon at her place—and a coveted introduction to the illustrious Miss Lucy of the famed Mink Kitty.

CHAPTER SEVEN

NEWPORT BEACH. CA
2014

"I WAS PRETTY NERVOUS AT THE prospect of meeting Lucy DuMont," La Costa explained to Felicia, as she gingerly opened the cover of a heavy scrapbook stuffed with Polaroids, bar receipts, and ancient drink menus, yellowed from the press of time. "I had never met a real Madame before, let alone one as beautiful and wealthy as Lucy. Here she is in this photo—third blonde on the left."

"Are you in this shot?" Felicia asked, studying it intently.

"No, I took this picture. Not knowing that my time would soon come. She was a guardian on my journey, for sure, but Lucy's story, as it was, could fill a book of her own. She was something of a legend."

Lucy DuMont's reputation preceded her, La Costa explained. Born and raised in Utah to strict Mormon parents in the early nineteen forties, Lucy and her family ironically lived in a culturally diverse neighborhood on the west side of town called Rose Park. Lucinda Hansen, as was her given name, ran away in the fall of her sixteenth year with the son of the church's pastor, Caleb Jones, in a raucous scandal that prompted a privately funded man-hunt for the two across eleven states over two years' time. They landed in Little Rock, Arkansas, where they laid low for several months. Eventually, Caleb's father called off the search when the two minors had inevitably turned eighteen, just two weeks apart from one another. They were legally free, and so they set out to make their way in the world.

Quickly, good intentions turned to hard luck, and Caleb's aspirations of preaching and starting a church of his own in Little Rock vanished as soon as funds dwindled, and the recession offered no chances for Lucy and Caleb to find decent work in town. They resorted to having to steal fifty dollars from a friend whom Caleb knew trusted him. The guilt eventually turned out to be too much for him, and one day, he just up and left. He returned to Utah the wayward Prodigal's son, where his family welcomed him back with open arms. Lucy, however, chose not to join him. Instead, she headed North, running as far away from convention, formality, and religion as she could, seeing as how it did not work out for her the first time.

She landed in Canada, where she soon fostered a love for performing and studied acting in Quebec, while working as an interpretive dancer in Community Theater. She auditioned and won a part in a local American production of a nude musical called *Slip Skin*, remaining on as a regular cast member for the next two years. When the show traveled to London, Lucy stayed on with the troupe until the final curtain call. She then married the show's director, Bernard DuMont, just three weeks after his divorce from an American screen actress. Lucy and Bernard decided to stay on in the city and call London their new home.

Repressed by years of stoic moral upbringing, Lucy had been unleashed at long last in a wonderland of sin and delicious decadence, following her husband's unbridled artistic aspirations as a producer and novice filmmaker, with erotica being Bernard DuMont's singular specialty.

The two enjoyed raucous trysts with multiple partners from time to time, and soon began filming themselves engaging in lurid sex acts and selling the amateur movies on the black market. They threw wild parties, serving up dangerous drugs and plenty of experimental sex—love fests, as they liked to call them—inviting off-beat actor types and prostitutes into their home, and oftentimes, into their bed, fast becoming consumed with their own visceral vanities and pleasures. Lucy especially found the mystique of woman-on-woman love to be a delightful addition to her own sexual repertoire; enough so to change things completely, and ultimately chart her course for different horizons.

After several tumultuous years, Lucy lost her call for the theater life and her taste for Bernard. She hooked up with a transgender stripper named René, called her marriage quits, and once again, moved on.

As a result of the profits from the DuMonts' film company, Lucy was provided with a sizable settlement, which she promptly sank into a multi-unit brownstone in Soho, a colorful section of town frequented by tourists and transient looking for a little action.

By this time, Lucy had cultivated a keen business sense and had a growing vision on how to turn the certain pursuit of sinful pleasure into cold, hard cash.

The brownstone housed four separate flats, which she had immediately converted into a single dwelling manor home featuring three sitting rooms, a main parlor, two functional kitchens, a dining hall, five bathrooms, and ten sleeping rooms—"boarding rooms," as she marketed them, one of which served as her own private quarters and working office. At any given time, Lucy was known to have anywhere from six to twenty young women residing at the DuMont Manor, a local boarding house advertised for female students of the nearby University who were seeking an off-campus alternative to campus living arrangements. In reality, DuMont Manor was nothing short of a modern-day brothel.

Within ten years, by 1977, Lucy amassed enough revenue to sell the manor and return to the States, where she moved to LA and later invested her fortune into some modest California real estate. She bought into the prosperous rise of the Wall Street boom in the early eighties, trading on the promise of huge stock swings garnered from "tips" acquired from associates in the know, enabling her to acquire The Oasis, a once-famous but now failing nightclub about to go under—for cold cash.

A Saudi Arabian businessman, had previously owned the club. He took three hundred thousand dollars for the exchange of worn-out cabaret tables, a code-hazard kitchen, a slanted bar, and a gravel-pocked parking lot.

"What will you do with this old heap of metal and moldy carpet, Ms. DuMont?" the man asked, smiling smugly through his gapped teeth.

Where skeptics saw garbage, Lucy saw potential. "Ain't nothin' a little spit and lipstick can't mend."

No truer words were ever spoken. It was the proven mantra of a millionaire maven who coined the very phrase with pride, which no doubt, would grace her tombstone someday.

That spring the new club, renamed The Mink Kitty after her prize Persian cat, Pigette, opened its doors, putting all naysayers and disbelievers to shame. Lucy never looked back.

CHAPTER EIGHT

LOS ANGELES, CA
JANUARY 1989

IT WAS ELEVEN THIRTY A.M., and Panther led La Costa through the empty club, which looked peculiar in the morning sunlight that streamed in through the streaky windows that were covered. The heavy opaque scarlet drapes were open, swagged elaborately from the ceiling to the floor. Gleaming marble cocktail tables dotted the entrance area, each with a set of high-backed leopard-print lounge chairs.

The dining rooms were dormant but ready. White-topped tables and plush velvet booths with black leather and chrome stools were aligned perfectly in front of the sleek mahogany bar that spanned for miles. Locked liquor cabinets in matching mahogany housed rows of fine wines, liquors, and bottled spirits; rows of gleaming goblets and champagne flutes hung upside down from brass glass racks in the ceiling.

The artwork was stunning. Large, bold oil prints of erotic scenes splashed onto huge canvas scrims, hung in gilded frames along the walls.

"They're all hers," Panther explained of Lucy's personally painted art collection. Apparently, she had a knack for oils. La Costa reacted with shock and curiosity at the contorted nude figures melting into one another in what looked like a Greek orgy. The females depicted in the abstract, appeared to be actual felines, with claws and tails protruding from their bodies.

"It's *high art*, all right." Panther chuckled at her own joke. "The old bag had to be trippin' on something when she painted them!"

Together, they rounded a mirrored corner. La Costa followed Panther up a winding carpeted staircase to the VIP loft that overlooked the entire club below. It, too, was filled with unnaturally bright sunlight peeking from behind heavy blackout curtains, which hung from the windows behind the stage. A collection of low black tables created a cabaret feel to the loft, which was really a showroom where the top customers received "special" private entertainment.

The showcase stage was a small motorized dais, atop which only the choicest Kittens pranced and posed beneath the spotlight. These were professional top-line strippers. Some girls flew in nightly from cities like Houston, Miami, or Chicago, just to perform their two shows—one at nine p.m., and the other, at midnight. They were highly paid dancers, who made their fortunes jet- setting to all the top clubs in the nation. Other dancers lived locally, like Panther.

Those who lived in Lucy DuMont's apartment complex had the best units in the city, along with fat charge accounts at all the local shops and boutiques. The Showcase Dancers parked their sports cars with the valets and walked into the finest restaurants anytime, where they received the choicest tables. Salons and day spas were at their disposal year-round, and each senior-level Kitten had a personal trainer, aesthetician, and her own Beverly Hills personal shopper. Not to mention a bevy of plastic surgeons, cosmetic dentists, nutritionists, and/or drug suppliers.

Panther was not yet a senior Kitten, but she did strip twice a week on the VIP stage. The crowds were not as large, but the tips were hefty, and working the "stage" as it was called, was the next step on a Kitten's way to the good life. At senior-level status, a Kitten could earn more money in two to three nights than most people made in an entire month. Attaining this was Panther's singular purpose and goal.

Mentoring and training the new "recruits" was one significant way of earning merit points toward senior-level status. Panther was a natural, and men gravitated to her lively and pleasant nature and drop-dead looks. She was hot and wore her sensuality like a pair of well-worn jeans, with natural ease and sexy confidence. One could not be in the same room with Panther and her fabulous body and not take notice. It would just not be possible.

The reality of this made La Costa wonder if she had what it took to do the job. Panther seemed to think so. The more time she spent with Panther, however, the more self-conscious La Costa became. The Mink Kitty was big league.

They toured the rest of the building. Next, the lounges and then the kitchen, and finally, the Kittens' Den—a dressing area in the basement of the nightclub, where the girls prepared for work each night. Upon seeing it, the decision for La Costa was cinched right then and there. The bank of lighted mirrors, rows of pink lockers, array of makeup caddies, and bounty of hairsprays, lipsticks, and perfumes were incredible. Satin and lace teddies, G-strings, bras, and panties were hung like tiny doll clothes on each girl's locker on fancy hangers. Rhinestone "cat collars" were also worn by each Kitten, complete with a tiny metal tag in the shape of a heart with their Kitty names engraved on the front—*Jezebel ...Tinker ... Samba ... Cleo.*

"Yours is purrrfect!" Panther teased. "Keep your name. La Costa is great!"

They exited the Den and walked a little farther through the back of the house.

"I'll introduce you to her now. Wait here." Panther disappeared behind a heavy steel door, leaving La Costa standing in a service corridor just off the kitchen. A Sous Chef was busy chopping salad vegetables on a cutting board with quick flashes of a huge knife. Soups and sauces were bubbling on the enormous stove burners, and Spanish-speaking dishwashers eyed her, chattering and rinsing and scraping dirty plates and arranging them noisily into industrial-size racks.

A moment later, Panther reappeared and led La Costa through the same doorway, up a back stairwell to Lucy's office. It was different than she had expected. Far less ornate than the interior of the club. The small room had no windows, and the walls were covered completely with hundreds of framed photographs. The tiny office was a bit stifling. It was obvious that Lucy was a chain smoker. Ashtrays overflowed with lipstick-marked butts everywhere. She was seated at her desk like a queen on her throne, with a phone pressed to her ear, motioning for them to come in.

Lucy was a large woman with huge, billowing bosoms. The kind that greeted you well before the rest of her. And from the looks of things, she was quite proud of them, displaying her mammoth-sized chest prominently within a too-tight corset blouse, which had flowing scalloped sleeves that came to a point at her pudgy elbows. The rest of her rotund frame was concealed beneath a gauzy black skirt that extended all the way to her ankles and back up, with a sassy slit revealing a beefy white leg with grotesquely puckered flesh around her thigh. Her stomach protruded prominently, and the waist of the tight blouse threatened to pop loose at any moment. She was not wearing any shoes and appeared to have matching tattoos, one around each ankle.

Lucy's hair was a chemical wonder of peroxides and processes, which had stripped it quite completely of its natural color. It was a course texture of frayed blonde curls swept upward and fastened at the crown with a ridiculous-looking plastic barrette that was intended for a little girl to wear, not proprietors of trendy night clubs. She was, in short, a piece of work.

Her desk, like her hair, was a confusion of possibilities, strewn with photographs, binders, and register tapes. La Costa simply stood mesmerized, taking it all in.

"Tell Mr. Honeycutt that the next time he pulls that, he'll be back in Wales so fast his head will spin!"

La Costa tried to make out the peculiar accent as Lucy spoke into the phone, picking her front tooth with a white-tipped acrylic fingernail. It was sort of proper, yet decidedly street savvy.

"Don't fuck with me, Harlow. I don't have the time to dick around. Just let him know, aye?"

Despite the two of them standing there, Lucy continued with her phone conversation for several minutes more. Panther studied the photographs on the walls, while La Costa's eyes were helplessly glued to Lucy. She may have been born piss-poor, but La Costa did know tacky when she saw it. The woman just did not fit the image that she had imagined. White rich folk were typically more put together than Lucy DuMont appeared to be. She had never seen anyone like her.

Lucy's eyes were a pale blue, void of eye shadow, and her sparse blonde lashes were spiked with clumps of thick black mascara that made them appear like two tarantulas fluttering on her face. A rosy glow, compliments of body heat, created red patches on the apples of her cheeks and along her white neck like a rash, and a smudge of frosty pink gloss had migrated from her thin lips to the outer corners of her mouth.

Lucy walloped and then bent over, choking violently, causing the chair to squeak and lurch beneath her. It was a common thing—these coughing and hacking fits of gasps and wheezes that no doubt, were a direct result of the carcinogens she was sucking into her lungs at a rate of three packs a day. She turned bright red in the process, and Panther hurried back into the hall to fetch her a glass of water.

What seemed like an eternity later, Lucy dropped the receiver back into its ancient cradle and stood up. Not only was she fat, but she was short too.

"Lucy," Panther began, as she shoved La Costa forward from the spot she stood frozen to on the floor, "this is La Costa Jackson. She's got *experience* . . . worked for Günter up until about six months ago. She was answering phones at Sophisticate for a while. Now she's cocktail waitressing at a bar near the airport and crashing with me. Thought we could use her here."

"Pleased to meet you, honey." Lucy stepped forward to shake La Costa's hand, treating her at the same time, to the distinctive sour odor of bourbon on her breath. "So, you are interested in working here, are you?" She hoisted her hefty frame onto her desk.

Lucy's words curled peculiarly at the ends, like they were fancy loops in the air. As it turned out, Lucy picked up the dialect in London from the many years she lived there. Some people said that the accent was fake. Either way, it was as much a defining part of Lucy's essence as the milky-white skin that she wore.

She reached into a drawer and extracted a brown cigarette. At first La Costa thought it might be a cigar, but once Lucy flicked a slender gold lighter and touched the tip to ignite it, it emitted a strange, fragrant smoke that reminded La Costa of burning leaves, only sweeter. It was a clove cigarette, Panther later explained. Another of many signature props that Lucy relied on and never was seen without.

The largest and most coveted one being her 1975 Cadillac Coup DeVille. It had gold-spoke wheels and red leather seats. Her license plate simply read: LADYCAT. It was a gift from a Lieutenant Governor from one of the dreaded states that starts with an *A*. Panther could not exactly remember all the details.

"He visited her every chance he got when he came through town. He had, among other

things, connections. His generosities kept the Mink Kitty going for a time when she almost lost it during the goddamn Reagan recession. Theirs was a well-known, poorly concealed, eight-year affair. Most people really didn't care, except, of course, for Mrs. Lieutenant Governor, Deidre Richardson, who could do little about her husband's philandering.

"Rumor has it that Lucy and Deidre actually met once, when Mrs. Richardson visited the club with an entourage of goons from the state department. She was trying to catch Lucy in breach of code or some such shit. Tried to have her shut down, but nothing ever came of it, though,"

Panther explained. "Once word got back to the governor, Lucy was never harassed again."

"What ever happened to Deidre Richardson?" La Costa asked anxiously.

"*Dead* . . . of course. Isn't that cozy? She swallowed enough Percocet to choke a horse."

La Costa got the job. Her interview consisted of balancing a cocktail tray filled with water glasses over her head, while negotiating a maze of low lounge tables, while wearing three-inch heels. No contest.

She then had to parade in front of Lucy in a flimsy silk teddy worn by all the Kittens in the club.

The final test was a two-minute dance routine, in which the head busboy, Arturo, posed as the customer. La Costa was required to perform a scintillating table dance for him, stripping off her dress down to only her panties. When the straps of her lace brassiere released and her bouncy thirty-eight Ds sprang loose with large, luscious Hershey's Kiss nipples at the ready—everyone in the room took notice. Arturo blushed at the instant erection it elicited in his pants.

Lucy squealed with laughter, embarrassing him into a quivering pool of Jell-O. "Okay, darlin'. You're in! You passed the jalapeno test!"

The first thing La Costa did was quit her job at the sports bar that she had held for the previous three weeks. She would need all her free time for more lucrative pursuits, like teaching herself new dance moves, jogging religiously each day, and memorizing the stack of training manuals and drink lists provided by the club. There was so much to know. Kittens had a code of behaviors that had to be followed to the letter. Rigorous dictates about their costumes, footwear, hosiery, interaction with patrons, drink service—even the way they were allowed to stand while working on the club floor.

La Costa wore a red nametag on her "collar," which meant that she was a trainee Kitten. It was the most beautiful thing she had ever seen. The costumes were glorious and expensive customized lingerie created by an in-house seamstress, who measured La Costa for her debut outfit, a lavender and lace teddy with a tiny matching apron. When she first put it on and peered into the mirror, she could hardly believe what she saw.

No one had ever taught her a skill, nor had anyone ever given her anything. Thanks to Panther and Lucy, she was being given a real chance to make something of herself. The feeling was foreign, but fantastic. And most unbelievably of all, she liked what she saw in the mirror looking back!

CHAPTER NINE

LOS ANGELES
1989

WITHIN THREE MONTHS, LA COSTA was working four nights a week and making more money than she ever imagined possible. She was serving cocktails in the show lounge and waiting on tables in the club's restaurant. The tips were flowing, and so was her self-esteem.

Immediately, she had moved permanently into Panther's apartment in Century City, along with five other girls from the club. The apartment was owned and managed by none other than Lucy DuMont. Rent was reasonable, and it had all the makings of a sorority house—with a twist.

The west side two-flat walk-up was no great shakes, but it was palatial compared to the rat holes that she had grown up in. It was more than adequate. Most of the girls from the club roomed together, sometimes three, four, or five of them all crammed into two- and three-bedroom units. They used the place on a "rotation" basis like flight attendants or traveling nurses would do, but these were the other kind of "working girls" who came and went at all hours—sometimes staying away for days at a time. There always was an available bed, a refrigerator filled with wine or beer, and enough drugs floating around to make every day a party.

La Costa decided to room with some of the other new girls rather than the more established Senior Kittens for fear of being taken advantage of. Newbies always got stuck with the worst of everything—mattresses, household chores, last use of the laundry facilities. It was a sorority all right, and at The Mink Kitty, all Kittens were expected to pay their dues.

La Costa was able to afford her portion of the groceries and rent, and still have a little left over for an occasional new outfit or a fancy meal from time to time in one of the trendy restaurants downtown. The girls most liked to hang out after work at a posh hotel bar called Braxton's, which always seemed to draw a fun nightly crowd of the area's movers and shakers. The dance club Trax was also a favorite haunt, where Kittens could be found hobnobbing with the likes of would-be actors and musicians, politicians, and movie producers. From time to time, a sports celebrity or screen icon would rent out the place and hire the Kittens to mingle with a few hundred of their closest friends and guests. The girls could usually be found at Trax following their shifts, dancing until dawn.

Not all Kittens worked for Lucy DuMont's "side business." It was referred to as simply *Escorting*, and none of the girls were forced into it. They had to come to it of their own accord and simply let Lucy know if they were interested. She handled things from there, first by putting them on the VIP stage, which enabled patrons to choose their escort companion by name, style, and type. Once a selection was made, Lucy would make the connection.

The club had several suites reserved in various posh hotels throughout the city, where one call to any of Lucy's contacts provided a choice room and accommodations for her ladies to meet with clients discriminately.

Insiders portended quite truthfully that the side business of Lucy DuMont's escort service was far more lucrative than the strip club alone, but neither the truths nor the rumors hurt business in the least, and The Mink Kitty was definitely purring.

Being a Kitten required much dedication for the Kitten to maintain her figure. La Costa and the others would be given demerits if their weight should increase by as little as three pounds once they reached their "Kitten weight." La Costa worked out every day at the gym, melting away a remarkable total of twenty-three pounds in just three months' time, revealing a svelte, lean knockout beneath her curvaceous exterior. She would hold steady at a lean one hundred twenty-two pounds. The transformation was shocking, to say the least. Now, at five foot eight, she did have a striking figure that won her the privilege of spotlight status performing center stage in the VIP lounge not six months after she first arrived. She performed two shows nightly, stripping down to panties and pasties for the elite crowds of rowdy tourists and businessmen who passed through, filling her garters with tens, twenties, even hundred-dollar bills as she gyrated under the hot white lights, making it ever so impossible to imagine the life she left behind. On stage, La Costa's well-crafted face showed no signs of the tired, frightened mask she wore beneath.

Relaxants took the frizz from her hair, which she kept cropped at the chin in a flirty bob. Dramatic eyeliner, false lashes, and smoky shadow played up her rather small, inset eyes, making them appear larger than life. She was a beauty. Her lips stenciled to perfection, featuring a doll-like pout dabbed in the center with a touch of sticky pink lip gloss. A tiny raised mole (an ingenious creation of eye pencil and pressed powder) floated on her left cheek. "Every girl should punctuate her style," she was known to say. La Costa's beauty dot, as she liked to call it, became her signature trademark.

In the years that followed, no one ever looked for her. She thought about the possibility of someday going back to Arkansas. Of walking into Tallulah's kitchen in a fine silk blouse carrying a designer beaded purse, prancing in her pricey pumps that cost more than her mother would have paid to Mr. Davidson for two months' rent. She fantasized about walking on the choppy linoleum floor, across the speckled worn tiles that bowed in the center of the trailer, in those shoes, just to imagine the sound they would make, and then the look on Tallulah's face when she would waltz right out again without saying a word.

And what, she wondered, became of the boys? Her brothers, Eli and Rufus? She sent checks back home of whatever she could spare from time to time, which were promptly cashed and gratefully received. She had hoped, since they were boys, that they were able to hold their own in the minefield of Tallulah's precarious life. Sending money made La Costa feel a little better knowing that even at such a distance, her brothers would know that she was thinking about them. Telling them that she cared. It was not for Tallulah that she sent the money. It was for the boys.

She had prayed for them so often. Every day, in fact, when she remembered to pray. It seemed to have been so much easier to find the time before—when she was down and out, frightened and alone . . . hurting. The days and nights were a blur of activity and denial now. Life in the fast lane, so to speak. She was certain that the face of God was indeed watching, and, no doubt—*frowning.*

It wasn't that there were not hard times anymore; times when she truly felt sad. Loneliness and isolation were her constant companions, despite her glamorous lifestyle that seemed to thrive only in the night-time hours, leaving her quite tired and spent in the light of day. It was not unusual for the girls to sleep in until well past two p.m. after working in the club until two or three a.m., partying well into the early morning hours, and then, when the drugs and the booze and the debauchery dissipated with the dawn they would stumble home—four to a taxi—and pass out from sheer exhaustion.

Oftentimes, La Costa would awake to find strange men who had spent the night leaving the apartment, their rumpled suits and shoes in hand, crawling to the elevator while crafting their alibis and patting down pockets for their car keys.

More than once, the stranger would be next to her in bed and she would panic frantically until she could find the crumpled latex discarded in the bathroom—assurance that even though her body was buzzing, a part of her brain still functioned on auto pilot, watching out for her. Protection first and always was her driving mantra. She was all she had.

Never did a day go by that she did not think of her own boy. The one she buried in the ocean. Still, she could not bring herself to admit how she was completely responsible for his death. She was reckless and stupid. Still. She pushed the thoughts away. Kept them buried. This was La Costa's way of coping with truths too horrible to face. She simply shut out the thoughts from her mind and forged ahead.

The drugs and booze had done their work over time to age La Costa duly. It became harder to maintain a fresh, youthful look and a well-toned body when the only thing you fed it was a steady diet of sleeping pills to wind down and a smorgasbord of uppers washed down with champagne cocktails to stay awake, night after night.

Both La Costa as well as Panther were heavy smokers, finding that it helped curb the appetite and kept them at their ideal Kitten weight. But the practice merely masked an inventory of more serious addictions that followed. They shot up frequently before going on stage, for an extra "boost," coming down slowly with the aid of barbiturates and pot, a steady supply that was as available as chewing gum around the club where everything was at their disposal—for a price. Soon it became progressively harder to keep up with their costly habits. And sleeping with the regular patrons for money, the ready answer.

Lavish parties lasting for days were hosted by top photographers, dealmakers, entrepreneurs, stockbrokers, CEOs, club owners . . . a never-ending holiday with rich, powerful men footing the bill and vying for the chance to be alone with them. Kittens were a commodity, and on any given night they were liable to attend any number of extravagant, high-profile soirees, where the only invitation necessary was the smile that they wore. The drugs and the booze and the money were free flowing. A never-ending carnival ride where behind every door another admirer was there to meet one of Ms. Lucy's girls and enjoy for themselves, much more.

Staying high was the mechanism that kept La Costa numb to the realities of her fate. But, unfortunately, it also blinded her greatly to the truth—that she was also numbing her soul. A feeling that frightened her to the core whenever she allowed it to surface.

CHAPTER TEN

1995

I T WAS WELL PAST SEVEN one morning when La Costa noticed that Panther had not come home the night before. The last she had seen of her was at some screen-director's place in Woodland Hills, diving into a crystalline heart-shaped swimming pool fully clothed, while a coked-out cadre of partygoers looked on.

Was she all right? La Costa wondered. *Panther had been pretty messed up.* It wasn't like her to just leave a party without checking on each other's whereabouts. *She remembered vaguely stumbling into the game room, where a man and a woman were arguing, trying to settle a bet. She staggered past the billiard table, where another couple was copulating right there on the green felt. Someone was tugging at her arm, and, wasted out of her mind . . . she followed. The tinkling of ice in his rock glass made her giggle . . . they waded through a hazy crowd of burnouts and junkies, leaning against the living room walls and stretched out on the floor. She remembered seeing two other girls from the club that she knew, Shana and Goldie. They waved her over. Shana was waving a champagne glass, and then the four of them stepped out onto the patio. That's where she saw Panther, plunging out of the pool, running to the garden shed, peeling her skirt and blouse off as she ran; her straight black hair flowing down her back. She was laughing and falling down in the grass beneath a gigantic summer moon.*

That was all La Costa could remember. Nothing more. The rest of the memory went dark. She couldn't remember how she even got home. Thankfully, she awoke in her own bed—alone. She was wearing the same outfit from the night before.

Panther's bed, however, hadn't been slept in.

The telephone razzed her brain from a deep sleep. "La Costa . . . it's Shana!" She was frantic and breathless. "It's Panther—we're at County General. Jesus Christ, she wasn't *breathing!* We found her this morning, lying beside the pool—out cold. They're trying to pump her stomach now or some shit. Oh, God—Lucy's gonna fucking freak out!"

La Costa didn't bother changing. Dumping the contents of her purse onto the bed, she grabbed her keys and was out the door. The five shared a racy Corvette that was parked up the street. La Costa ran the four blocks to the garage with her high-heeled sandals tucked beneath her arm. Then she jumped behind the wheel and sped to the hospital, holding her splitting head all the way. At any moment, she feared, she would lose focus and hurl the red rocket into an oncoming lane. Tears streamed down her cheeks, burning her lips. The stale, rancid taste in her throat was a mixture of whiskey, cheese dip, and bile. She blew her nose on a fast-food napkin from the floorboard and prayed aloud as the wind rushed through her as she sped fearlessly and recklessly along the freeway. "Please, dear God . . . don't let her die! Please don't let Panther die!"

La Costa bolted through the emergency entrance doors

and was instantly hit with the unmistakable stench of the trauma ward, mixed with the stale tangle of smells that always permeate hospitals. Sour wafts of air, antiseptic . . . sterile . . . full of fear. Of death.

Residents in lab coats and blue scrubs hurried in and out of doors, and orderlies in green uniforms wheeled carts and gurneys in all directions. La Costa sprinted to the large reception desk breathlessly.

"I'm looking for a friend, Panther—I mean, *Phyllis St. James*. She was brought in this morning."

The attendant coolly checked her computer screen, pecking at the keys while she cracked her gum, with little regard for the chaos that was erupting in all directions around her. Just another day at the office. The gold hoop earrings that swung from her earlobes were enormous. She eyed the polyester smock the woman was wearing and noted the cluster of tangled chains and crucifixes that covered her plastic access badge around her neck. It read: "HI—I'M DESTINEE. HOW CAN I HELP YOU?"

On the other side of the counter, Destinee saw a hooker. A dirty whore. Fearful and frantic for any news about her hooker friend. La Costa read this in her eyes. It was common. Outside the world of the club, people didn't see things quite the same way.

"Released." Destinee drawled the word languidly.

Destinee looked a lot like she knew things. Like how to fry chicken, sew a quilt, raise a bunch of children—do what was expected of her in the real world. She grabbed a hospital brochure and pointed to a phone number with an enormously curved gold fingernail and tapped it on the page. "This here's the outreach center. Give them a call and have your friend see someone for follow-up counseling."

La Costa nodded fuzzily. She had been crying a lot, and her nose was still dripping. A skinny white nurse next to her handed her a tissue. "She'll need to see a physician in two weeks for another evaluation, if she wants to get clean, that is," Destinee continued, all business. She whipped a business card out of nowhere. "Have her contact this place—it's expensive, but it's good. Public aid won't pay. So, if she can't swing it, then see to it she gets help *someplace*."

Destinee looked at La Costa long enough to surmise the answer but asked anyway. "Are you a . . . relative?"

"No, ma'am. Just a friend."

La Costa had never had a friend before. She never really thought about it. It never mattered before. The thought of standing by and watching Panther slowly kill herself was more than she could bear. She was the closest thing to a sister she had ever had.

What are we doing? La Costa ruminated. *Night after night . . . the parties. . . the drugs?* It was an incessant cycle of destruction, and although La Costa managed to teeter on the brink of its whirling gravitational pull just barely getting by unscathed, Panther, however, was not so fortunate. She was quickly going down, and would soon be swallowed up. This, La Costa was certain, if she kept up the reckless pace, would be the fatal outcome.

La Costa knew it. Destinee, the emergency room attendant, knew it, but how? How would she attempt to convince Panther? She was her friend, that's all she knew. Panther had given her a break in life that helped her to get out of her ghetto apartment and into a better place. A place with a new family of sisters and a sort of crazy den mother in Lucy DuMont. It was a strange type of family indeed, but it was a family, nonetheless. She had Panther to thank for it. Now it was time for her to give something back to her—whether she liked it or not.

This was a wake-up call if there ever was one. La Costa vowed then and there that she would figure out a way to save both of them from the wrecking ball that was hurling straight toward them. She had twenty-one hundred dollars saved in an empty peanut butter jar beneath her bed. That, along with tips from the next two weeks, would amount to enough to check Panther into a local hospital's rehabilitation program.

All the way back to the apartment, La Costa rehearsed her speech and how she would convince Panther that she needed help—they both did. How she would tell her she would get help too, and that she was only doing this because she loved her.

When she arrived back at the apartment, she was stunned to find that Panther still was not there. *Didn't Shana bring her home?*

One of the four house Kittens, Jizzy, had reported seeing Panther run through just a half hour prior. "She flew in and out of here with her loser boyfriend, AJ, about an hour ago. Said something about going to Vegas and not to worry. She'd see you at the club on Friday. By the way, rent's due tomorrow. She didn't happen to give you her share, did she?"

La Costa puzzled. "Vegas?" A frightening jolt pitched her stomach one full rotation. *Shit!* She rushed to her bedroom and felt frantically beneath the bed for the plastic jar. She knew it would be empty even before she looked at it.

When Friday came and went with no sign of Panther, La Costa was worried. An emotion that quickly turned to anger when she learned that Panther had called in sick for her weekend shifts.

"Sick, my ass!" La Costa fumed when she read the roster and saw Panther's name crossed out in red. Panther's name had been struck for "illness." The other girls nodded and shrugged their shoulders incredulously.

"What's she up to now? Scared us all out of our minds!" Shana said.

"Who knows? That girl does any old crazy thing she pleases," said Jizzy. "How fair is that to us, who have to pick up her slack? Ungrateful *bitch!*"

They all agreed, chiming in with nods and *tsks* as they primped their lashes and brows in the dressing room mirrors.

"Yeah, and why'd she leave with *him?*" Goldie said, slamming her locker.

Everyone knew that AJ was bad news by anyone's standards. At just twenty-one, he was a Jamaican giant, mean as a snake, and disliked by most everyone. He was known to be violent and controlling, but somehow, he had convinced Panther to run away with him and La Costa's money. They were probably blowing every cent of it at that very moment in the casinos.

"Well, she'd better be winning—that's all I can say," Jizzy quipped as she fastened the hooks of her sequined bra. "She's gonna need it to get her room back. She stiffed us again on the rent. Frankly, I'm sick of her shit! Girl's gotta learn how to manage her cabbage. I say, we kick her ass out and let Monique come live with us instead. She's been looking for a place for weeks."

The bevy of scantily clad beauties agreed.

Monique brightened. She was a rookie recruit with butt-length auburn hair and mile-long legs that went on for days. Shana had brought her in from a club in Dallas. She did not strip, but she would make enough serving cocktails to pay for her share of the rent. In the fall she would be starting up at the university, majoring in—what else? Theater. It was all smoke and mirrors.

"Monique could have a place closer to campus, and believe me, this one won't piss away her pay!" Shana added. "It's fine by me," she told the others.

"It's yours if you want it, honey," Goldie chimed in.

Monique nodded, smiling.

Jizzy examined her reflection in the mirror. She was one of the more seasoned Kittens with mounting seniority. She was a living Barbie doll if she ever there was one—all beach-blonde hair and five-hundred-watt teeth, right down to her over-baked tan. Everything about her competed for attention, making one wonder what was and what wasn't real. She looked positively plastic. It was always La Costa's practice to stay as far away from the girl as possible. In fact, she hated her type.

"It's settled, then," Jizzy said, lifting her serving tray, rearranging the pens and matchbooks inside the rock glass that served to anchor a stack of pink-and-black-striped cocktail napkins. Then, she looked squarely at La Costa. "Anyone got a problem with that?" she said, her fake baby blues all a-blink, knowing full well about the friendship between La Costa and Panther.

La Costa nodded morosely and said nothing. No one else seemed to care, nor did they believe that Panther would be coming back. And so, it was done. Panther was officially OUT.

Five weeks passed without so much as a phone call or a post card from Panther. La Costa thought she might know how to find her family. She knew that her parents were split and that she might have a brother who lived in Denver. She could not remember. Panther had been vague on her family details and could have high-tailed it to Colorado, or anywhere in the world by now. La Costa thought better of trying to track Panther's brother down. What would she say? "Hi, I'm a good friend of your sister's . . . we stripped at the Mink Kitty here in Los Angeles and serviced gentlemen clients. I was wondering if you have heard from Panther lately?" *Right!* She didn't think so.

Monique moved into the apartment and took over Panther's side of the room. They were six living in a three-bedroom unit. It was ample enough, as someone was always coming or going at all hours. Best of all, it was located just blocks away from the club. The shared apartment was the nicest digs La Costa had ever lived in. But now, with her best friend having betrayed her trust, she liked the setup a whole lot less. *What was she doing?* she wondered. *Wasn't everyone just out for themselves?* Why did she even think she could trust anyone? In the end, it was the disappointment in losing a friend that mattered more to La Costa than the money. She could find a way to make more.

She sighed heavily when she finally made up her mind—staring into the makeup mirror was when she did her best thinking. She was exhausted. She was sick and tired of men hungrily eyeing her from a distant chair in the smoke-haze darkness of the dingy club. Tired of the charade that lured them to come in, night after night . . . helping themselves to her. The money was meaningless, she decided, after all. If the act of earning it did not kill any ounce of decency she had left inside, then surely spending it on drugs, booze, and fast living would. She would end up like Panther, gambling with her very life one way or another if she stayed. This would not do. Not anymore.

It was not going to be easy to walk away from it all—the money, the attention, and the thrill of being a Kitten. It wasn't the noblest of things, but it was something. Something that wasn't serving her quite like she had hoped. In a world that valued sex and beauty seemingly more than being chaste and invisible, ordinary girls did not receive the perks in life. She knew this. "Ordinary" did not open doors or influence powerful people. She was smart enough to realize that she had gotten all that she could from Lucy DuMont's world. It was over, and time to move on.

La Costa had a stack of business cards that were tied with a large rubber band and buried in her lingerie drawer. One hundred seventy-seven of them, given to her by various patrons from the club over the years—business executives, modeling reps, porn scouts, born-again Christians, nearly somebodies and truly nobodies—everyone had a calling card, it seemed. They loved to slip her their pitch with the flick of a wrist: "My card. Call me if you ever need 'whatever.'" Just fill in the blank.

There was one in particular, though, that she was searching for. It was a patron she knew who lived in Nevada. He was a nice gentleman, a "regular" client of hers, who visited the club at least every couple of months when he was in LA on business. She shuffled through the stack and located his card with ease. It was white with gold metallic raised lettering that looked like a playing card. The Ace of Diamonds. It read: *Gerald W. Hildebrand, Executive Vice President, Nevada Chamber of Commerce.* On the back was a hand-written promise, sealed in blue ink: *If ever you're in Vegas, Lucky La Costa, look me up. You're aces with me, kid!"*

She smiled when she remembered Gerry and his funny way of always talking in clichés. He was a throwback from another era, like a character from an old black-and-white movie. He was in his late fifties, a tan, lean, and silver-haired white gentleman who was an heir to the Hildebrand hotel dynasty. He often spoke to her of the promise to get her a job if ever she was ready to hang up the garters and glitter.

That was, *if* she wanted it. He called it "respectable work," like in an office or department store. She had his word, and she knew that with him, it was as good as gold. The card was her ticket to a new beginning.

She placed the call.

Three weeks later, La Costa packed all her belongings and bid a teary goodbye to Lucy and all the girls. They had thrown her a little farewell party in the club's kitchen just before opening the day before she left. Manuel had baked her an extraordinary cake in the shape of breasts, with pink and red sprinkles around the gumdrop nipples. They all signed a gag card that was so raunchy, it made her blush to read it in the presence of the entire staff who made their living around elevating titillating sex to an art form. Colored condoms were inflated and tied to her locker, made to resemble festive balloons. The crowning moment came when "Al" a blowup male doll was presented to her with a chorus of hoots and applause.

"He'll be your driving companion, La Costa! Not a single word all the way to Vegas! Just prop him in the passenger's seat and go!" Monique giggled.

And Lucy was quick to point out, "Yeah, and his *wanger* points north, so you'll never get off course . . . unless you *want* to, that is!"

Everyone howled. They were guzzling champagne and trying not to peel away the layers that would show their own true feelings, envying La Costa for having the guts to leave.

"Say hi to Panther, when you see her!" Jizzy piped sarcastically.

"Yeah, if you can find her!" Shana tossed.

"I will." La Costa smiled, secretly hoping in her heart it

was possible. Vegas was a big town, and there was no telling where on earth Panther and AJ could have ended up—or even if they were still together.

Someone handed La Costa her name moniker from her locker before she took off. She tucked it into her purse. She promised them all that she would keep it forever and never, ever forget them. It would be the only thing she would take from that life. That, and a shoebox filled with photos and few pieces of memorabilia from the club. The lead bartender, Scotty "Rocks" Renior from the club's main bar, loaded her down with swizzle sticks, ashtrays, and matchbooks for the memory vault. "Have a sweet life, Miss La Costa," he said with a shit-eating grin that always made her smile.

"I'm gonna try," she said, forcing herself not to cry. All the extra attention made her feel strangely vulnerable. The Mink Kitty had been for her, a true family.

It was five forty-five, and soon would be time for the club's doors to open. Everyone scurried to their stations around the bar, the lounge, and in the main dining room, throwing kisses her way as they waved and bid La Costa all the best.

She took one more lingering look and then turned for the back service door, leaving the Mink Kitty's illustrious VIP show lounge and stage that night and forever, with one less Kitten.

CHAPTER ELEVEN

NEWPORT BEACH, CA
2014

L A COSTA AND FELICIA BROKE for lunch on the deck, beneath the bright summer sky and a commotion of beachgoers, vacationers, and residents dotting the shore with their colorful towels, umbrellas, and watercraft. There was a simple lunch consisting of a spring greens salad and croissant sandwiches with spicy deli meats, basil, and melted provolone. Fresh fruit—a medley of melons and berries—accompanied the meal for good measure, but the highlight, La Costa's famed peach pie, was cooling on the kitchen counter for later.

"I thought you'd enjoy a change of scenery, so I've had our lunch set out here," La Costa said as the two walked onto the gray-washed planks of the stunning deck, greeted by the screams of seagulls and children laughing. A large patio table and two chairs were waiting. A handsome young man in his twenties had just finished pouring the ice waters and placing the pitcher in the center of the table.

"Thank you, Florian," La Costa said.

He was her personal assistant, an intern from USC with aspirations for a major in musical arts. As it was, it took a small army of individuals behind the scenes to help her do what she did with seemingly effortless ease. La Costa called on him whenever she could, to delegate the necessary mundane tasks that would otherwise eat up her precious writing time. "Enjoy your lunch, Ms. Reed," he said. "Coffee is brewing. I'll check back with you to see if you need anything done for the book promos running tomorrow."

Felicia's eyes widened. "Does he cook?"

"No, this is all catered. But he is a *whiz* with technology and keeps my calendar and my social media presence humming, as they call it. I'd be dead in the water without him!"

Felicia smiled, and La Costa handed her a plate. "Dig in."

The tape recorder was turned off as they enjoyed a delicious meal, talking about things like motherhood, demanding work schedules, and slipping into middle age with as much aplomb and grace as possible. Felicia, a seasoned sixty-something, regarded her short-cropped platinum hair as a badge of honor. "You just come to know things, don't you? I mean, by the time you come into a certain age," Felicia said wistfully as she surveyed the vast horizon where the water and the sky met perfectly, uncluttered, with not a single cloud in sight.

"I do believe that you're right. However, I would like to think that life still has much to teach us, no matter what manner it has brought us to where we are today," La Costa said. She drew in a long, full breath and exhaled. "I have nothing but gratitude for my scars, you know? Wouldn't change a thing if I could."

Felicia pressed her palms together and sighed. "Exactly!

And that, my dear, is what people want to believe for themselves as well—what you write about in your books, your heroines—they speak to women and encourage them."

"I truly hope so," La Costa said, modestly.

"Shall we continue, then?" Felicia said, reaching for the recorder and her notes. "Out here, or inside?"

"Let's go back inside," La Costa said. "I have some more photos I'd like to show you."

Moments later, the two were seated at a large oak dining table, where La Costa had scads of photos strewn about, taken from photo albums, faded with age. A few framed photos were taken from a wall in her den, and a stack of notebooks and journals lay about like old friends, in neat piles that were arranged in chronological order.

"Coffee or tea?" La Costa asked Felicia, whose eyes widened at the colorful array of artifacts and memorabilia on the table and the sheer magnitude of the care that La Costa had taken to collect and preserve her memories.

"Tea, please. Thank you. I can't wait to jump into all of this. Where do we start?"

La Costa chuckled. "Well, with what came next—there's always another chapter waiting around the corner. Mine was when I met my guardian angel."

CHAPTER TWELVE

LAS VEGAS, NV
1995

L A COSTA READ THE SLIP of paper that had grown moist and soggy in her clenched fist. The climate was brutal, and felt like a blast furnace breathing in her face. It was only eight a.m., and already, her makeup was melting. At least in LA, there was the occasional breeze to save you. Nevada, it seemed, just stayed hot; so hot in fact, she feared that she would just morph into a puddle right there on the sidewalk.

She could feel the thin fabric of her silk blouse grow wet beneath her armpits. She pressed the intercom at the main entrance door, and a woman's voice answered from the tiny speaker.

"Prestige . . . who's calling, please?"

"It's La Costa Jackson, ma'am. I am a friend of Gerald Hildebrand here to see Mrs. Byrne."

Gerald Hildebrand's secretary, Evelyn, had given La Costa the street address, as well as a list of available apartments in the area. She was temporarily staying at the MGM Grand, compliments of Gerry's generosity, just until she could land a job and a place of her own. Evelyn had made the arrangements, no questions asked, as was her practice in keeping her employer's secrets, and his business humming. La Costa appreciated the woman's candor, especially when she had referred to La Costa as being a favorite "associate" of Gerry's from the West Coast. "Mr. Hildebrand is out of town just now on business," Evelyn had said. "However, Ms. Jackson, he has asked me to assist you in getting settled. He'll be back on Friday from Phoenix, and he can meet with you then. Oh, did a package arrive at your hotel room?"

"Yes, thank you. I got Gerry's . . . *gift.*" She had stopped herself, and cringed. He would be expecting the usual. A naughty romp with whips and toys and playthings, the likes of which would make a dominatrix flinch. The box of "goodies" had arrived, all right, ready for action, along with two dozen long-stemmed roses. Gerry was a pervert, but at least he was a gentleman about it. She would be ready for him when he came to claim her appreciation for the whopping favor. That's just the way it worked with Gerry.

The intercom crackled, and La Costa was melting by the second in the blasting heat.

"Oh, Miss Jackson, yes. Please do come up."

A moment passed, and then the buzzer sounded, unlatching the door. La Costa slid gratefully from the sidewalk into the cool foyer, out of the punishing heat. The interior of the building looked a lot like an old warehouse that had been converted into several separate office suites. It turned out to have been an old canning mill at one time, reminding her of a John Steinbeck novel.

An open freight-type elevator was waiting not two feet in front of her. It resembled a large open cage, looking odd and out of place in the stark brick building. It had a red painted gate and no solid doors. She stepped into it, and a feeling of excitement washed over her, along with a rush of coolness from an open-air vent. The elevator lurched upward with a jolt, shaking a little on its ascent. Waiting there at the top of the second floor was an attractive middle-aged woman in a Chanel suit. She had an inviting smile and two tall glasses of iced tea, one in each hand.

"Hello, La Costa! I'm Georgia Byrne. It's hotter than Satan's house cat, wouldn't ya say?"

CHAPTER THIRTEEN

(TWELVE MONTHS LATER)
LAS VEGAS, NV

THE AGENCY WAS NOTHING LIKE Sophisticate, where La Costa had worked as a temp nearly five years prior, with its gleaming high-rise windows and labyrinth of cubicles, wardrobe rooms, and massive photo studio. By comparison, Prestige was much smaller; a one-woman business not keen on competing for the high-dollar clients. Rather, Georgia ran her little agency like a cherished vocation, in which she hoped to refine young girls into ladies that she could be proud to represent.

A relic from another time, Georgia valued manners and propriety. She had once taught high etiquette to young debutantes in her home state of South Carolina, which would later become the basis of a budding talent agency that she and her beloved husband, Macklin, would run years later on the East Coast.

It had been nearly a year since La Costa had left LA, and the club life, behind. She was embracing a new life now, thanks to the generosity of Georgia Byrne. She had been gracious and patient with her new employee, teaching La

Costa how she liked to arrange the composites—client lists, accounting ledgers, and computer files. La Costa was a quick learner and had buckets of common sense in her very pretty head. Georgia didn't mind having to show her how to format a memo or process a new model into the system. She had a keen eye for fashion and proved invaluable, helping in preparing new young models for their first photo sessions and go-sees.

La Costa was, herself, a natural beauty. Smart, conscientious, and loyal—a virtue not seen very often in the business. She was creative, too, and eventually began drafting rough ads for some of the agency's best customers. Clients enjoyed her pleasant banter on the phone, and it was La Costa's helpful idea to change the look of Prestige's brochure to attract more business from the local corporate sectors.

Most of all, La Costa had a real sense of gratitude toward Georgia, for taking her on with little clerical experience, and for trusting her and not asking a lot of questions about her past, or anything else she didn't want to talk about. La Costa was certainly striking enough to model herself, but declined at every turn, as she had other aspirations, it was clear. Georgia was as pleased as she could be to be able to help her along.

The job paid for a modest one-bedroom apartment in Henderson, just fifteen minutes from the Strip. No one had her address, especially not Gerald Hildebrand, whom, as it turned out, was Georgia's brother-in-law by marriage. Little did Georgia know of her dear relative's proclivity for young black women with whom he wanted to indulge his every perverse fantasy—which included tying him to bedposts and beating him with jump ropes and other childhood props. Once La Costa moved into the Double Aces Courtyard complex, she never heard from him again. She was certain that except for rare and infrequent occasions, neither did Georgia.

Not one for surprises, La Costa got a big one the day that she looked up from her desk during a casting call and saw Phyllis Jean St. James, a.k.a., Panther St. James, walking through the front door of the reception lobby! There Panther was, in the flesh—coming to apply to model for Prestige.

La Costa couldn't believe her eyes. She had searched every dance club and scoured every strip bar twice over, for the past year, asking around and combing the internet for a lead, any clue as to where Panther might be. Unfortunately, after meeting with nothing but dead ends, she had decided to give up. After all, there was no guarantee that Panther was even still in Las Vegas anyway.

Then, this one ordinary day, Panther simply walked into Prestige.

La Costa could not help but see it as a sign. Their paths, which had once crossed, were about to cross again. In a moment of panic, La Costa wondered, what she would say to her. Did Panther even *know* that she was working there? What if she didn't want to be found?

Panther looked starved-thin and gaunt. Her once-gleaming caramel skin was sallow and ashy. She did not look, in the least, like herself. A deluge of time and troubles, along, no doubt, with too many collective years of substance abuse had taken a toll on her natural attributes, finally robbing her of her light and vitality. She appeared to have aged at least five years in the span of one. La Costa could hardly believe it.

Still, Panther held her head high and proudly flipped her licorice-black hair with the Cleopatra cut—choppy bangs and long strands that fell past her gaunt shoulders. She tossed her chin when she spoke, enlisting the heart-stopping power of those amber eyes that were swathed in smoky shadow, duly concealed beneath a curtain of sweeping black lashes. She was, it seemed, hiding much beneath the surface, but the camera would forgive an indubitable number of grievances, and on some level, she still had what it took. If anyone had the power to salvage and redeem herself, it was Panther.

La Costa watched as Panther was ushered into the conference room to meet with Georgia, who would be seated at the head of the table to oversee the consultation.

Not ten minutes later, Panther emerged from the room, bypassed the reception desk, and headed for the exit. It was La Costa's moment to make her presence known. She caught up with Panther at the elevator. The hallway was otherwise deserted, as Prestige was the only business on the second floor. *No better time than the present*, La Costa thought, swallowing hard and reaching out to tap Panther lightly on the back.

"Hey, Kitty Cat!" It was La Costa's nickname for her. Nobody else called her that, so the words did more than stop her in her tracks. Panther positively squealed with joy, when she spun around to find La Costa beaming back at her.

"Holy shit, girl! What are *you* doing here?" She gasped, letting her gym bag slip to the floor and throwing her bone-thin arms around La Costa, wrapping her in a skeletal embrace, smelling like *Shalimar*, her signature scent. And only then did La Costa truly believe that it was real. Panther was alive and well and standing right there!

Up close, La Costa could see that Panther had acquired a tiny scar near her mouth and had tried to cover up a bruise on her left forearm with stage makeup. She wondered if

Georgia was able to detect it during the interview and assumed, she likely had, as nothing slid past her. Panther was wearing a white cotton blouse, a short floral skirt, and red stilettos. Her bare legs were still as long and lean as a racehorse.

"You look great, as usual," La Costa said.

"You do too!" she said. "Are you modeling here? With the agency?"

La Costa smiled. "No, I work here—for Georgia Byrne. I'm her office assistant. I love it."

"That is so cool. I mean, you can take care of me, right? With the old lady? I could really use the money. I'll do just about anything, right? Trade show work, fragrance promotions, you name it. They have my comp."

"Yeah, sure. Of course. I'll see what I can do. But I'm just her gopher, you know. Georgia does all the hiring."

Panther nodded.

They both laughed nervously, and then Panther added, "I'm teaching jazzercise at the YMCA near I-15 twice a week and on Saturdays. You should come by sometime."

"Sure, maybe," La Costa said, noticing that Panther was not looking her in the eyes. The obvious issue was hanging in the air between them. Finally, La Costa blurted, "I thought you were gone for good, the way you took off and all."

Panther dabbed her forehead. The air in the hallway was stifling, and the heat index rising by the millisecond. "Yeah, well, I didn't actually *plan* it that way. But sometimes . . . you know, shit happens. That reminds me—I still owe you guys money for back rent. I'm intending to send that off to Shana back at the club in LA as soon as I can get caught up."

Who was she kidding? La Costa thought. *Like that would ever happen now.* It was evident that Panther had selective memory about what she had done—if she had even been in her right mind when she split. It was obvious that Panther had no intention of acknowledging the level of betrayal that had preceded her exit from La Costa's life. In spite of all that, it was good seeing her old friend. What did it matter what happened back then? It was all in the past. *People change, don't they?* La Costa thought, placating her own skepticism. She only really knew one thing for certain: it was pure fate that they had ended up in the exact same place—again.

"I heard that Georgia is the best in town. So, when I decided to pick up some modeling work, I naturally wanted to check Prestige out. Girl, I'm so glad I did," Panther said.

The truth, though she chose not to share it, was that none of the dozen other agencies in the area would hire her on. She had seemingly lost her stride.

"I'm glad you did too." La Costa beamed. She was happy, yet beginning to feel a little uneasy by the strained awkwardness. "Well, I gotta get back to work," she said, checking her watch. "Give me your number, and I'll call you."

"We don't exactly have a phone. AJ says it's a useless expense. He carries a pager. If anyone needs to get a hold of him, he hits up a pay phone."

La Costa cringed. That explained a lot. Maybe everything. *She was still with that abusive loser from the past?* "Well, here's my phone number," La Costa said, writing it on the back of one of the agency's business cards. "I'm living at a complex called the Double Aces in Henderson."

"No way, girl. You shittin' me? That's where *we* live! Unit two twenty-four—wow! This is amazing. We're neighbors!" They sprang into a fit of laughter mixed with incredulous head wagging. "What are the chances of *that?*"

"Serendipity, I think they call it," La Costa said. "I'm literally only a few doors down from you two." She scrawled her apartment number on the card. "Is the world a small place, or *what?*"

"I'll say," Panther said, slipping the enormous gym bag onto her bony shoulder. She held up the card and smiled widely.

"I can't believe this," La Costa said as she headed back to the cool office through the glass door.

Panther echoed the sentiment with a *"Whoot!"* as she stepped onto the waiting elevator. She pressed the bottom button on the panel, causing the ornate red gate to slide shut, and the ancient elevator to slowly make its descent. "Me either," she said, exhaling. *Me either.*

CHAPTER FOURTEEN

PANTHER WASTED NO TIME IN reacquainting herself with her old friend and called the very next day to suggest they have lunch, an event that quickly turned into a weekly habit for the next several months. They met every Tuesday for sandwiches near the park just up the street from Prestige, at a row of picnic tables beneath a shady awning, located across from a shopping strip.

La Costa could not believe that she was actually able to share a part of her new life with someone who knew her past—every horrible and wonderful detail of it. She remembered how the two used to sit up all night talking or passing the time during slow shifts at the club, trading painful and regrettable childhood stories. Panther's life, although not as volatile as La Costa's, was really not all that different. It was most likely the reason that the two had connected so strongly in the first place. The Mink Kitty was their bond and always would be. But now, it was a million miles behind them, as so much had changed seemingly overnight. Neither mentioned what had happened, or spoke of Panther's chucking it all into the wind and making a run for it, leaving responsibilities and everything behind. For La Costa, just having had the common link was enough. Besides, in so many ways, Panther seemed to have changed, yet again, from her wild and reckless ways. La Costa was sure of it, and the feeling of gratitude for both of their transformations was what she intended to focus on.

"Sorry, I've only got thirty minutes today. Georgia needs me for an important client meeting at one o'clock," La Costa explained, while unwrapping a chicken salad sandwich on her lap.

"Look at you! Miss hot-shot junior executive," Panther enthused. "Client meetings at the boss's request. Snap! That's big time!"

"Right." La Costa's voice dropped an octave. "Well, I guess it beats taking off your clothes and being gawked at by perverts all night—" She caught herself and stopped abruptly.

Panther's pained look told all.

"Oh, I'm so sorry, Panth. You're not still dancing, are you?" Of course, by *dancing* she meant *stripping*. And by the dead silence, she knew the answer before Panther could confirm it.

"Well, only in between the side jobs. Modeling for Prestige and teaching classes at the Y is nowhere near enough to keep afloat. It's just until my *real* career takes off. Don't tell Georgia, okay? She can't know."

La Costa nodded. Of course she would not tell Georgia, and also would not tell the fact that the agency only took Panther on as a favor to her. But, in fairness, it wasn't as if La Costa's life played out like a Disney movie. Who, after all, was she to judge? She felt foolish and sorry for implying that Panther could not do better.

"I know this guy, he's a friend of AJ's. Anyway, he knows some people who make films in Hollywood. I could introduce you to him. He's great. His name is Zander. He's the reason we came out here in the first place, to try and get me into one of his movies. He's gotten me a gig at Baby Dolls off the south end of the Strip—just until things pop."

La Costa nodded. Her mind was anywhere but in the ballpark in which Panther was pitching. Those days were behind her. Vegas was Sin City, all right, but she did not come there to fall prey to the trappings of making an easy buck. She wanted to do things right, earn her way, for once in her life. Working for Georgia at Prestige gave her something that stripping never had—pride in herself.

"No thanks, Panth. I'm fine, really."

The once-exotic beauty smiled. "Of course you are, hon. I am so happy for you, and grateful for all of your help in getting me signed on here at Prestige and all. You're a doll, and I am going to find a way to pay you back. I promise."

La Costa smiled. "Eat your sandwich, girl. I gotta get back to work."

Over the next several months, their lunch visits dwindled. La Costa saw less and less of her friend around the apartment complex, or at the agency. Sometimes she would run into her and AJ getting into their car, or checking the mailbox. AJ, otherwise known as Alfred James Williams, was a towering black dude with deep Jamaican brown skin, a shaved cue-ball head, and a ratty goatee. He drove around in a red Eldorado convertible with white interior and wore mirrored shades all the time, day or night. He was a shifty, mean misogynist. La Costa remembered Panther telling her how he once served eighteen months for dealing cocaine when he was a teen. It was a woman who tipped him off to the cops, a woman who prosecuted him, and a female judge who put him in a hellhole in Joliet, Illinois. His rap sheet filled three binders with everything from harassment complaints to assault cases from a litany of convictions and charges brought about from past acquaintances, neighbors, and ex-girlfriends too numerous to count. It was clear to anyone with eyes that he flat-out despised women, as he was often heard to say, "They's all whores and bitches to me." He blared offensive Hip Hop and Rap lyrics unapologetically from the booming speakers of his car—a soundtrack to his twisted, vengeful, brooding persona. He wore several gold chains around his massive neck, and large, fake diamond studs in his enormous earlobes. He had huge tatted-up fists. He wore a jagged, brown scar on his forehead like a badge of honor, acquired from a prison fight. He had played Russian roulette more than once and lived to tell. A control freak to the core, he feared no one. AJ was a bold gambler, a sore loser, and a bully. He used people to get ahead, drifting from one deal to the next, hoping to score a quick buck and gain *fuck-you-world* fame. Hooking up with Panther was the worst twist of fate that could have befallen her. Trouble was, she just couldn't see it.

Whenever La Costa saw AJ, he made her skin crawl. Plain and simple, he was bad news.

Panther and AJ liked to frequent a dance club where La Costa went on Friday nights herself, called The Copa. It was a neighborhood haunt just off the Strip, where she could let loose and dance without anyone bothering her. It was a chance to get out on the shiny-lighted dance floors just like everyone else, to get lost in the pulsing strobe lights and heart-thumping dance tracks of the seventies-style retro discothèque. There, in a crowd of hundreds of people, nobody knew her name. That's how she preferred it.

On occasion, La Costa would run into Panther—late, presumably after she had worked a shift or two at one the casinos or highway strip-clubs. The venues where she worked were constantly changing. Strung out and still with her stage makeup packed on, Panther would stumble into the dance club with AJ, who led her around by her coked-up nose.

Oddly, their presence always instantly commanded a table to be cleared, when there was barely standing room to be had in the lounge or on the crowded dance floors. An entourage of eight or more would soon join them. Shady-looking goons like AJ, and their stripper girlfriends in flimsy halter tops and hot pants.

La Costa knew a porn actress when she saw one. And, frightfully, Panther fit right in, making a drug and drunken display of herself on more than one occasion.

That was always La Costa's cue to leave.

The night that La Costa heard shouts—once again—coming from outside Panther and AJ's apartment, was for her, a turning point. La Costa approached the door once they were inside to see if Panther was okay. She had not seen or heard from Panther in days, which was not unusual. But when La Costa heard Panther's desperate screams and bursts of shattered glass that sent every dog in the complex barking, she could not ignore it. She high-tailed it back to her own apartment unit and called 9-1-1. Who knew what AJ was capable of? She dialed the police and waited, praying that they would hurry.

Through the peephole in her door, she could see AJ back on the balcony, shouting obscenities and delivering violent kicks to their apartment door. The sound of Panther's pleading cries emitted from the parking lot, where she had since run frantically for cover. Legions of squad cars met them on the hot asphalt with their sirens blaring and lights flashing.

La Costa sighed with relief and then turned out her porch light. It would be over and forgotten by the morning.

Until it started up again.

It was always about sex, or drugs, or both. Either Panther was not putting out enough, or just physically could not keep up with AJ's reckless escapades. But when AJ had successfully put Panther in Urgent Care with a fractured wrist and multiple contusions, La Costa could not stand idly by any longer.

"Leave him, Panth. Leave the bastard, or die. It's as simple as that."

"I . . . can't," the defeated young woman said, wincing from searing pain that was far stronger than the paltry drip of Tylenol that she was hooked up to. "I have nowhere to go. Besides, he's my acting agent. He's representing me."

"Acting? For skin flicks? Panther, he's *pimping* you. Don't you see that?" La Costa said. "You'll move in with me. You'll get a steady paying job. Forget all about the men's clubs and this porn acting that he's pushing you into. I'm serious, Panth, but I'm only offering this if you promise to quit all of it. *Everything.*"

Panther did not know what to say. She simply blinked back the tears that burned her swollen, bruised eyes. No one had ever showed her such unconditional kindness. *No one.* La Costa was not just anyone. She was a true friend. "I can pay you back. It will take some time, but—"

La Costa smiled. "Hey, you helped me out once too, remember? If it weren't for that, I wouldn't be here. I mean it. Now it's my turn to help you out—all the way out."

They were the exact words that Panther wanted to hear. Fortunately, she didn't lose the baby through it all. She would be needing her dear friend's kindness more than ever. More than La Costa could ever begin to imagine.

CHAPTER FIFTEEN

SPRING 1997

WHEN AJ FIRST HEARD ABOUT the baby, he delivered a beating so severe to Panther that she ended up at Valley Medical for injuries incurred while attempting to flee from his pounding fists and unremitting verbal assaults.

She had been packing her things to move in with La Costa, and he caught her.

"Where do you think you're going?" he said, standing like a mountain, blocking the path from the bathroom to the bedroom door.

She had just finished zipping up her cosmetic case when he pushed her hard against the bathroom sink, causing her forehead to hit the mirror.

"I'm going away! Me and my baby are leavin' here and ain't comin' back!"

"You're *what?*" AJ was incredulous. He stood, stupid and silent at first, and then saw the suitcases stacked by the bed. His lips quivered and then broke into a grin. "Naw." He chuckled, eerie and manic. "Aw, *HELL NO!*" he said, pounding his giant fist into the wall.

Panther slid beneath his massive arm, still stuck in the drywall, and ran in the opposite direction of her belongings, toward the front door.

"Stupid, goddamn bitch! You whored yourself to someone else—that's what happened! Didn't it? Fucking liar! You think I would *want* you to have my kid?" He grabbed her arm with a gigantic hand and twisted until she begged for him to stop. He could have easily snapped it off her body like a twig. "Fucking garbage! That's what you is, whore! Now you've gone and done it. Well I ain't payin' a fucking dime for your bastard-dick runt, I'll tell you that!"

He lunged at her with a broad-sided kick and struck her squarely in the chest, just missing her abdomen. She went down with a wail. "It's *yours*, AJ, I swear!"

"There!" he said, kicking her in the back. "It's probably a retard anyway—I'm just helping its vegetable ass out a little." AJ rearranged his pinky ring and smoothed his trousers because brutally beating pregnant women caused things like pinky rings and pant creases to move out of place. He grabbed his car keys and sped out of the complex, leaving Panther writhing on the floor, coughing up blood.

She tried to pull herself up but collapsed back down onto the worn-out carpet in a heap. Luckily, La Costa, having heard the commotion and shouting, ran up the cement stairs to find her. Someone in the complex had already called the police.

"Jesus Christ, Panther!" La Costa screamed when she saw her there, broken and bleeding. "Hold on, Panth. Help is on the way!"

Miraculously, the baby would be all right. But Panther had decided that once she moved in with La Costa, she would be careful to keep mention of it under wraps, just until she could decide exactly what to do next. Telling La Costa would only complicate things. In spite of everything else uncertain, she did know that paternity could be determined, and that when it was proven that the baby was AJ's, maybe he would feel differently about it—about her—and her potential to make bank with her talent and acting skills as planned. If all else failed, she figured, she could always sue the bastard for child support. Either way, she couldn't lose. The baby was her *meal ticket*, and she wasn't going to do anything to jeopardize that stroke of luck!

CHAPTER SIXTEEN

PANTHER WAS THIRTY THOUSAND DOLLARS in debt from maxed-out bank cards, a number of unpaid personal loans, and a severely overdue car note on a nineteen ninety Corvette that she wrecked not three weeks after she drove it off the lot. Not to mention, thousands that AJ claimed that she owed him for "business expenses." It was more money than she could ever make waiting banquet tables at the Crystal Palace Hotel, a job she had taken at La Costa's urging. She was issued a matronly waitress's uniform and was instructed to purchase comfortable white shoes.

"Ugh!" Panther lamented. "I've never worn a pair of comfortable shoes—ever! How am I supposed to serve people dressed like a nun?"

La Costa laughed. They had a deal. Panther would be schlepping trays of roast beef and spaghetti dinners at weddings and corporate shindigs for the hotel's catering department, where the only cheesecake served would be on dessert plates, and La Costa would provide a safe home.

Panther agreed in exchange for the room and board, but in a word, she hated it. During the week, she also worked in the hotel's gift shop selling T-shirts, plastic playing cards, dice sets, and little shot glasses that said: *Welcome to the city of Lost-Wages!*

Soon she would have to quit teaching the fitness classes at the Y on weekends, as she would be beginning to show. *Pregnancy was so inconvenient!* A strong, healthy baby, however, would be her ticket to Easy Street once AJ was proven to be the father. Then, he would owe her, and she would have no problem using her little "trump card" to apply the pressure. Other than this aim, the thought of becoming a mother was the farthest thing from her mind.

La Costa enjoyed having her old roomie around. In fact, it was, at first, just like old times, minus all the booze and wild parties. There was a second-hand sofa on which Panther slept in the living room, and La Costa emptied a few dresser drawers and halved some closet space for her to hang her things. They shared the bathroom and divided the real estate in the fridge right down the middle.

La Costa introduced Panther to the economics of shopping second-hand thrift shops and yard sales for everything from canned soup to clothing. "Living on a budget sucks," Panther complained, missing the seven to fifteen hundred dollars she had pulled in on weekends spent at Baby Doll's, the last gentlemen's club where she had made serious bank in her post-Mink Kitty heyday. This was so much more complicated than she had ever imagined. Plus, she was utterly exhausted—all the time. She especially hated living on mac and cheese and canned chili all the time.

"But at least you are safe and well and free to do what you please," La Costa reminded her. "So, life here is not exactly brunch at the Bilaggio these days, but nobody's bustin' you in the face either. Doesn't that make you feel empowered?"

Panther persevered, feeling nothing but tired and trapped, while La Costa spent more time with her bible and taking English composition classes, nights at the University.

It was all just a means to an end for Panther. She had heard through the grapevine that AJ went out to California with Zander, the film guy, to put together a film crew. They were to begin shooting a series of adult videos for the promoter of E-Rotica, an outfit out of West Hollywood, who was selling to the new cable markets. A film that she had been promised the lead in at one time.

As soon as she was free of this scene, Panther vowed, she would be well on her way to the West Coast herself, where, she was certain, her future awaited her. She would get back into her groove after the baby was born, and then show the world what she was really capable of doing. She wanted to be where the money and connections were happening, not hopelessly stuck in the hellhole she was currently in.

She was going to be a screen actress, and nothing—and no one—was going to stand in her way. The trick simply being, to bide her time until then.

CHAPTER SEVENTEEN

PANTHER CAUGHT LA COSTA OFF guard not two
months later. They were in the supermarket picking
through the produce, stocking the cart with the usual
weekly allotment of frozen entrees, corn chips, and diet
soda. The fruits and vegetables were a vain attempt to
balance out the otherwise trash diet of quick-fix foods like
pizza and toaster-tarts they existed on. La Costa had noticed
as of late, however, that Panther had taken a particular
liking to eating in great and astounding quantities. At
first, La Costa decided that depression had to be the cause,
making Panther overindulge, but as the weeks and months
passed, she just kept on gaining. Soon, however, it became
apparent exactly *why*.

"How many months?" La Costa asked, picking over
the skins on some sickly tomatoes. "Three or four, I'm
guessing?"

Panther shoved her hands into the pockets of her denim
overalls and shrugged at the watermelon. "Yeah, I guess it's
more like five, though."

"*Jesus Christ!* Panther!" The outburst startled a small
child, who was staring at the two of them curiously from
the basket seat of his cart.

Neither said a word at first, just glancing around at

anything but each other. La Costa struggled to force down her fury. "First, I rescue you from that bastard, and then I take you in . . . help you get a job. And this is how you thank me? By keeping secrets?"

Panther feigned tears. It was easy. She felt like shit, and so it was easy to cry. Her bottom lip quivered, and she buried her face in her hands. She looked like a broken doll.

"I'm so sorry, Cos. Oh, God, I just don't know. I don't know what I'm going to do. I've never been so scared in all my life."

La Costa felt Panther's anguish, more than she could say. But, at the same time, she chastised her for slipping up. "Where was your head? Why didn't you use protection?" She pushed the cart and launched it down the soda aisle, Panther following along like an obedient puppy.

"We did," she lied. *That's what HE thought too!*

"This is great . . . really great, Panther." It was all she could do to not simply repeat the obvious, like a mother of a teen daughter who had just broken the unbelievable news, standing there with doe eyes holding a bag of potato chips.

Silently, they moved over to the deli counter, Panther with tears now dripping down her cheeks. La Costa ripped a number from the dispenser. It was going to be a long wait.

"It *is* AJ's, isn't it?"

She knew that La Costa hated AJ and would never have anything to do with him—under any circumstance— let alone helping to raise his child, so she lied again. "No. It's a guy at the gym. At least, he *was* a guy at the gym. I told him about the baby and never saw him again. Word has it that he has a wife and family out in Tucson." Then, Panther delivered the hook. The words that would clinch the deal. "I don't think I'm going to keep it. I'm trying to build up the nerve to—"

La Costa's heart pulled in her chest. All she could think of was the day that she sent her baby boy away on a cool breeze, into the ocean, writing his name on a cross in the sand, wondering if his tiny body might have been carried by the current to—who knew where? It was more than she could bear to imagine. She was young then, and scared. Panther wasn't afraid, she was wasteful, and as usual, she was just looking for an easy fix.

The emotion, which had been previously locked deep in the vault of La Costa's soul, seeped into her now, prying the bolts and forcing the hinges of her memory to burst open. She would not allow it. Not ever again, and certainly, not now.

It was all La Costa could do to hold her tongue. She had enough money saved to register for another semester of night classes at the University in the spring. Her plan was to take a creative writing workshop and try her hand at fiction writing. She had kept a journal for the past two years and loved the therapeutic release of spilling it all onto the page. Be that as it may, this was far more important, and she would just have to find a way to convince Panther to let her help her. That's all there was to it.

That night Panther awoke to the sound of La Costa's muffled sobs coming from her bedroom. She slipped from the couch, wrapped a blanket around her shoulders, and crept in the darkness. Tentatively, she paused at La Costa's door and peered in.

"*Cos*—?"

The crying stopped.

Panther stepped into the room and saw La Costa sitting up in bed, her knees folded close to her chest. She was clutching a small piece of cloth, stroking it pensively, and seeing something both heart-warming and devastating in it at the same time. Panther approached her friend and said nothing, letting the moment give way to a flood of emotion. La Costa's grief was unsettling. In that moment, she too, felt the sudden and uncontrollable urge to cry.

Panther reached to touch what she could now see was a receiving blanket. It was perfect and unused. Together, and for friendship's undefined reasons, Panther came to immediately understand more than La Costa's pleading eyes could say. No further words were needed.

Finally, when they both finished hugging and crying, Panther leaned back and spoke toward the ceiling. "I'm sorry, Cos—I didn't know. Do you want to tell me about it?"

She shook her head. "It doesn't matter now . . . not anymore. But I'll tell you, Panth, not a single day goes by where I don't think about him." She choked on the words that grew dry in her throat.

Panther touched her hand to assure her that she did understand.

"I'm really scared," Panther said, biting her thumbnail and waiting. She was more frightened than she had ever been in her freewheeling thirty years. "I can't have no kid, you know what I'm sayin'? I ain't the mothering type. And alone? We'd never make it."

"Hey." La Costa had already pulled herself together. "You mean, *us*—you and I. We'll do it! We'll manage this like everything else we ever have. Look, I don't know that much, but I do know that you can't go killing your baby and just do away with it. Hon, it doesn't work that way. Trust me, it won't be over."

Panther shook her head in disbelief. "Oh God, Cos. I don't know . . . it's so much to ask. You have no idea how much I *want* to do the right thing." She had large tears dripping down her face. "That's all I want."

"And you will." La Costa smiled, handing over the blanket. "I promise, you won't be alone. I am going to help you."

Panther took the blanket gingerly, as if it were a thing of gold.

In the big picture, it was easy for La Costa to do the right thing. After all, Panther was her only true friend in all the world. And while it could never bring back the loss of sins past, La Costa had faith in the future that doing this promised. She had a good feeling about it.

"It won't be easy," Panther warned, almost more for herself than to La Costa, wiping her face with the back of her hand, warming to the idea.

"I'm used to 'not easy,'" La Costa countered. "That never changes!"

"Thanks. You're like a sister to me." Panther smiled, relieved.

"You're welcome, Kitty Kat." The words lifted her in a way that assured that she had just done the right thing.

It wasn't a large price to pay for true friendship, she thought. Not in the least. La Costa would only need to help Panther and the baby until they could get on their feet. She could sacrifice a bit more and make that happen.

Panther, on the other hand, saw things much differently. She could not believe how fortunate she was to have a friend as gullible as La Costa. She was like no friend Panther had ever had, all right. And that was *exactly* what she was counting on.

CHAPTER EIGHTEEN

A T FIRST IT WAS EASY, but soon got progressively harder. Panther's addiction to cigarettes and weed was compelling. She needed either just to get up and through the day. She only permitted herself to drink wine instead of the hard stuff and rationalized that was "safe" for the baby. Pot was her "natural" solution to sleep deprivation and nervousness, she reasoned, averaging a minimum of three to four sober hours during any given day. Consequently, the baby was growing slowly, and she did not even start showing until well into her fifth month.

Once La Costa was on to the situation, she was rightfully fearful for the baby's chances of coming to full term with a mother so hell-bent on self-destruction. She had seen it a thousand times back home when she was growing up. Crack babies and preemies born of booze-infused indigents and junkies. Things far worse and horrifying than that even, in the filthy shelters and halfway houses she was forced to stay at when she left home. Panther was no different than many of the others, just a good measure prettier, and that counted for something in life. But it wasn't everything. She was frivolous and fearless in the face of danger, and used everything she could to numb the pain of having to face herself—her real self—in the mirror each day. La Costa reasoned, well aware of her friend's inevitable demise, *If I can't help her to change for the better, then maybe God can.*

So, she prayed for Panther's soul and begged for Him to protect her unborn baby while Panther was doing everything in her power to destroy it, along with herself.

"Come with me to church next Sunday and talk with Pastor Mark," La Costa pleaded, until Panther was loath to refuse.

The worship was at Second Baptist, otherwise known as the "Miracle on Madison Avenue." Eventually, La Costa persuaded Panther to come along with her on Wednesday nights as well, for bible study. It was all part of La Costa's plan to rescue Panther's wayward soul.

Surprisingly, Panther found that she actually liked the services. She found the hymns peculiarly sensual and ancient; seeming to soothe a well of emotion buried deep inside. And in a strange way, the church did make her feel welcome.

As a result, Panther began to frequent the church with La Costa on Sunday mornings, no matter how rough of an evening preceded the eleven o'clock service. It was Pastor Mark's sermons that interested Panther most. His flamboyant gestures were menacing, but the message of God's unconditional love and forgiveness was enthralling.

While she wanted to believe that a heavenly God had a plan and purpose for her life, Panther found it far more difficult to accept for herself. The "high road," she reasoned, was for the chosen ones, like La Costa, who found the secrets of happiness, which she continued to grapple for. It was like God was a powerful and mighty entity who wagged his finger at her in disgust, much like the ominous images she held of her own father, an avowed atheist, who later became Born Again, and who chastised her for her doubt of the divine deity and for the wayward lifestyle of which she had embraced—wearing short skirts and listening to the devil's music. He died when she was fifteen, proving to her just how merciful cancer could be on a man who followed his religion, at the end, at least, to the letter, yet ended up dying well before his time. A father who ended up leaving them hard up on one hundred twenty acres of a failing farm and unpaid notes to satisfy. When her mother suffered a nervous breakdown from the trauma, Panther dashed before social services could find her. She had not stopped running ever since. She rode her thumb all the way from Missouri to LA, until a trucker deposited her in front of a posh hotel, where she had said that her father was waiting for her. Then she walked from there, straight to the very first gentlemen's club she could find—Lucy Dumont's Mink Kitty, which was still being renovated at the time.

"So that's how you met Lucy?" La Costa once asked, curious as to life's penchant for serendipitous parings.

Panther shrugged. "It was meant to be. I just walked in off the street, and she hired me to dance. No audition. No questions. I guess she just saw something. She said, 'Yeah, sure. You can start tomorrow, hon.'"

"You've got a guardian angel, Panth. Don't you see?" La Costa said, right there in the church pew. "Someone out there is watching out for you, no doubt. So, please, I am begging you. Stop the partying—the booze, the drugs. Give this baby every chance to be healthy."

Together, they gazed up at the cross, and Panther squeezed La Costa's hand and vowed, "I will."

Two months later, Panther gave birth to an incredibly small but perfect baby boy with flawless mocha skin like

Panther's, and a mane of frizzy dark hair. His lips were heart-shaped like Panther's, and thankfully, he had escaped the curse of acquiring AJ's broad, flat nose. It was, instead, small and pert, and he had a perfectly round head, giving him an edge over the bevy of smashed-faced newborn infants.

Panther named him Louis, after her grandfather, who smelled like Copenhagen cologne and whom she loved, but hardly knew. He had died when she was nine, but held a huge place in her heart, redeeming in some small way, the belief that not all men were disappointments.

It was no ordinary premature birth, and no coincidence that Panther labored twenty-nine hours—just long enough to push the clock into the early morning hour, causing Louis to be born at exactly twelve ten a.m., Christmas Day. An appropriate statement in testament to the miracle of birth. The birth of a seemingly perfect child in spite of dicey odds and the most adverse conditions imaginable. It was truly a miracle.

The baby's lungs required the assistance of a respirator, and he would have to remain on a machine for a short duration of several days, just until they would be strong enough to function on their own.

La Costa served as Panther's coach through it all, having attended the prenatal sessions. She talked to Panther confidently through the merciless torment of mounting contractions with commands to breathe like a steam engine, while La Costa massaged her enormous swollen belly and hoisted her back from the mattress when it finally came time to push.

Not two hours after giving birth, Panther was out of bed, fumbling through her purse for a cigarette, already thinking about how she could score something stronger. Louis was down the hall in the NICU.

"Aren't you breastfeeding?" La Costa asked in an accusatory tone, addressing the pack of menthols in her hand. "And, incidentally, where are you planning on smoking that? This isn't exactly a bar, you know."

Panther smirked, pulling her blue jeans on beneath the crumpled hospital gown, clenching the unlit cigarette between her pale lips. "I know." She masterfully slipped into her bra beneath the gown, then gathered and tucked the excess of it into her jeans. "*Damn!*" She had forgotten to pack a spare T-shirt as the one she had been wearing when she came into the hospital was nowhere to be found. Hospital chic was not her best look.

She slipped her bare feet into her athletic shoes and fumbled for her jewelry from a Styrofoam cup on the bedside table. She fished out her cheap gold hoop earrings and gave La Costa a disregarding glance.

"Oh, R-E-L-A-X, Cos! I'm just going to be more comfortable at home. I hate hospitals. They give me the creeps. Let's go."

AJ had disappeared, seemingly for good. Panther's letters were returned "undeliverable." Each month she grew more and more desperate, frantically calling contacts and acquaintances throughout the West Coast in hopes of finding him. He was Louis's father, and he was in the wind.

Word on the street had placed AJ in a small import/export business down in Miami, but Panther could not know for sure. Any hopes that she previously had for cashing in on AJ's paternity, earning her at least child support, dissolved, as harsh reality quickly took center stage.

Her job at the hotel had been replaced, and sporadic trade show work and modeling stints from Prestige were hardly enough to keep the baby in diapers and formula. La Costa did what she could to help, but she was already paying the rent and utilities for all of them, along with the weekly grocery bill and incidentals. She even watched after Louis on weekends, when Panther supposedly was waiting tables again, this time at Nickel Buck's, a local casino just off the Strip.

La Costa was suspicious of the fact that, in spite of all the extra side work she was able to get for Panther at the agency, along with her tips from the bar, Panther was almost always flat broke. It was not evident at first that Panther's evenings spent at the bar working, was simply a cover for a mounting obsession growing more serious by the day, *gambling*.

Every chance she got, Panther fled to the casino, to the shiny bank of blinking, clinking, mesmerizing slot machines to gorge her obsessive fixation with the silver demons, which had fast turned into her newest replacement-addiction. If AJ's paternity would not provide the means for her to breakaway to LA and her dream of becoming a celebrated film actress, then she would just have to find another way, she reasoned.

Gambling with more than her paltry paychecks, she began risking everything she had, week after week, of hitting the jackpot—just once—and claiming for herself the gold, so to speak. For the chance of winning enough money to free herself from the mess she had made of her life. Somehow, in her delusional, self-effaced insanity, she figured that La Costa and her son would understand. They would be, she figured convincingly, much better without her.

Panther continued to gamble recklessly, taking large, uncalculated risks, sinking an incredible seven thousand dollars into the local casinos, betting primarily on the cyclical returns of the dollar slots and the law of average probabilities that governed the gods of the lucky sevens and triple cherries. When dividends reigned high, she placed her winnings judiciously at the blackjack tables, where four to six hands most typically doubled her money. And, most critical to her success, she stuck to her number one cardinal rule when she was winning. She would then stop and walk away for the evening. A practice that proved truly lucrative, as in just six months' time, Panther had amassed and managed to stash away nearly thirty thousand dollars—enough for an airline ticket to LA, and a brand-new life—for one.

Phyllis Jean Baker left a photograph of herself in Louis's crib, along with a stuffed toy black panther and the receiving blanket that La Costa had once given her. The note left for La Costa on the kitchen table contained a hollow apology and a one thousand-dollar bill with simply the words, *You'd be a better mother than I could have ever been. God knows this too. I ask you both to forgive me.* It was simply signed, Panther.

CHAPTER NINETEEN

FALL 1999

THREE MONTHS BEFORE LOUIS TURNED two, Georgia announced that she was shutting the doors to Prestige forever. A larger firm out of New York had bought the agency from her for far more than it was worth, according to Georgia's lawyers, so she took the money and ran.

"I'm going to try my hand at writing a memoir." Georgia threw a waft of smoke from her ultra-thin cigarette, of which too many over the years had permanently pummeled her vocal cords to gravel.

"Oh?" La Costa seemed surprised at her soon-to-be former boss's newest ambition. "And what are you going to write about?" She asked this, while continuing to pack a large cardboard shipping box with stacks of files that would soon be sent to the new agency.

"Why, my life!" she trilled.

The company who purchased Prestige was a conglomerate called Imperial Casting, and they represented some of the most famous faces on the New York runways and in fashion magazines throughout the world.

Georgia could have never competed with such muscle. "The independent businessman is a dying breed," she would say dishearteningly, as she smoothed the creases on her skirt. Ever proper, ever perfect, that was Georgia. A lovely and cultured creature from a time where little girls went to charm school instead of to the mall, to learn how to do things like balance teacups and saucers on their knees; how to extend one's hand to a gentleman, curtsy like a lady, and of course, to master the finer art of blushing.

Georgia was a dinosaur, and she knew it. Prestige did not even have a computerized system of operations. They did everything the old-fashioned way, by hand. That's what made Georgia so remarkable. She kept everything in her head. All the figures, clients' names . . . their needs, preferences, models' names and stats . . . wages, dates . . . trends.

She knew it all, and despite the rise of big-name outfits through the years, such as Kelly Enterprises and Ramerez Modeling Agency, out on the West Coast, she managed to hold her own in the trade show and pageant markets. Until now. After thirty-seven years, Prestige was finally and officially, closing its doors.

Now, Starlight Publishing wanted her story, and a tenacious agent named Leo Monk had been pressuring her for months to consider writing it after seeing her featured on a local news segment about the agency. It was Georgia's biography and unique back-to-basics approach to life in modern times that most interested the publisher. A candid and feeling memoir on the life and times of former charm schoolteacher-turned modeling agent. A former beauty queen herself, Georgia then was a Southern Debutante heralding from none other than the Palmetto State, where her family, the stoic Applewhites, raised, among citrus and cotton crops, four generations of daughters—two of which won the crown of state and national pageants. Georgia was one of them.

"Why'd you do it, Georgia?" La Costa had to know. "Why sell the agency?"

"Because, my dear, and you should know this yourself by now, it becomes time to do the next thing. To move on. To turn the next page, so to speak."

La Costa seemed satisfied with the answer, but nonetheless, unsure as to where her own "next life-page" was going to take her. Little did she know just how poignant Georgia's words would turn out to be.

La Costa knew she wasn't young and ignorant anymore. She was wise beyond her years, and now, she was not alone. She had Louis to think about, and that made the prospect of starting over again more than simply a matter of self-survival. She had choices to make that would affect both of them. She had a family to protect now. Because of this, and how far she had come, La Costa knew that they would be all right, thanks to the good graces of Georgia, who would keep her secret of how Louis had come to be hers. She was sure of Georgia's loyalty. Georgia had given her so much, enabling her to prove her skills and talents as an invaluable assistant. For once in her life, La Costa now had a solid resume and marketable skills. She would have some control of the future, or so she'd hoped.

Most unexpectedly, Georgia, once again, decided to throw a curve her way. "Come join me, won't you? There's plenty of room in the beach house for you both. Louis would love the ocean!"

La Costa could hardly believe her ears. Was Georgia seriously inviting them to move with her all the way to South Carolina? "Thank you, Georgia, but I—we couldn't."

It was unthinkable. Being that close to her old stomping

grounds again was not in the cards for La Costa. She liked Nevada, but thought about the possibly of exploring New Mexico, as good a place as any, to start over and raise a son.

"What? You couldn't use a job offer to be my editorial assistant? I need one, La Costa. You know how bad I am with punctuation and spelling. Dreadful! You once said so yourself." Then, she closed in for the kill. "And you know, dear, I'm not getting any younger. With so much to do— the shopping, the cooking, driving from here to there . . . it's all so very much for someone like me, you know. Not to mention the memoir. So much to research and to write. I was thinking about investing in one of those desktop computers. You know, on which to write the manuscript. Only, I don't know the first thing about such things. But, you do, right?"

She knew full well that La Costa had been taking English classes at the University, and also classes in computer fundamentals. That, plus she was a voracious reader. La Costa had edited all of their marketing materials and collateral on a regular basis. Georgia knew first-hand, and better than anyone, La Costa's gift for words.

"This publisher—can you believe it? She's interested in my life story. It's all very flattering, but in just three months' time, she's expecting to see an outline, and frankly, dear heart, I don't think that it's possible to work such a miracle without one's right arm. So, what do you say? I'll give you a twenty percent raise, room and board, and all the bad fashion advice you can stand. I have a place in South Carolina, right on the beach—in Hilton Head. It was a family home passed down among my parents' siblings throughout the years. In nineteen ninety, it became ours when my then last-living aunt passed away. It has been boarded up since Macklin's death, but I'm ready to go back there now, for good. It's beautiful, La Costa. Nothing but green trees and blue water. Not a neon sign in sight. No one to bother or even find you, if you wish to remain unfound. What do you say? Please say yes."

La Costa grimaced. *Was it that obvious that she needed to run somewhere safe?* Louis was nearly two, and the thought of Panther appearing out of nowhere to rip him from her life was one that kept her up at night. Plus, the thought of working with Georgia on creating a book for publication seemed like a dream come true. It was La Costa's secret wish to write books of her own someday. Those were not the thoughts of single black women, especially unemployed ones!

Georgia watched La Costa's eyes slowly begin to flicker with excitement at the possibility, quickly adding, "It would be such a blessing to me, dear, if you and Louis would accompany me. It would be a perfect arrangement. I'm leaving on Sunday at dawn. Everything that fits into the U-Haul, goes. Everything else is yesterday's news and can be left behind."

At that, she tossed a stack of useless modeling headshots into the trash bin with finality.

La Costa glanced at Louis. He was a joyful little boy, playing contentedly with his building blocks on a blanket on the office floor. What if Panther came back? What if she wanted to take Louis with her? What, then?

She thought about the odds of probability around the prospect and suddenly realized that Louis was now completely her reason for breathing and for the very life she was living. He was immutably, *hers*.

What purpose would Panther's coming back to reclaim her son have, other than to simply and undeniably kill La Costa dead. No, she wouldn't have it! Not again—not ever again! There was no way she could ever trust Panther with Louis. There was no telling how he might be treated, by

Panther, or her newest no-good boyfriend—she could never let that happen. Louis was *her* son, and he belonged with her, where he was loved and safe.

She secured the last box with a strip of packing tape, and then sealed the deal between her and Georgia with a handshake, and then a hug. "We'd be honored to join you, Ms. Byrne. Yes! Thank you so much."

The Sunday morning dawn broke in the dusky Nevada sky. Georgia clapped with delight when she saw that La Costa hadn't changed her mind and was rattling onto the driveway with her Nissan Sentra loaded to the gills with all of her and Louis's worldly possessions.

"I don't know if this ole clunker will make it all the way to the coast," La Costa said, concerned.

"We'll pull it, dear," Georgia cajoled. "I don't think you want to cross the country in a sardine can. I think I can wrestle up a hitch."

La Costa smiled, relieved in more ways than one. She was excited, scared, but duly prepared—for anything.

The old house was a historical landmark. It was over one hundred years old, but it had a kind of charm that beckoned one to sit on its massive broken-planked porches and stay a while. Georgia and her late husband, Macklin, had started remodeling it just two years before he died. Georgia had used it less frequently than she originally expected, which amounted to once every few years, not wanting, for the most part, to stir up memories of the past. That was now all about to change.

It was originally owned by the heirs of a Charleston family dating back to the late nineteenth century, when it was built during the Carolina Cotton boom just after the devastating Sea Island Hurricane of 1893. Georgia did not want to part with it after her husband's death, but she couldn't imagine ever being able to enjoy it in her retirement, as had been her and Macklin's plan. He had loved the ocean about as much as any man was capable. His dream was to rest in the tranquility of his golden years at the tip of the pier, baiting hooks and working in the shed, restoring his old fishing boat to pristine glory. They had started to renovate the house summer after summer and dreamt of the day when they would call it their permanent home.

But Macklin had succumbed quickly after the prostate cancer was detected, dying later that fall in 1992. The old house remained shuttered and silent for three years before Georgia could finally bring herself to return to its paint-chipped and weathered porches and begin salvaging the vacant rooms and overgrown gardens.

In 1995, she hired an architect to renovate the house top to bottom. She redesigned the kitchen, built a second bathroom, and expanded the rear porch into an exquisite sunroom. Georgia had every intention of restoring the old museum into a livable showplace, and then she planned to sell it for a king's ransom.

"So why didn't you?" La Costa asked as she stroked Louis's cheek. He was lulled into irrepressible sleep not twenty minutes after they rolled onto the interstate, propped snuggly in his little car seat.

"Because . . . oh, it's silly." Georgia lowered the window to flick an ash. The Lincoln Continental felt sturdy and powerful on the road, pulling the heavy trailer and La Costa's tiny car in tow. "I had this dream about a month after he died. In it, I see Macklin, and he's standing by his boat. He's just standin' there in the sunshine on the dock, frowning like, I don't know, like a little kid, I guess. I say, 'Hey, Mack! Why are you so blue?' Now I get closer and see that he's got big ole crocodile tears in his eyes. He's pointing out behind me, toward the house."

"What did you do?"

"I ran over to him to say that I would—" Her eyes misted over as she choked on the words. "I said that I would never let it go. Our house. It was our dream. He smiled. I swear, he did. Just like he was so pleased, and then he turned back to his boat. That's it. That's all I remembered when I woke up. But a promise is a promise, and so I'm keeping it. Been renting it out to friends and tourists over the years. Our old neighbor, Lisle Teeters, has been looking after it for me. He lives in Beaufort just twenty miles away. He says I won't believe what transients can do to a place."

"I'm sure it's just beautiful," La Costa assured her.

"Well, I hope so, dear." Georgia patted her chignon, which was pulled up high on her head and wrapped with a Hermes printed scarf that matched the aquamarine-beryl tones of her eyes. She looked striking, like a once-upon-a-time movie star.

Georgia was a first-class lady, all right. Perhaps the classiest person La Costa had ever known. Once, she had seen photographs from Georgia's old modeling album and could not believe how truly stunning she had been in her prime. Thin, yet curvaceous, with those hypnotizing eyes, high cheekbones, and flawless ivory skin. Her ash-blonde hair cascaded in thick, silken curls down her shoulders and back, swept off her forehead with a thin velvet bow. Even now, at sixty-nine, Georgia had the style of a well-preserved beauty.

La Costa had no doubt that she and Macklin's dream

house would have withstood the assaults of time, emerging somewhat better for the journey.

Just like Georgia.

CHAPTER TWENTY

L
A COSTA LOVED THE WAY that Georgia could turn a phrase. She had a unique and delightful way—a grand Southern way of expression that was very different from the way folks in California or Nevada spoke. Georgia was a master storyteller and treated La Costa to hours of wonderful stories about growing up the last of five children on a stately plantation in South Carolina, recounting her own grandmother's patchwork quilt of folk tales and fables; life lessons and captured dreams, every last sentence and detail of Georgia's captivating memoirs.

Sometimes, they would just drive without talking, and that's when La Costa would stare out of the window, imagining the people and places in her mind that Georgia put there. Rich, complex histories of real people with hopeful hearts, triumphs, and tragedies. At a rest stop in Leupp, Arizona, La Costa purchased a collage-ruled composition book in which to capture notes on everything she could from Georgia's wonderful tales. It gave her the most terrific idea for a story of her own.

La Costa excitedly scribbled random and fragmented thoughts onto the pages from the back seat of the Lincoln, seated next to Louis as he played contentedly with his picture books.

"What's that?" Georgia said, peering curiously into the rearview mirror. "A journal?"

"Sort of. Sometimes I just like to write down things I think about, or see, so as not to forget. I've got nearly twenty-five binders like this filled with notes. I'm keeping track of things for Louis now. Someday he can read it all and make of it what he will. Maybe even learn some lessons from my life mistakes and those of his mother." Her voice trailed off awkwardly.

"*You* are his mother!" Georgia declared sternly. "And that makes him one very lucky little boy."

"Louis lucky boy!" a fervent little voice interjected, causing Georgia to nearly bust a gut. Louis giggled too, quite pleased with himself.

"Oh, that kid is a stitch, La Costa! We're gonna have some FUN, aren't we, Louie?"

La Costa smiled.

"Show me those notebooks sometime?" Georgia said. "Or better yet, *write* something from them. I'd bet your life would make a wonderful story."

This made La Costa recoil inside. *If she only knew!*

But that was the thing about Georgia. It wouldn't have mattered in the least, La Costa would later relay in her memoir. The woman was a catalyst to everything yet to happen, and La Costa could not have been more grateful for this incredible guardian angel ushering her to her dreams.

"Maybe someday I will." La Costa's voice trailed as she watched the green trees go by. "Someday . . . "

Georgia drove until her bad knee got the better of her and La Costa had to take the wheel and continue until sundown, when they reached New Mexico and pulled off the interstate to find a room for the night in Albuquerque.

The next day, they drove across the Texas panhandle, to

Little Rock, Arkansas. It would be the longest of the three-day journey, and the two took turns in three-hour shifts. Georgia spent her back-seat time either entertaining Louis or catnapping.

Georgia rose with the chickens, and so they were repacked and back on the road by four a.m. the following morning for the final leg across Alabama, nearly eight hundred miles, down to Savannah, Georgia, and finally into South Carolina.

By five-thirty that night, road-weary and excited, they arrived at the spectacular shoreline of Hilton Head Island.

The first several days were dedicated to cleaning up the clutter, dust, and debris time and abuse had accumulated in the halls and rooms of the once-stunning beach house. Time and neglect, however, did little to taint its truly impressive aura. In La Costa's eyes, it was magnificent.

There was light painting to be done and brass fixtures to polish. The entire garden had to be cleared of weeds and years of overgrowth. The soil had to be re-tilled, and new seedlings planted. Bleached-out curtains came down, and fresh new ones went up. Bed linens were replaced, a youth bed erected for Louis in La Costa's room. Carpets were beaten, paintings and fixtures were dusted, and windows were shined to perfection.

The cupboards were filled with parcels of food from a local food-mart, the pilot light on the range lit, and soon the smells of home cooking permeated the air.

It took them three full weeks to transform Georgia and Macklin's dream house from an old boarded-up weathered beach house into a home.

Georgia hung a framed photo of her with Macklin in the entrance hall. It had been taken on their wedding day, in front of a small chapel in Richmond. She also displayed several more throughout the house. It was sort of sweet and sad at the same time. La Costa soon learned that Georgia talked to Macklin at night—as if he were really there, in the house with them all. Since she and Macklin had never had any children of their own, La Costa imagined that Georgia was lonely, and probably had been for a very long time.

CHAPTER TWENTY-ONE

(ONE YEAR LATER)

WEEKS AFTER A FULL AND carefree summer and
months well into the turning of the new century,
La Costa began to wonder when she and Georgia would
begin writing the manuscript. They had done nothing but
work on the house since they arrived. Figuring it wasn't
right to pry, La Costa simply said nothing and continued
to be a helpful assistant to her eccentric boss, who charged
her with mundane household tasks, such as food shopping
and sorting laundry. Georgia did not touch her ancient
relic of a typewriter one time. Instead, she spent long,
languid hours in her gardens, rocking blissfully on her
wicker glider on the front porch, reading trade magazines
and sipping iced tea.

It had been a welcome reprieve from the bustle of the
agency with its ringing phones and whirring fax machine.
Yet, somehow, La Costa couldn't help but feel slighted.
Why, then, did Georgia bring her here? To be her paid
housemaid? Louis was restless too, and keeping him quiet
and content was a challenge. She worried constantly that
his high-spiritedness and natural curiosity was making
Georgia tense or annoyed.

But the more La Costa apologized, the more reassuring Georgia was. "It's all right, dear. Really, I enjoy Louis tremendously. The question is—are *you* happy here?"

"Yes. I mean, who wouldn't be? It's more than beautiful. The house is extraordinary."

"I'm thinking about re-doing the bedrooms on the second floor and adding four more on the north side of the house," Georgia said, her thoughts whirring.

"What for?" La Costa was incredulous. "Why on earth would you want so many bedrooms? Are you thinking about opening a hotel?" La Costa chuckled.

Georgia grinned. Her blue eyes twinkled as she twirled around to catch La Costa's reaction.

"Oh my God! You *are*! You are planning on running a hotel!"

"A bed and breakfast, dear. They're all the rage. I've been waiting for my accountant to finalize the figures. He says we're ready anytime now to begin further renovations. The place should be completed and ready to open by this coming fall. Just in time for the snowbird tourists."

"And the book? What about your contract with the publisher? I thought—"

"Oh, La Costa. That's why you're here, remember? I'll surely need your help with getting the B&B up and running, but in the meantime, *you* write it. I've seen your journals. They're full of terrific ideas and story lines. Really, La Costa, you're bright and talented. You could finish writing it without half-trying."

"What? Those are *your* memories. Georgia, I can't just—"

Georgia cut her off by delving into a pile of tapestry samples, which were slated for the new guest rooms. "These just arrived today. Let's take them upstairs and look at them in the natural light. C'mon!"

La Costa was stunned. Just like that, she asked her to write the manuscript! What did she know about being a biographer? La Costa was not at all comfortable with the charge.

"Can't you get someone else to do it?" she pleaded, following Georgia upstairs from room to room as she darted around purposefully, eyeing ceiling heights and paying heed to door moldings. She held out one end of a measuring tape across an imaginary wall, where a window seat would go. "Nonsense, dear. Grab the other end of this, won't you? You're the one I want to be my ghost writer."

"Thanks, Georgia, but—"

"But, *nothing*," Georgia said, releasing the lever and causing the tape to recoil with a sharp snap back into the dispenser. "Case closed."

Two days later La Costa woke early one morning and was shocked to find Georgia seated at the kitchen table, pounding on an old manual typewriter, next to which, a full ashtray suggested that she had been at it all through the night, and was still there, greeting the dawn.

"Manuscript?" La Costa asked, hopeful, from the kitchen doorway, looking on with her arms folded smugly across her chest.

"Naw ..." Georgia spat a shot of smoke. "Business plan," she growled in her gravel-tinged morning voice. "By the way, we're out of decaf."

Then she produced a notebook from a teetering stack of papers and charts in front of her. "Here, I did jot down some of my thoughts. Notes, for the book. I thought it would be helpful."

Georgia's "notes" eventually filled five spiral binders.

CHAPTER TWENTY-TWO

DECEMBER 2002

WITH THE WEST WING SLEEPING rooms now finally finished, and all things holding to schedule, the B&B would be ready to open in summer of two thousand three. The kitchen still had to be expanded to accommodate another range and a large utility sink and a refrigerator and freezer unit. At first, Georgia and La Costa would be doing all the cooking, until the need to bring someone on full-time was warranted. One of the downstairs bedrooms was converted into a working office, from which Georgia would keep the financial books, register logs, and supply inventories. She invested in a high-speed computer processor with a laser jet printer, a fax machine, and a small copier. She had a separate phone line installed in the sitting parlor, as well as in each of the guest rooms.

Georgia named the charming respite, Splendor Bay. Her dream was, within four or five years, to expand the bed and breakfast's offerings to include full-service spa quarters with meditation rooms and a sun solarium and exercise room. "You think big—you do big things," Georgia was always fond of saying. And in all her life, La Costa had never before or since, met anyone more capable of doing just that—big things.

The weekends were already booked solid June first through winter of two thousand four when rugged vacationers would trickle in after Indian summer for one- to two-night stays sporadically, keeping Splendor Bay's warmth and hospitality brimming when ocean waters chilled and boats and their owners spent more time tethered to their docks and the mainland. When winter skies settled over the water and jackets and hats were the order of the day.

La Costa missed the arid desert climate of Nevada that she had come to love, not unlike the endless summers of California. South Carolina embraced the slight change of seasons as it calmed her moods in new and mystical ways. She often found herself from time to time, drifting into tranquil thoughts; calm and peacefulness washed over her for the first time ever in her life of thirty-one years. The sea air and sunshine . . . life . . . honest work . . . the home she and Louis had made there with Georgia, was a bliss as near to perfect as La Costa had ever known.

Throughout the previous fall and winter months, La Costa had worked diligently editing Georgia's manuscript, conducting phone interviews, diving into research archives—past press releases, photographs, and memorabilia; rewriting and proofing countless drafts, all of which ultimately withstood the rigorous scrutiny of the subject of the biography herself. Now, when she was not busy preparing for the arrival of an overnight guest, or designing or sending out scads of marketing collateral, Georgia worked over La Costa's shoulder to coach her on the project.

By Christmas, the final draft was completed. It was

entitled, *Southern Peach—The Story of Fashion and Business Maven Georgia Byrne*. La Costa insisted that her name not appear anywhere—on the cover or in the acknowledgments. It was her gift to Georgia, and she had preferred to leave the matter at that.

The milestone, along with the completion of the guest rooms for the B&B, was celebrated with grand jubilation. Georgia made an event out of everything. She had purchased a bottle of French champagne months before, and she had been saving it for just the perfect occasion to open it.

She was particularly known for her lavish extravagances when it came to birthdays. Louis, who was turning five, received from Georgia, an imported train set from Germany, a five-foot stuffed panda, and a healthy savings bond for college.

Georgia also gifted La Costa with her own personal computer, saying, "You've more than earned it. My publisher loved the manuscript and is already talking about book number two—a quick guide on the lost art of 'etiquette revisited' in a modern world. And it's all thanks to *you*, my dear. You did it!"

"*We* did it!" La Costa said, knowing that she could never have hoped to accomplish such a task without the encouragement and guidance of such a savvy mentor and subject as Georgia. It had been a joyful task for La Costa to write about Georgia's life. It was a story easy to tell. In the process, La Costa had discovered that she enjoyed telling stories as much as she loved reading them. Writing was a newfound passion. Later, she would recount in her memoir, *I knew then that more than anything, save from being Louis's mother, I finally knew what I wanted to do—to be a writer.*

And unbeknownst to her, *Southern Peach* was just the

beginning of sweet things to come.

Just when La Costa thought that things could not get any better, a wonderful thing happened. A referral came in the form of a phone call from New York City. Georgia's agent, Leo Monk, had pitched La Costa as a hip, young, debut writer with edgy urban themes and streetwise moxie.

Apparently, Georgia had copied several rough drafts of a piece La Costa had been working on in her journal, tentatively titled *Invisible Girl*, and presented it to Monk and several publishing contacts with the expectation that someone might be interested.

Bold, truthful, and uncensored, La Costa wrote with raw human emotion, as if she herself had experienced the very realities of her heroine. Little did anyone know that the material was the very fabric of her soul, and that the streetwise character, Vivian Dunn, was really Mayella Jackson. Or, if Georgia did know, she never let on.

Leo Monk was impressed enough to pitch it to his colleague, Tess Kardamakis, a very high-spirited and hungry new agent who was overflowing with gumption and tenacity. And, who, at eight months pregnant, spent her weekend in Vail glued to a chair in the resort's lodge, riveted by the compelling unabashed saga of fifteen-year-old Vivian Dunn and her poignant search for rescue and survival on the tumultuous streets of East LA.

Within three months, La Costa had an agent and a signed contract with Gaylord Publishing for a projected completion date for the story, and a deal regarding the delivery of two future manuscripts, *on spec*. She was given a small advance and instructions for re-working the plot to involve a chance meeting with the story's heroine and an integral secondary character. The publisher was pushing for the manuscript to have a fairy tale-*esque* ending, turning her gritty exposé into a genre-lucrative modern romance that would change everything for the vivacious character of Vivian Dunn—and not least of all—for La Costa herself.

CHAPTER TWENTY-THREE

NEWPORT BEACH, CA
2014

"THAT IS WHEN EVERYTHING REALLY just turned around for me," La Costa said, gathering the loose photos and scrapbooks back into neat little piles. "I was about to be a published author—a romance author—as long as I turned up the heat a bit. I said, 'I can do that!' It was then that I settled on my new pen name, *La Costa Reed*."

"Can you tell me, is there anything behind your having chosen *Reed* as your pen name?" Felicia asked, flipping through her notebook for a page that wasn't already covered with notes.

"I picked *Reed* because I simply loved the sound of it. It seemed strong; like a name you would continuously have to earn. My agent, Tess, said that it was a durable author name. It was going to appear on the cover of a book— *many* books—so I knew that I had better like it. And so, I've been going by *Reed* ever since."

"And what does your son, Louis, think about all this?" Felicia asked gingerly.

It had been agreed early on that mention of Louis Jackson, La Costa's son, would be limited in the exposé, and that no pertinent details about him be divulged. La Costa remained guarded and tight-lipped when it came to the subject. She was extremely careful in relaying to her interviewer details of her life in the past few hours that she *chose* to relay. Louis, for the most part, was strictly off-limits to the press and public. Certain details concerning the truth remained an omission in her own memoir as well, out of respect for Louis's privacy and safety. Felicia and the magazine had agreed to work around the subject, as they were litigiously buried in a mountain of binding non-disclosure agreements that forbade them from divulging any details about La Costa's son—except for what she agreed to share.

"Oh, you know, he is your typical sixteen-year-old high school kid, I guess. He plays varsity basketball and is a whiz at math. He loves video games and is allergic to doing chores. Let's see, have I forgotten anything?"

"I'd say that you are pretty proud of your son," Felicia said.

"I am," La Costa agreed, smiling. "I'd add that he is my best work yet."

No longer would Reed have any connection to her past self, Felicia would later write about the acquiring of La Costa's pen name. *She was, by then, indeed a long way from little Mayella Jackson from West Memphis, Arkansas. La Costa Reed had shed her old name and earned a new one, by choice. Bought with pain, struggle, and much sacrifice, it was a tribute of sorts to her newfound self-worth.*

"I could hardly believe my eyes when, a year after I had submitted the finished manuscript, I saw the galleys, and then the cover for my first book," La Costa said, grinning at the memory. "Large letters spelling out my name on a glossy book cover. It was so surreal. It was really something."

"I'll bet it was," Felicia said.

"Would you like to see it?"

Felicia nodded. "Can I?"

La Costa ushered her down a short hall, past a teenage boy's room, into a small but brightly lit room just off the master bedroom. It was La Costa's writing den, and it, too, faced the ocean. The east wall was covered with chrome-framed book covers encased in glass, proudly on display, along with a desk full of family photos.

A feeling of reverence washed over Felicia as she stepped in to get a closer look.

"That's it, there," La Costa said a bit coyly. "My first bestseller with the original cover design—it really was awful, actually!"

The cover graphic looked like the blurred colors of speeding cars on an endless highway of city lights, and a young girl's silhouette loomed in the distance. The well-preserved cover featured the title: *City Vixen*, the first book in the four-book, Vivian Dunn, "Vixen" series, with the typesetting appearing larger than La Costa's name. Later, it would be changed to feature her name front and center in large, bold font across the cover and spine, once LACOSTA REED became synonymous with bestselling romance.

"Wow," Felicia said. "I had not seen this original version. It's really something."

"I bawled when I held the printed copy in my hands for the first time," La Costa said, shaking her head at the incredulous reality that had become her life. It never ceased to amaze her and fill her with gratitude. "I could only hope back then that at least *one person* in the world would want to read it."

Felicia laughed at the understatement. "Do you mind if I take some photos of you in your workspace here?" She had her digital camera at the ready.

"Sure," La Costa said, removing two framed photos of Louis and safely placing them into a drawer. "Ready!" She was glad that she had her hair and makeup girl by earlier that morning. The formal photo session for the magazine would be days away, but she knew that her readers preferred the candid, real-life shots. "Let's put these new hair extensions to good use!"

La Costa smiled, directing her poses toward the wall of her honored backlist.

"Just great!" Felicia said as she snapped a few gems. "Perfect!"

"Okay, but afterwards, I am going to see about slicing up some of that pie for us," La Costa said. "What do you say?"

"Deal!" Felicia said, clicking away.

Twenty minutes later they were back on the patio, the afternoon sun was high in the sky, and the beach was filled with tourists and locals frolicking in the sand along the shoreline. The cool breeze off of the ocean and rolling waves tossed the paddle boarders about like little tub toys. La Costa brought two china-patterned plates from the kitchen, each with a perfect triangle slice of lattice-work pie. "The plates are from a collection that belonged to Georgia," La Costa said, placing them on the patio table, along with two sterling forks, each wrapped in a linen napkin. "And so is this recipe. It's old-fashioned—two-crust peach pie, made with fresh peaches, of course. The secret is to use a cast iron skillet and dark brown sugar, as opposed to the light. That way, you can really taste the molasses."

Felicia's eyes widened when she got a whiff of the still-warm blend of nutmeg and cinnamon.

"I never knew that I could bake until I met Georgia," La Costa said. "She taught me how. I swear, every time I make this pie, I think of her—every time."

La Costa disappeared back into the kitchen, laughing, and then returned with two mugs of steaming coffee.

Felicia was already two bites into the heavenly pie crust and warm, gooey delights dancing on her tongue. She lingered over every forkful. "You are quite the baker, I would say. This is amazing."

"How do you think I got these curves? Girl, I do love to eat what I bake! That was a rule of Georgia's too," La Costa said, folding herself into the deck chair. "And let me tell you, what Georgia gave to me in sugar, my crazy agent, Tess, gave to me in *spice*! Got your recorder ready?"

CHAPTER TWENTY-FOUR

JANUARY 2003

LEO MONK HAD BEEN WORKING with Georgia Byrne for the previous four years in persuading her to write the book, which was finally slated for launch that spring. He was more than happy back in December to help champion her protégé, La Costa Jackson, with a swift referral to an agent more "suited" to novice fiction writers seeking representation. Leo had known Tess Kardamakis from previous days in 1988, when the two worked at the same real estate firm, and co-listed a home in Virginia Beach, where they each were living at the time. Both shared a love of books. Monk had jumped ship from the real estate circus soon after that to join on with a boutique publishing house in Central New York named Starlight Publishing. Five years later, he broke out on his own to become an independent agent on the Upper East Side of Manhattan, representing high-profile authors in the non-fiction market. Namely, the influx of self-help books, memoirs, and tell-all tomes reminiscent of the mid-nineties' appetite for quick-fix remedies and inside gossip. Georgia's biography was soon to become one of the many jewels in his crown, and to which, he would owe her plenteously.

Monk had arranged for La Costa to meet with Tess Kardamakis, who had become a literary agent for her own start-up agency in early two thousand, and was always on the hunt for new clients. The meeting was set for the first Friday in January, at a busy deli in Millburn, New Jersey, where La Costa would be arriving straight from the airport for the one-day round-trip interview. Tess was seated at a table near the entrance of the bustling neighborhood landmark. La Costa could smell the pastrami wafting in the air as soon as she walked through the venerable threshold to behold a cacophony of sights, sounds, and colors. Tess waved at her from a nearby table enthusiastically. "La Costa! Hello—you made it!"

La Costa wriggled out of her coat and gloves and placed them onto the back of the chair, freeing her hand to extend to Tess. The woman was like a ray of sunshine with a wide grin, impish auburn eyes, and a riot of ginger curls run amuck, parted and gelled in a face-framing blunt bob around her cherub face. She looked like a dead ringer for Bette Midler. Her Jersey accent matched the woman. "How was the flight? Short, but brutal, right? I, myself, hate to fly."

"It was fine, Ms. Kardamakis, thank you. I have never flown to another city for a lunch, though, I'd have to say. I feel like I'm missing something not having a single piece of luggage. Nice to meet you."

"Oh, call me Tess, please." She chortled.

The two shook hands, and Tess gave La Costa a slow, earnest stare. Her cheeks were ruddy and puffed like a chipmunk. It was obvious at first pass that the woman was pregnant. *Very* pregnant.

Tess missed nothing, quickly acknowledging the

elephant that was her abdomen in the room. "Eight and a quarter months, God help me—this one's huge. And I gave birth to twins once already. I'm thirty-seven, for Christssakes. I told my Demitri, no more after this—I'm closing shop. I haven't seen anything below my boobs in a zillion weeks. I'm lucky if my shoes match. And *can* you get a bikini wax at thirty-seven weeks? It's crazy."

La Costa smiled, trying to take it all in. She did not really know how to respond. Her stomach was rumbling now, less from nerves and more from the incredible mélange of aromas dancing in the air. She had been up since dawn preparing for the trip and could definitely eat.

"Oh, and *do* believe the hype. They have the best grinders in town. Maybe in all of the East Coast. You're going to love this place! I'll bet you're starved. Of course you are! I always am."

La Costa relaxed a bit as the moments passed, and she felt like she and Tess had begun to click, settling into a fast and easy conversation about Leo Monk, and Georgia, the new year, and life living on the coast.

It was well after their order was placed and their iced tea glasses were filled a second time that Tess got down to business, although everything that came from her buoyant persona seemed to float like champagne bubbles in air. "I am just so delighted to have had the chance to read your manuscript. Leo said that I was going to love it."

"Oh, thank you," La Costa said, feeling a bit relieved.

"Well, I don't love it, *yet*. But I do see its potential, and that's why you're here. Two words for you, my dear— DEVELOPMENTAL EDIT."

La Costa stopped cold. "What? I'm not sure . . ."

"No matter. It can be fixed. The format, the grammar, the structure. What you can't fix are the intangibles, and you have those, for sure. You check all the boxes. Tell me, is the character of Vivian Dunn based on yourself?"

"She is," La Costa demurred. "I mean, is that okay?"

"Sweetie, it's okay if it sells books."

The food arrived, and Tess switched gears. "No shop talk for now. I want to get to know you better, and, of course, you need to know who I am and what I can offer. Do you have any questions for me?"

"Only a million," La Costa said. "Starting with, how do I eat this sandwich? It's huge!"

Within two and a half hours and a pitcher of iced tea later, La Costa had learned more about Tess Kardamakis than she knew about herself. Namely, that Tess and her husband, Demitri, fifteen years her senior, met in 1994 in Virginia Beach, after she sold his home in a real estate transaction. They fell in love, and she followed him to New Jersey, where the two were married in 1995, and she continued to work selling real estate up until the birth of the twins, Reyce and Sienna, who were now seven. Tess drove a Volvo station wagon, had a nanny, a housekeeper, and a chocolate Lab named Hershey. Her husband, Demitri, was a Greek businessman, who owned a restaurant service equipment business. He was sweet and kind and was the love of her life.

Tess loved knitting and reading, hated hospitals, Pilates class, and pompous query letters. She drank five-dollar lattes, had a quick, musical laugh, and looked at herself with a self-deprecating humor. She was of Jewish and Greek heritage, her mother hailing from a small town in Western Greece and her father, from Tel Aviv. She often joked about her prominent nose, compliments of her father's Israeli heritage, saying, "At least these days it's not the first part of me to enter a room!"

La Costa learned that Tess was born and raised in the Williamsburg section of Brooklyn in the late sixties. It was the very same part of town where her legendary idols had risen to fame from—in her own words, "Babs and Barry came from Williamsburg, now how cool is that?" Who hadn't heard of the famed Barbra Streisand, or the pop icon Barry Manilow? Certainly not Tess, as she was on a first-name basis with the two, whom she might have vicariously shared a similar zip code with at one time. La Costa had to smile. She wasn't worldly by any means but did agree that she loved a good throwback seventies ballad from time to time.

"Do you know why those artists were so freakin' successful back then, and still sell to a loyal fan base of baby boomers and every-other-generation through to today?"

La Costa did not.

"It's because people love a good love song, like they love a good love story. *That's* the reason. When you are selling emotions, you got your audience by the *kahunas*. Trust me, my first two were conceived during a Manilow's Greatest Hits loop on my iPod one slow autumn weekend afternoon in—are you ready for it? In *New England*. No lie. I swear to God! That's a true story."

"Does Barry know that?" La Costa asked, laughing out loud, and suddenly noticing that the busy restaurant had since cleared out, and they were the only two still lingering in a conversation that La Costa felt could go on for days. She simply adored Tess.

Tess laid it all on the line to convince her that she was the real deal, and although she had not been representing top-known authors for years like the winning track records of agents with the big publishing houses, she was still worthy of nurturing La Costa's talent and earning her a viable book deal.

"I got my start right after the twins turned two. I was going out of my mind, looking for something to do that would help me find my mojo again and didn't involve listening to mind-numbing Barney videos on repeat. I had been bedridden for the last trimester and had gotten through it by reading everything I could get my hands on. I ripped through whole collections and box sets of every genre from kids' books to erotica. You name it. The good, the bad, and the ugly. I read them all. Every trope, every variation on a theme, no stone unturned. No lost galaxy unexplored. It was then that I realized what I most loved to do was what I could do best—find the diamonds in the rough and help talented writers launch their careers. I had a calling, you might say. A knack for knowing what would sell out there. I just needed a chance to prove myself and get my feet wet in the industry."

"So, what did you do?" La Costa asked, riveted.

"I took a job as an assistant for a literary agent in the city and learned all that I could. I was a quick learner. I paid attention to the agent's duties and learned the ropes. One day, a manuscript crossed her desk that she was not interested in, but I had read it and knew its merits. I arranged to meet with the author on the sly, as I just had fallen in love with his story. It was unique and yet timeless in so many ways. I went over my boss's head and presented it to a publishing house on her letterhead."

La Costa gasped.

"I know, right? A big no-no."

"So, what happened then?"

"It was picked up by that publisher all right. And I was promptly fired."

"Oh no!"

"Oh, yes. But I was thrilled! I learned what I needed to know. I *did* have what it took, and so, I opened up shop in a spare bedroom in the house, got some business cards printed up, and began soliciting manuscripts in writers' magazines and publications everywhere. Even in bookstores and libraries. I attended writers' conferences, eager for the scraps that other agents passed over, and soon came to find that much of the work was 'pass-worthy,' but that I only needed to find the gems in all that rubbish. I was so diligent and critical about every submission that came my way. I had to be. I was hungry for the promising unknown."

La Costa noticed that Tess's demeanor had sobered a bit.

"That's where you come in, La Costa. I have been searching for that one great gem, and I do think I found it in you."

"I don't know what to say, Tess. This is all so new for me. I honestly don't know if I can do this."

"Tell me, truthfully. Did you ghost write Georgia's biography?"

La Costa nodded.

"Then you can do this. I know you can. All you have to do is say yes, and I'm off to the races for you. Trust me, you have something extraordinary, and the world deserves to see it."

Just then, her cell phone rang, and she broke into a tirade of Greek expletives mixed with English—"Maaaaaa! Óchi do not let Papa get up there. Demitri will come by tomorrow. *Anaméno.* Yes? Okay, love you, Mitera—*antío.*"

Tess shook her head. "My father is a maniac with the house repairs. I don't like him to climb ladders. I'm sorry for the interruption. If you don't think this is all too much, I would love to represent you."

La Costa was more than certain. "Okay then, let's do this. You've got yourself an author. How do you say, 'let's do this' in Greek?"

"*As to kánoume!*"

La Costa laughed. "What you said! You'll have to be patient. I do not know the first thing about any of this. It's definitely all Greek to me," La Costa said, slipping on her coat.

"Just don't you worry, sweetie. Do the work. Make your deadlines, and let me worry about the rest. Lucky for you, I speak Greek!"

CHAPTER TWENTY-FIVE

2003

WITH THE SPRING CAME THE launch of Georgia's book *Southern Splendor* that sent Georgia on a multi-city book tour and a schedule packed with signings, television and radio interviews, and personal appearances. La Costa was left to hold down the fort with the final renovations, in which she had claimed a small section of one of the smallest guest rooms as a working office. Splendor Bay was set to receive its first guests with the grand opening, in just three short months. Georgia would be back by then, and things would hopefully move ahead with the Bed & Breakfast, and Georgia's book sales humming in the background. La Costa now had a deadline of her own to meet with Gaylord Publishing, a fast-growing publisher squarely in sixth place standing in the shadows of the top-ranking behemoth trade houses in New York. All it took for a company to rise in the rankings was a significant spike in unit sales due to a healthy list of bestselling titles and authors. It was Tess's belief that her client could do just that. Finalizing the fourth draft of *City Vixen* was a process that made La Costa's stomach queasy every time she sat at the computer and stared at the blinking cursor. *What if Tess hates it?* she wondered. *What if the publisher made a mistake and the whole thing was really just a sham? What if she was a sham?*

Fear and uneasiness permeated her thoughts, and yet, she pushed on. Filling her workspace with outlines and index cards; hundreds of notes and drafts that it took to get a single close-to-perfect, three to five thousand-word chapter. In her heart of hearts, she reasoned that giving birth to an elephant would be easier. Yet still, she wrote. Every day, without fail. Finally, early that fall, she had reached the end of the best draft she could write, and the feeling in doing so, was euphoric.

"Here's to you, my dear! Another great milestone for La Costa Jackson—or should I say, *Reed*! The world is going to love your book, I'm certain of it!" Georgia said, raising her glass of Merlot over the dinner plates in the brand-new gourmet-style kitchen with its gleaming granite counter-tops and sparkling new appliances.

La Costa smiled. "That remains to be seen. Along with Tess, that makes two of you who think so—three if you count my publisher. Fingers crossed," La Costa said. "And here's to you being back, and to more happy guests at Splendor Bay!" It was now early fall, and with the B&B up and running, it was good to have Georgia home, and all three of them together once again for a scrumptious meal. Georgia's baking was only rivaled by her way around a skillet of fried chicken, cornbread, and white beans.

Louis was sitting in the chair like a little man, with his napkin tucked neatly in his collar and elbows off the table, as was Miss Georgia's stern directive at any meal setting. He had just started kindergarten, already well ahead of his classmates in proficiency of the academic basics and growth ratios. He would be turning six in the winter, by which time, La Costa was certain, he would tower over his classmates in more ways than one. Louis was wildly smart and athletic—qualities that burst forth as soon as he could walk and talk. La Costa could not have been prouder of him.

"Mr. Jennings is staying on another day in the Palmetto room," Georgia said, "and we'll need to move the Mackays to the Port Royal suite for this coming weekend."

"Got it," La Costa said. They had been steadily busy since the start of the summer season, keeping up with the preparations and details for the heavily packed weekend guests, who often checked in on Friday afternoons and stayed on through Sunday evening. Georgia had to hire additional help to ramp up the housekeeping, and a part-time breakfast cook to keep the patrons in fanciful and delectable morning meals that met with Georgia's high standards. She, of course, oversaw the creation of all the sweets and pastries; delights of all manner that were ever-present for the taking, and on display in pretty glass domes on fanciful cake pedestals on the large dining table just off the kitchen.

On occasion, Georgia would need to break away to a promotional appearance or signing and leave La Costa at the helm. She didn't mind, really, as having the stability such a lavish home, a business to manage, and her own debut writing career about to take flight, made her feel useful, needed, and wonderfully *validated*. Of course, nothing mattered more to La Costa than Louis's happiness and stability. They were a family of sorts, and it didn't matter if they matched the traditional definition of what a family should be. It was hers.

Stan Petty studied the weathered photograph that the woman had left of the infant boy, along with the envelope with the retainer she had given to him six months prior for his "services," which had been fat with small bills, all twenty-five hundred of it, and of which, was now, empty. She had been anxious to know the whereabouts of her son, and had promised to produce the balance upon delivery.

She showed up again, unannounced, looking pretty, but strung-out. Not unusual in cases like these. She still, however, refused to provide any contact information in order to reach her. "I'll contact you," was all that she ever said.

"Where are we?" she asked, unable to keep her jittery nerves in check, fishing a cigarette from her purse.

"These things can take months, or even years," Petty grizzled, trying to feign optimism. "And it'll cost more moving forward. I think I got a good lead on La Costa Jackson's whereabouts, so I would encourage us to keep searching."

"How much?" Her tone was low and tight, like she hadn't taken a full, deep breath in days.

"At least another two grand," Petty said, unflinching. With what was at stake, he held all the cards.

"I'll get it," was all she said. And then quickly left.

Petty spun around in his dilapidated office chair and chuckled, watching through the broken blinds as she drove away.

He tossed the manila folder back onto the messy pile on his desk.

It was not three weeks later when a raid on a crack house in the Wholesale District yielded a bust in which his client was shown on the evening news, being shoved intothe back of an LA police patrol car, kicking and screaming. Petty later confirmed her conviction for a myriad of offenses, ranging from drug possession to prostitution to an aggravated robbery charge that placed her at the scene of a botched hit at a quick mart in Watts. She wouldn't, he reasoned, be returning anytime soon.

He retrieved the then-buried file folder from the bottom of stack that was simply marked: PANTHER ST. JAMES – MISSING MINOR, and pitched it, along with all of its contents, into the wastebasket.

CHAPTER TWENTY-SIX

JANUARY 2006
(THREE YEARS LATER)

A T THE SUGGESTION OF HER agent, and with her first four-book series completed, La Costa and Louis moved from South Carolina to New York City, into a small but comfortable garden apartment in Manhattan, where La Costa could be closer to her publisher and the writing market.

It was beyond thinkable to be leaving Georgia and Splendor Bay, but the writing, so to speak, was on the wall, and the move was what was needed for La Costa to progress with her calling, which was writing salable romance fiction in a highly competitive market. She simply could not continue to divide her time between her writing deadlines and the B&B. She needed to be in New York, in close proximity to her agent and publisher as her career was beginning to pick up momentum. Plus, the time had come for her and Louis to stand on their own feet.

"You know, I am going to miss you and this place like crazy," La Costa said, holding back tears that rivaled nothing in the world she had ever felt. No other job change or life move had ever packed the punch that leaving Georgia and the business that she had helped to build did.

"It's just another chapter, my dear," Georgia had said. "It's yours for the taking. You must follow that path wherever it leads. You've *earned* it. I couldn't be prouder of you."

La Costa could not recall a time in her life when she had ever heard those words. It was as if she had been given a second chance in life to rewrite her story. Georgia had given her that gift. How would she ever begin to repay her?

"I just want you to go out there and *slay it*, dear heart. Go show that big ole world what you've got. There is so much more, I know!" Georgia smiled, and then enveloped her with a hug that smelled like Chanel No. 5 and felt like home.

"Thank you—for everything, Georgia. We are so grateful to you."

"It is I who is grateful, my sweet. Go! Be a fabulous success. I expect nothing less," Georgia said with that twinkle in her eye that never failed to make La Costa believe that anything *was* possible.

La Costa and Louis climbed in the Town Car that would take them to the airport. The movers had an easy load with just the packing of her and Louis's personal possessions. It would be a new start, indeed.

Life in New York City was an adjustment, at best, but it was where La Costa needed to be as her career began to take flight, closer to her agent, publisher, and the movers and shakers in the publishing market. At times, promotional and publicity appearances, to which she was contracted, had La Costa traveling from coast to coast, which often compromised much of her scheduled writing time during the week. As a result, she would have to then make it up in the evening hours, after she and Louis had eaten dinner, when she then helped him with his homework, piano practice, or just grabbed some free time to play a video game or two. Once Louis went to sleep, La Costa would make a large pot of coffee and get to work writing into the early morning hours to get her word count done. It was blissfully grueling, but she loved it. Time spent with Louis was precious, and she was not about to take any more away from him than necessary. Her agent, Tess Kardamakis, was as resourceful as she was dedicated to La Costa's success. She arranged to lend out her nanny and let Louis stay with her family, whenever La Costa had to travel. Tess's twins were one year older than Louis, and they got along famously. It was truly a group effort to keep everything moving in the right direction. Weekends were kept free for Louis's extracurricular activities or for fun romps around the city exploring new foods, cultures, and neighborhoods that fed La Costa's muse and ignited Louis's own curious spirit. When able, La Costa volunteered at Louis's school in the classroom or library, which allowed her to spend additional time with him both before and after school.

La Costa completed her fifth novel—the first in what would be a six-book series—just as Louis finished the fifth grade. The first book in the series, aptly entitled *Steele and Ink*, brought in a decent stipend in advances from Graylord and paved the way for more to come. It was a contemporary romance featuring a strong-willed modern-day heroine named Rebecca Steele. In the heady novels, Rebecca, the protagonist, is a young tattoo artist who owns a shop in the middle of Harlem, and who is not only gifted with the ability to ink stunning and beautiful tattoo motifs, but—lives as well, through her dynamic and addictive blog postings that promoted fierce and inspiring takes on life. With a bent for beauty and expression, Rebecca's exploits often put her squarely in the path of diverse and unpredictable adventures of the heart that, like fresh ink, forever leave their mark. In subsequent books, Rebecca meets and falls in love with a chancy race car driver who is as elusive as he is handsome, a drifter songwriter, a politician with presidential aspirations, and a police detective who exploits her sensibilities, using her studio to crack down on a dangerous drug ring, of which he is secretly involved. In the sixth and final installment, the self-assuring and lovelorn Steele finally lands her true love in a twist no one would see coming.

As the books were published and launched, La Costa was expected to travel several months out of the year to meet contractual obligations at press interviews and promotional appearances. She had a clause added to her publishing contract that would see to it that such appearances would coincide with Louis's academic schedule. She refrained from attending book signings or readings in the summer or spring months, when he was home from school during his middle school years. For the most part, La Costa and Louis were inseparable, soul-locked companions who shared an intrinsic bond that transcended traditional ties of the DNA brown eye-brown hair genes. They were the best of pals. La Costa raised him with every bit of unfailing love and sacrifice that any natural mother would have for her child.

Remarkably, with the release of the fifth book of the Rebecca Steele series, in 2010, Georgia's memoir, *Southern Peach*, which had been optioned for a made-for-TV movie, was finally given the green light for production after an eighteen-month hold, thanks to the adroit sales finesse of Leo Monk, who had garnered top dollar from a premium cable network, hot for the winning bid. The success of the long-awaited adaptation taken from the imprimatur would not go without further tribute to La Costa, who was given public and screen credit for the film featuring Georgia's life story and marriage to Macklin Byrne, as being co-written by the incomparable and emerging author, La Costa Reed. The modern-day romance of epic proportions, having garnered an Emmy nomination to boot.

The fact that the network banked on the project, further catapulted La Costa from the ranks of emerging writer to celebrated awarded author was all the confidence needed to affirm La Costa Reed's standing as one of the most successful breakout writers of the decade. By the time the movie aired in the spring of 2011, and her second series was complete, she was fast becoming a household name, whose must-read, binge-worthy novels topped everyone's list.

CHAPTER TWENTY-SEVEN

NEWPORT BEACH, CA
2014

"THAT'S ALL OF IT IN a nutshell, I guess," La Costa said, gathering up the plates and offering Felicia a refill on her coffee.

"Oh, thank you, but I believe I have reached my limit and have taken up enough of your time," Felecia said, content from the pie and the riveting conversation. She was satisfied that she had gotten what she had come for, as evidenced by the stacks of copious notes she had taken and the recordings that would more than fill a three-page spread in the magazine about the famed author.

La Costa smiled.

Just then, footsteps approached, and the front door swung open. A young, handsome teenage boy bustled in, wearing earbuds, oblivious to them at first.

"Oh! You will get to meet my son." La Costa brightened. "Louis, please mind yourself—we have a guest. This is Ms. Hayden from the magazine. Felicia, this is my son, Louis."

The boy quickly removed the earbuds and reached zealously to shake her hand.

"Pleased to meet you, ma'am."

He was a sight to behold, Felicia thought. Rail-thin skinny with a broad, honest smile and a gleam in his eye for his mother and for the pie he spotted on the counter. Felicia collected her things and stuffed them into her large leather portfolio. "I have just spent the most marvelous afternoon interviewing your mom. She is a great lady and a fantastic author, but, of course, you already know that."

"Yes, ma'am," he said with an awkward wag of his chin, and then looked for La Costa to release him.

"Go on, then. Those waves won't wait. It's getting late," La Costa said, and then, turning to Felicia. "He is quickly becoming an ace surfer. Who knew? Ever since we moved out here, he has embraced the water like a fish!"

Felicia recalled from her pre-read of the memoir that Louis was enrolled in a high school for gifted children, showing prodigy-level aptitude for music composition. By age fifteen he was already an accomplished pianist, but much preferred the hustle of the basketball court in which to shine, with an eye on UCLA for college admission the following year, ahead of his classmates. La Costa had written that she would have much preferred Julliard but would be happy to let him follow his passion wherever it would lead. It was obvious that she gave him rein to follow his dreams.

"He is quite an accomplished young man," Felicia said, once she heard the door to his room bump shut.

"He is dead-set on that scholarship," La Costa said, removing the plates and cups from the table. "That's why we moved out here. Thanks to technology and frequent flyer miles, we manage to close that cross-country gap, and I'm able to fly coast to coast when needed to see my publisher. Our main home is located in the Wilshire Corridor—twenty-one stories up. It's near the country club and away from the bustle of LA, but close enough. Also, that's why I bought this little place here on the beach. It's the perfect escape for when things get too crazy in the city. We really love it."

"So, why now? Why write *your* story at this time? Surely you have many more novels left to write," Felicia asked, almost as an afterthought, as she made her way to the door.

"I don't know," La Costa said, walking her out. She gazed dreamily at the afternoon sky that would soon be giving way to evening breezes when the beachgoers would be packing up their towels and ice coolers and heading home to dinner. "It just felt like the right time, you know? I wanted to be transparent and real for my readers. I wanted to say some things that story-telling alone, could not allow."

Felicia nodded. She did know. "Well, La Costa Reed, you are as brave and enduring as you are beautiful. Thank you for a wonderful interview. The magazine and its readers are going to love this feature."

They exchanged goodbyes, and Felicia was off, scrolling through her phone, which had been buzzing with missed messages.

Later she would write: *Now, as La Costa Reed unwrapped her own story, book number eleven,* No Secrets, *she had established herself not only as a celebrated contemporary romance writer, but through the pages of her own superlative memoir, as a true and spirited survivor as well. As one of the bravest and enduring, the world had ever seen.*

CHAPTER TWENTY-EIGHT

2012

HENRY PAIGE WAS A SIMPLE man with pale white skin, a bristly mustache, a broad, genuine smile, and sparkling grey-blue eyes. He stood only a moderate five foot nine, but had a deep, soothing voice that was striking when he spoke. He was Scotch-German and was proud of it. He had, above all else, a gentle disposition and a tireless heart. That's what most people liked about him.

A former running back who played for Minnesota State in 1981, Henry studied business and horticulture at the university and dabbled in mystery writing on a part-time basis. He moved out West when he was twenty-three, and received his doctorate in business in the spring of 1989 from UCLA, while working as a bartender. Soon after, he took a job working at a small family-owned winery run by an extravagant entrepreneur named Dustin Gabriel in the summer of 1990, at which time he met and married Gabriel's niece, Lynda. The two were anxious to start a family right away, which they did. The would-be novel he had been tinkering with all of his college years was relegated to the bottom of a forgotten drawer.

Henry worked for Gabriel for several years, first as a sales rep, and later, helping to run the operations of the five thousand-acre vineyard, which came to yield year after year, the region's choicest Sauvignon grape harvests, producing some of the Valley's finest wines.

In 1995, Henry became the head of marketing, selling to retailers, restaurants, and hotels throughout the East and West coasts. Then, later, as vice president of operations, where he assisted the seventy-two-year-old Gabriel for the next several years, until illness rendered the old man too frail to attend to the affairs of the business. The winery was eventually handed down to Gabriel's children in 2002, and Henry was out.

His viable stock interest in the vineyard, yielded a rich and bountiful take for him to share with Lynda, which he promptly dumped into the stock market. Within two years' time, they had enough funds to purchase their own business.

On his forty-third birthday, after a surprise party thrown by Lynda and their young teenage sons, Zachary and Grayson, Henry found himself driving alone in the night. Confused and angst-ridden, he sat contemplating his future, staring at a glass of watered-down gin, at a bar seventy miles away from their sprawling home in San Rafael. He had no idea how he had even gotten there. All he knew was that he did not want to invest in a business— or one more day of his life—with Lynda. And that's how he knew that the marriage was over.

In the end, Lynda got the kids, the house, half of all of their assets, and plans for the new business, a start-up vending service, of which he had no interest in championing. She even took their incorrigible yapping Yorkie named Barkley. As far as she was concerned, she had the right to everything, and she took it. The marriage was a sham. He could not go on pretending. He simply didn't love her, and feared, perhaps, that he never had.

Henry spent the next two years of his life rebuilding. He quit drinking the hard stuff, learned to become blissfully addicted to the taste of coffee and the exhilarating rhythmic trance of the tapping of the computer keyboard. He managed to resurrect his manuscript from obscurity and decided to give it some sort of resuscitation. Pulling the old, abandoned manuscript from the bottom of a storage box, he looked at it pensively. He was, by self-admission, hardly a wordsmith, but the practice of simply going through the motions freed him, in ways that he could not explain.

He drifted for a while in thought. Tried to write again. Gave it up.

And then tried once more.

CHAPTER TWENTY-NINE

AUGUST 2014

WHY ON EARTH TESS CHOSE to call La Costa to a meeting halfway across the country at, of all places, a yoga class, was anybody's guess. Trapped in an overcrowded storefront studio in Jersey, with steamy windows and floor mats that smelled like sweaty feet, Tess persevered. It had been over ten years, and an equal number of books representing La Costa Reed's illustrious career. Now, La Costa was about to release *No Secrets*, number eleven, into the world. Tess's last-born was now ten years old, and Tess was still trying to ditch the last twelve pounds of "baby weight."

"I just thought this would be fun to do instead of a Skype call," Tess said, moving ungracefully into downward dog. "Besides, the ice queen wants to see us, and we have to bring her something big for this launch. You know how she can be."

Tess was referring to Patrycja Claypoole, better known as "Patty" by the drones who did her bidding from the large mahogany-desk-filled offices high in the sky of one of New York's most prestigious testaments to traditional publishing known simply as Gaylord. Patty's permanently planted humorless expression was no match for her take-no-prisoners approach to beating the competition.

"She actually kind of scares me," La Costa said, folding into child's pose, which was her favorite because it signaled the end of the torturous machinations. "That's why I have you—to deal with her. Me, I just write the stories."

The class ended, and a chorus of *Namastes* filtered above the ancient wooden floor up to the exposed-beamed ceiling. After which, the bevy of young and middle-aged moms and nannies, who had been staring at La Costa, broke into conversations about their days, their weeks, their husbands/boyfriends/lovers, she had guessed.

"It's all so predictable," La Costa said, reaching for a towel. "Patty will just push me to write more, faster. Wait until the article by Felicia Hayden comes out in *High Style*. Then maybe she will not be so worried about the sales of the memoir hurting anything."

"Hurting anything?" Tess said. "Take a look at that." Suddenly, someone broke away from the crowd of spandex and Lycra. She had recognized La Costa, and soon a crowd of women encircled her with accolades and requests for her autograph.

"Ms. Reed! Is that really you?"

"I think it is! Yes, it's her!"

"Would you mind signing a copy of the article? It's just in my car—"

"We love your books!"

Tess smiled. "The article hit this morning. These are your people."

La Costa was pleased, and a bit perplexed. She didn't usually garner such a reaction. She remained and chatted with the women, agreeing to sign their magazines and posing for photos. One fan even asked La Costa to sign her yoga mat.

"The numbers don't lie," Tess later said. "And when you connect with these types of women—like you did in that interview, they are going to react this way."

"I guess something worked," La Costa said. "I've never been recognized outside of a book signing. That was incredible!"

"Yes, but we can do better. We can do *more*. Let's get changed, and then I want to show you something."

A half hour later they were back at Tess's house, a sprawling twelve thousand square-foot mansion in Englewood, just five miles from Manhattan, that once was owned by a hip-hop rapper. It had eight bedrooms and a movie theater built on the first floor. Tess's favorite feature was the ultra-private office that was once a music studio located adjacent to the house. It was all hers, and even though it was windowless, she loved it. Her husband, Demitri, had the colossal double-door den just off of the dining room, with a view of the massive winding driveway located in the front of the entrance of the palatial home. The rest of the house was free-range paradise for their three children, live-in housemaid, and bevvy of shelter dogs that pretty much ran the roost.

Tess ushered La Costa into her chic but efficient office and dropped her yoga bag on the floor. She readily bent over her computer and brought the screen to life. It was fixed on a spreadsheet from the publisher.

"Come take a look," Tess said, backing away so that La Costa could view the bright screen.

"What am I looking at?" La Costa asked.

"That right there are the figures for the pre-orders of *No Secrets*. They are at forty percent greater than the figures you have been pulling with each book in the Rebecca

Steele series. This interview you did with *High Style* is resonating with men *and* women in the demographic, and particularly with a broader age-range. I'm telling you, you are crossing over completely into another level here, *Bubbi*."

"Wow!" La Costa said. "I mean, that's good, right?"

"That's freakin' fantastic—and we need to bounce on this momentum right away. As soon as the book drops, you're guaranteed to be sitting sweetly at the top of *all* the lists—*Publishers Weekly*, *USA Today*, the *Times*—and it's going to be my job to *keep* you there."

"And how do you propose we do that?" La Costa hedged, fearing that Tess had something bold up her sleeve, as usual.

Tess glanced at the crystal clock on her desk, and then reached for the remote. "Let me show you." She powered on the giant television monitor suspended across from the insanely expensive custom-made leather couch. The screen came to life with a glowing happy-faced talk show host named Kristen Michaels on the set of a lively, midday talk show that followed the local news with high, gleaming stools, and over-produced stage lighting.

"I'll give you the answer. We are going to get *you* booked on that, and every little morning and afternoon news show in the country—that's how!"

La Costa's stomach dropped. While she couldn't be happier with the pending success of the memoir, she was not so sure about live television appearances. She never signed up for *that*. In fact, the thought of it gave her the jitters. "Up until now, things have been comfortably private. Book signings were one thing, but . . ."

"I've got a press release going out this afternoon, and several more in the week ahead. I wanted to run this by you in person before you head back to LA. Clear your schedule, La Costa, this is going to be huge—it's really going to put you front and center. That little fan-fest back there at the yoga studio was nothing. There's plenty more where that came from. Are you game, my *Ketzel*?"

La Costa nodded. She trusted Tess, and that was all that mattered.

"Okay, if you think it's necessary. But you're buying lunch."

"Deal," Tess said, grabbing her cell phone and car keys.

"Hey, what does 'Ketzel' mean, anyway?" La Costa asked.

"It's Yiddish," Tess said with that assuring glint in her eye that La Costa knew better than to doubt. "Yeah, I think it translates to 'little goat' or 'little kitten,' or something. Either way, we got this, *Bubbi*. No worries!"

CHAPTER THIRTY

2013

EVENTUALLY, HENRY PURCHASED A SMALL wine bar in La Jolla and named it Cork! He ran the entire operation on his own. In two years' time, he was able to add on a small retail store and hire additional staff. He had eventual plans to build an indoor-outdoor bistro slated for the following spring.

Henry believed in things like divine providence and cosmic destiny. So, it was no real surprise when the universe finally decided to serve him up a heaping dose of pure fate. The question being, was he ready?

The answer came not three weeks later in the simple serendipity of an old magazine left open on the chair next to his in the library, where he liked to steal away at off-times of the day, alone with his thoughts, and "puke in his journal," as he liked to refer to it. An advertisement caught his eye, with a bold proclamation, hyping the release of a sizzling new read, touting, *A novel so riveting, you'll not eat or sleep until the last page is turned!*

Henry chuckled to no one in particular. He was alone at his favorite table by the window, enjoying the solitude and the blissfully quiet, hushed tones of the sacred place. "What bunk! Who writes this stuff?" he wondered aloud.

He eyed the ad further. He was an avid reader himself, but of mystery thrillers, not the sappy, drama-laced cookie-cutter paperbacks and supermarket rags for bored housewives to binge on. He caught a glimpse of the author pictured above the book's cover. It was a stunning black woman posing on a deck with the surf and sand in the distance. She had a wide, familiar grin. Leaping from the newsprint in large script was a name that made him pause. *Another great book in the Rebecca Steele series by La Costa Reed!*

Could it be? he wondered, studying the glossy advert. *La Costa.* He had only ever heard that name one time before. It was during his bartending days in college, at Miss Lucy's Mink Kitty in Los Angeles—a long, long time ago. It *had* to be her! La Costa with the velvet skin and those stunning eyes. He never forgot a face, especially one as striking as hers.

Henry scooped up the magazine, walked out of the library, and headed home.

A college roommate who was the in-house deejay for The Mink Kitty club had referred Henry to Lucy DuMont back in 1987. Henry had just moved to Los Angeles, transferring from Minnesota State's graduate school, and was in need of a part-time job while he finished his degree.

"They're looking for a good bartender," he had said. "Why don't you check it out? Hey, man, there are WAY worse gigs you could land. It would be weekdays until close. If the hours don't kill you, I *promise*, the scenery will! You just gotta remember to keep your wood in your pants and ole Lucy will take care of you. Give her a call."

Henry took the number and the advice and was hired to work the VIP lounge. Hell-bent on earning his business degree, Henry remained focused, distancing himself from the tawdry temptations that came along with working in a strip club. Drugs, sex, and booze were ample and served up each and every night, all which could have easily been his for the taking. Instead, Henry shielded himself from the temptations. He studied voraciously on his breaks and remained as distanced from the self-indulgence and decadent lifestyle as possible. Which was to say, not the easiest of tasks.

Henry soon became the club's star bartender. He was quick and efficient. He never gave the girls a tough time, except for when their drink orders were called "out of order." As all things, Lucy had a set way that she liked things run, and deviating from any of the rules, simply meant lost time, and lost time meant less money to be made. On a bartender's wage, Henry had to work extra hard to pull down the tips that would fund his dream. He was focused and determined to own his own business someday. Every experience therein was a learning one for Henry.

He was quiet and a bit introverted, but he knew more than anyone everything there was to know about wine. He saved Lucy a ton of money in reorganizing the premium shelves and ordering and managing all the club's bar supplies by utilizing several new local vendors who were hot with discounts to win their business.

He wore a white tuxedo shirt and a bow tie—club regulations. And his nametag and lace-ups had to shine, or he would not be working that night. Lucy was just as strict with her help as she was with the showgirls who all worked to pack the house.

"The girls bring 'em in, and you see to it that they don't want to leave. Keep 'em deliciously drunk!"

On Friday nights, Henry co-bartended with Rory
Stevens, a muscular black body builder from down South,
who was, among many things, a former Chippendale's
dancer. The two made an odd team behind the glistening
massive bar. Rory, with his bulging pecs and biceps, and
Henry, short and preppy, a squeaky-clean Caucasian frat-
boy intellectual type in his aviator specs and mop of wavy
hair, cropped short at the neck and around the ears. He
had an earnest smile, though, and everyone loved his
quirky delivery—always cracking jokes while cutting up
the lemon zest and the limes.

The two learned to work the crowd as well as the girls
who served the cocktails, pushing booze and selling sexual
fantasy. It was all the same, it seemed, after a while. Henry
let Rory handle the female patrons who shimmied to the
bar with store-bought breasts and drug habits that could
knock a bull on its butt, and with agendas of their own.

They would order Kuris and Kahluas straight up,
slipping them their phone numbers, breathlessly touting,
"I'm a dancer . . . just in from Cincinnati." Or any such
other place. "Do you think you could put in a good word
for me with Miss Lucy?" In other words, "*Whom do I have
to fuck to get hired here?*"

Henry handled each situation with professionalism and
aplomb, leaving the hound-dogging to Spinner, his crazy
roommate and the club's best deejay, or to Rory, with his
thousand-watt smile and amazing dick. Henry had other
interests and plans that would take him far—better dreams
for himself than just getting by, or getting laid. He saw a
future for himself, far beyond all of the superficial bullshit.

Henry had always been aware of La Costa from the
day that she started at the club. He remembered seeing
Panther touring the new girl with the shy, sad smile. She
looked much like the other novices, with the exception,

perhaps, of being a lot less confident and slightly fuller-figured, which he found to be incredibly sexy. He had always secretly had a thing for the black girls. When she danced, though, all anyone noticed was the free-spirited way she moved to the music, entrancing her audience.

Over the course of several months, before leaving the Mink Kitty for his dream job in the vineyards of Napa, Henry might have said a total of three words to her—if that. Rarely did she waitress in the main lounge on the nights that he tended bar. And when she performed in the VIP lounge on weekends, her shift ended long before he finished counting out his cash drawer, after which he left for the night.

Sometimes, he, another bartender named Carlo, Rory, and some of the girls would all go out for breakfast in the early morning hours after work. La Costa never joined them. Once, he saw her at a producer's house party in Malibu, but she looked right through him, and he walked away, dejected, loath to ever try to catch her eye again.

Henry came to know the other black girl, Panther, quite well. But only regarded her as a wannabe zombie, always hanging on and flirting with anyone who was supplying the best drugs de jour. It didn't matter to her who had them—men or women. She would whore herself just to score a hit. Whoever had the best stuff got Panther's attention for the night. She simply gave it away, like so many of the others, who were also living crazed, dangerous, drug-induced comas until it was time for another evening, another show, another time to do it all over again. "Girls like Panther were like cocktail olives," he would say, "pickling in their own juices." Always hanging on, waiting to be devoured.

The whole scene was revolting, really. He had no idea if La Costa was anything like the others. All he did know, was that she lived with Panther and some of the "wilder" strippers, so what else was he to think? Besides, dating Kittens, let alone fraternizing with them, was strictly frowned upon. He was instead, quite complacent to just do his job. In his eyes, every last one of them was off-limits. Period.

He couldn't have been happier when Gabriel's hiring assistant phoned him at the club one night right out of the blue. He took the call in the back locker room just before the start of his six p.m. shift, not three days before the Christmas holiday. He grabbed a pricey bottle of champagne from behind the bar, popped the cork, and threw back a celebratory swig. Then, he swaggered through the kitchen, whooping and slapping high-fives with the bus boys and dishwashers along the way. He bounded into Lucy's office, where he promptly and exuberantly grabbed her and kissed her squarely on the lips, and said, "I love ya, Lucy. But I quit!"

CHAPTER THIRTY-ONE

NEW YORK CITY
SEPTEMBER 2014

LA COSTAS'S PALMS WERE SWEATING before she even reached the small, nondescript television studio in Midtown Manhattan. Tess was late, as usual, and La Costa was on her own to ferret her way to the lobby entrance that would lead to the set, which she was expected to report to in exactly seven minutes. The cab ride from the airport did little to calm her nerves, and all she could think of was being home, back in California, sitting in her favorite writing chair at her desk. That was her happy place, and where all the magic happened, as far as she was concerned.

Ten minutes later, she was sitting in a stylist's chair being given a short list of "talking points" that she would be expected to cover in the four-and-a-half-minute segment. Natalie, the androgynous-looking stylist, was quickly assessing the eyelash extensions situation when Tess finally walked in.

"Tess! I'm so glad you made it. I was beginning to think you stood me up!"

"What? No worries. I was on the line with your publicist. A radio station in town that wants you for a call-in interview sometime next week. We are definitely on a roll. Are you ready for Kristen?"

La Costa nodded, and then shooed away the accosting stylist with the lash glue and said, "I'm good, honey. I've been tending to my own for years—we're going to leave them be."

Natalie obliged and quickly dusted La Costa's silky skin with an iridescent cream along her neck and décolletage. She was buxom and curvy in all the right places, and the sheen only accentuated her assets.

"That leopard print blouse is perfect!" Tess said, having chosen the ensemble herself from Barneys. Nothing but class and style for her star author.

A dab of lip-gloss completed the touch-up just as Kristen Michaels bounded into the dressing room, all smiles.

"Hi, ladies, are we ready for a show?"

Tess and Kristen exchanged a near-miss air-kiss on each cheek, and La Costa rose from the makeup chair to shake the hand of her exuberant host.

"Nice to meet you, Kristen. Thank you for having me," La Costa said.

"Hi, La Costa, so nice to meet you. I promise, this will be painless. Just a few general questions about you, your writing process, and the new book. I will give you free rein to promote the memoir and any of your backlist titles. How does that sound?"

La Costa smiled. "You make it sound easy!"

"Like coffee clutching, really. Just be you and it will come off perfect, I'm sure," the Kathy Lee Gifford doppelganger said brightly. "I'll have my assistant, Topher, come for you two minutes out."

She waved them off with a fifty-watt smile in her perfect designer shift dress with zero cellulite evident on her stick-thin arms.

Just as La Costa managed to thank her again, Kristen was gone, clicking away down the hall in her Christian Louboutins with a bevy of production assistants in her wake.

Tess felt La Costa's tension and reassured, "It's just like talking to a friend. Forget the lights and the cameras, and the millions of eyes on you."

"You mean, the tens of thousands of eyes. This is just a local show," La Costa said, starting to click her acrylic talons together, which she did when she felt out of her depth.

"No, actually, this little segment is going live to all of the affiliates for the parent network. It is the quickest way to reach as many viewers as possible—coast to coast," Tess said, addressing the stylist. "Maybe a little bit more powder on her forehead? She's looking a bit *warm*. Jesus, La Costa, try not to sweat until it's over."

Just before La Costa could find the words to end the madness of what felt like a bad dream, the production assistant appeared in the doorway.

"It's time, Ms. Reed. They're ready for you."

La Costa took a deep breath, steadied her resolve, and prayed for the best.

It wouldn't be the first time she had to play to an intimidating crowd.

The interview went flawlessly. La Costa shone like the star that she was. Kristen was kind and affable, giving La Costa the spotlight, which made the four-and-a-half-minute interview seem like a friendly conversation with a friend. The camera loved La Costa. She settled into talking one-on-one with Kristen, just like she had done with Felicia, the magazine reporter back in her beach home. It was no different, really. She did not focus on the bright lights that bounced off reflector screens, or the steady blinking red glow of the two cameras that were trained on each of them; or the movements in the shadows off set of the technicians that scurried about, waving their arms, or some of whom just stood watching. It was a show, and La Costa was the star. It was her moment, and rather than shield herself with a wall of protective placidity, she let herself be completely in the moment. It felt wonderful to simply be authentic and to live her truth.

Tess stood proud and still in the darkness, looking on. *Take it all in, La Costa. You deserve it. Everyone is watching!*

Everyone, indeed, was watching. Clear across the country, in La Jolla, the East-Coast live broadcast aired sometime after seven a.m., streaming on the small television monitor that Henry had mounted beneath the oak cabinets above the kitchen counter. He had previously turned on the morning news before stepping out to run the dog around the block and to get the newspaper from the driveway. When he walked back into the sunny kitchen, he poured himself a second cup of coffee, reached for his reading glasses, and turned up the volume with the remote. He caught a glimpse of the end of the interview with Kristen Michaels featuring a beautiful black woman with a stunning wide smile and sparkling eyes. It was then that he saw it—the title font on the bottom of the screen, framing a closeup shot of her face, which read: LA COSTA REED – BESTSELLING AUTHOR.

The words stopped Henry's heart cold. *There she was again!* He couldn't believe what he was seeing. It definitely was *her!* Then he wondered, *What were the chances?*

And thirty-five hundred miles away, at a women's correctional institution in Brooksville, Florida, so too, did a gaunt, forty-five-year-old woman with a scraggly salt-and-pepper braid wearing a faded blue bandanna see that same image emanating from a television screen set up in the crowded recreation center. She watched with cold, blank eyes as La Costa nodded and smiled gregariously, bathed in the bright lights of the news studio and the interviewer's accolades.

The woman sat in silence as she dragged a ragged fingernail back and forth across the small tattoo of a black panther etched on her wrist, and continued to stare at the screen—slowly *seething*.

CHAPTER THIRTY-TWO

LA JOLLA, CALIFORNIA

FINDING LA COSTA WAS NOT going to be easy. When Henry phoned the publisher and asked for the name of the agency representing her, he learned that she actually had two, one for her books and the other, who managed her press and personal appearances. Months earlier, Tess Kardamakis had decided to hire on a publicist to help with visibility.

What was he doing? He scribbled down the numbers for the publicist but hit a dead end when he tried to ask for personal information. A helpful millennial-type receptionist suggested that he check Ms. Reed's website for a list of promotional appearances for the upcoming weeks. He did just that. All were at local bookstores and auditoriums in and around Manhattan. He deduced that the East Coast was most likely her home. Discouraged, he decided that would end the extent of his sleuthing efforts. What was he? A *stalker*? No chance!

Still, he continued to think about La Costa. He simply could not get her out of his mind.

Two months and seven well-worn La Costa Reed paperbacks later, Henry passed a big box bookstore in San Diego one afternoon and caught sight of something that caused his heart to skip a beat. It was that familiar smile— La Costa's smile, on a life-size poster of her in the window. The caption read: MEET LA COSTA REED, AUTHOR OF *NO SECRETS*. HER LATEST AND REVEALING BIOGRAPHY ON SALE HERE! *Special in-store appearance. Saturday, twelve p.m. until three p.m.*

He could barely believe his fate! Once he pulled himself together, and blessed the gods of unexplainable serendipity, he grinned all the way home, but not before buying her celebrated memoir.

He devoured the memoir in a marathon eight-hour read that lasted until dawn, making him late for work at the bistro that next morning.

What were the chances that La Costa Reed would be right there in California that weekend? In his part of the world, no less? And, most importantly, would she remember him? He was certain that he still had that tuxedo shirt and black tie stored away . . . *someplace.*

Henry was excited and apprehensive all at the same time. Even if La Costa did remember him, would she be at liberty to talk about the past? Obviously, it was not a deep, dark secret that she had blotted from her life, or she would not have chronicled her life story now, post-celebrity. A shameful stint as a nightclub stripper, one would think would be something she might have chosen to bend the truth about. Instead, from what he had read, she was owning it boldly.

Henry had done his homework. La Costa was forty-three, single, and had never been married. She had a sixteen-year-old son named Louis, whose last name was Jackson, her real surname, he presumed. She was now touting a fancy pen name that suited her well. La Costa's writing credits consisted of an early biography of Georgia Byrne, the modeling industry maven, which included a television movie, the four-book contemporary romance "Vixen" series, the six-book "Rebecca Steele" mystery/romance series, along with a handful of stand-alone steamy romance titles that were often sold in box sets by the publisher. These, added to her controversial memoir, rounded out her current catalog. In addition, La Costa also maintained a fan blog and frequently submitted exposés for several national women's magazines, including *High Style*, of which, she appeared in a four-page spread about her life with the release of *No Secrets* back in the August issue. A frustrated and closeted writer himself, Henry marveled at her unprecedented success. He truly could not have been happier for her.

Other than these publicly disclosed details, the other areas of La Costa's private life were non-existent. He was certain from the website, media kits, interviews, and back-of-the-book jacket biographies, that La Costa previously had never let the rest of the world—her public—know how very close to home her first central character, Vivian Dunn, mirrored her *own* past and background. At least, what he assumed it to be. Now he wondered, *Would she appreciate a reminder from a time in her life she might rather forget?* He wrestled with the dilemma until his gut reaction won the bitter battle waging within. Everything seemed to indicate that the time would be right. He would reach out to her.

From a street side window, Henry watched as La Costa greeted a never-ending throng of fans, some two to three hundred at a time, lined up along the aisles of the mammoth bookstore for over two and a half hours, for a signed book jacket, and to shake hands with the beloved author. She had the same expressive brown eyes he had remembered, and he could see the expert way she used them to entrance her admirers.

La Costa was a natural beauty. He knew it back then and found it to be even more true now, some twenty-five years later, as she sat there, strong, confident, and elegant, a far cry from the woman he had once known, who was a lost and frightened young girl, all of those years ago. He had decided not to approach her just then, or to intrude on her spotlight. There would be another opportunity. Still, there was, in spite of all the accolades and attention, the same spellbinding smile as she moved her attention from one person to the next, poised and perfect in her stunning black and ivory Chanel suit. He watched her from a distance a few minutes more, and hopped in his Jeep for the short drive back up the coast, unable to remove the permanent smile that had him grinning for the rest of the afternoon and into his dreams that night.

He would remember the image of her well. It would be just one of many such moments he would forever hold. And in retrospect, it was the *exact* moment he knew that he was going to fall all the way in love with her.

CHAPTER THIRTY-THREE

HENRY DECIDED THAT INITIATING CONTACT with La Costa would require a clever and non-threatening approach. In the spirit of romance and ingenuity, he took an active leap of faith and sent her a cheerful hand-tied bouquet of flowers through her agent, Tess Kardamakis, with the East Coast agency, but did not sign his name on the enclosed card. He had figured that he would follow up with an equally unassuming gesture, perhaps reintroducing himself to her at another book signing.

No one was more surprised than he was when he checked his phone for messages the next day and found that La Costa had called to thank him for the delivery. And moreover, that she actually lived right there in Los Angeles!

"How did you know I was the one who sent them?" Henry asked.

"My agent and I tracked the order through the florist," she later told him over a bottle of Cabernet at a quiet table in the middle of LA's busiest restaurant row. "I told them that the driver must have dropped the card, and they gave me your name. I mean, I had to know who it was. It's not every day that I get flowers—and from a curated flower farm, no less.'"

"It's definitely the ethical aspect of it all for me." Henry chuckled. "The wrapping they use to tie up the bouquets are actually recycled burlap coffee bags. It's all locally sourced and socially conscience."

"I really love that," La Costa said.

The two agreed to meet for dinner, once Henry divulged who he was, and that they were actually old acquaintances. They talked for hours, seemingly non-stop. "I can't believe it," she kept repeating, touching her face and blushing in the most delightfully shy way as she began to remember. "Henry, from the club! We used to time the end of our shifts by your unfailing bar routine: At one forty-five a.m., precisely, you began clearing all the condiments and shelving the premium bottles into the cabinets. Didn't matter if there were fifty patrons standing there. At two a.m., sharp, man, you were closed for business!"

They both laughed.

"Yeah, Lucy had strict policies, especially when it came to paying overtime. Besides, I really hated that place— no offense. I did my job, and BAM! I was out the door. Besides, I had a graduate course to muddle through," he said pensively. "I guess that's why we never really hung out." His eyes were fixed on the candle's glow, which, in the half-light, revealed a deep dimple in his left cheek when he chuckled.

"I guess so . . ." La Costa's voice trailed. "It is as if it all was another lifetime ago. Someone *else's* life, huh? At least, it is that way for me."

Their dinners went mostly untouched and were soon cleared away. They finished off a second bottle of wine, talking for several hours more that seemed to pass like minutes. The two, reminiscing about *the old days*, as Henry liked to call them.

"I remember you, though, so vividly." Henry sighed.
His voice was deep in tone and rich with texture. La Costa
was now transfixed by a tiny scar on his upper lip. She
had never really regarded Caucasian men any differently
from other races. Only insomuch as she did find their
demeanor a bit softer and their charm more subtle. Still, no
less appealing. *So many questions*, she thought. There was so
much that she wanted to know about him beyond his coy,
boyish grin; about things that she saw there in his gentle
leaden eyes. Strangely, she trusted him and the way, in that
moment, he made her feel as if she were twenty years old
again.

"I guess I was just too shy, or I felt too invisible to
approach you. I would have asked you out in a second,"
he said.

This made La Costa smile even more. A tinge of
excitement stirred inside of her. She didn't have many
friends, really, let alone a gentleman friend. It had just
always been easier to keep things at a distance. Connecting
with someone from her past made her feel oddly validated.
It was good that someone like Henry could see her today,
as a successful, accomplished woman; someone who had
made something of herself in spite of a troubled and sordid
past. Even though she didn't owe anyone anything. It was
all self-acquired. It was something to be proud of, and it
made her feel wonderful to be celebrating that fact there
and then with him.

When the check arrived, she let him pay. Not having
anticipated the possibility of spending adult time with
Henry, La Costa was especially happy that Louis had
previously arranged to spend the weekend with a friend
from school, whose family was taking a boating excursion
to Catalina Island. With this in mind, she surprised herself
when she asked boldly, "Would you like to see the city

from a modest high-rise overlooking the country club, Henry?"

La Costa's home was a work of art, perched nearly at the very top of the luxury condo complex on the twenty-first floor above Club View Drive in the Wilshire Corridor. Colorful abstract paintings lined the walls of the expansive loft-style gallery. Stone and metal sculptures dotted the built-in shelves, and pristine modern furniture created a cozy yet eclectic air to the pristine modern minimalist décor. Track lighting and marble floors spanned the thirty-eight-hundred-square-foot unit with walls of floor-to-ceiling sliding windows creating a passage onto a shelf balcony that looked out onto the Hollywood Hills, and offering a breathtaking view from the master bedroom of the city skyline and a crescent glowing moon in the distant sky above.

"High-rises make me happy," she explained. "But anything over thirty floors is enough for me."

"It's beautiful," he said, speaking directly into her shining eyes.

The wine was giving everything a dreamy hue, causing her to blush and giggle a little too much for her liking. She had a thought spring to her mind that made her light up even more, remembering an old photo album she had kept of the club, filled with color four-by-five prints and square Polaroids. She excused herself to go retrieve it from her work office.

After rifling through several storage boxes in the closet, she found the faded cloth-bound album, stuffed to the gills with loose photos and memorabilia. It had been her farewell gift from her roommates, the other Kittens, so many years ago.

When she returned to the living room, Henry had selected a John Legend CD and was adjusting the knobs on the stereo. "I can't believe that you actually have a CD player. That's so old school. I love it!" Henry said.

"Why fix what ain't broke?" La Costa said, reaching for a bottle of Beaujolais Reserve from the wine rack in the great room, and then retrieving two glasses from the lofty designer cabinets of the stunning Malibu-Modern kitchen galley. Tess had sent her the bottle as a gift for the completion of the final draft of her last novel in the Rebecca Steele series a few years back. La Costa had never had the notion to drink it herself, or an occasion to share it with anyone, until now. She uncorked the wine with expert flourish and poured the expensive liquid into the two round goblets, then handed one to Henry, who smiled. She settled next to him on the couch, and, together, they sank a little into the exquisite leather and more easy conversation.

Opening the photo album, she let the memories spill into her lap. They devoured the pictures with relish, curiosity, and good humor. Faces and names floated back to the surface, along with some memories better left forgotten. La Costa stirred when she saw a photograph of Panther striking a CoverGirl pose. Louis had her smile, no doubt. Anyone with eyes could see it. She grew suddenly tense at the flood of pain that seared through her veins, along with the numbing red wine. *Would Henry be able to tell if he met Louis?* she wondered. *Would he see it?* It had been so many years, but still, she feared ever revealing the truth to Louis, and the irreparable damage that knowing the truth about his birth mother, Panther, could cause. Louis knew that he had been "adopted" by La Costa from infancy, but nothing more beyond that. And La Costa planned to keep it that way.

"Hey, I remember her well. She called herself Panther,

right?" Henry said, his eyes bouncing from one image to the next, relishing the walk down memory lane. "You two were tight, right?"

La Costa glazed over the inquiry. "I do think we were, back then. Look, here's Lucy with all of us, posing for a group shot on New Year's Eve."

Henry let his hand linger on hers as they laughed and talked, exchanging war stories like old college chums, just the harmless, surface stories that somehow needed to be remembered; needed to be told.

"Look at those heels! A lot of the time, we would put our sore, blistering feet into the toilet bowl after a shift to soothe them. And then do you know what we would do?"

"No. Tell me. You didn't actually—"

"Oh, yes, we FLUSHED it! You bet we did. That was the best part. Very refreshing. An instant foot massage!"

He shook his head, imagining the scene of sixteen young women in G-strings, stilettos in hand, waiting in line to stuff their feet into the two working toilets. "No wonder they were always stopping up!"

"Do you know what else?" La Costa was now covering her face coyly with her hand.

"I'm afraid to ask."

"Sometimes, we took beer bottles from the cooler and rolled them under our arches. Anything to soothe our aching dogs!"

"So that's what that was all about!" He brightened. "You girls were always coming over to me asking for a cold brew, *unopened*. And come to think of it, by at least two thirty, every morning, the floor manager had us pack a couple dozen Bud's on ice, which were sent to the dressing room. I always assumed that you all *drank* them."

"Oh, we did—afterwards!"

Henry smiled. He looked handsome and inviting in his

black silk T-shirt and Italian blazer. A trace of aftershave wafted from his neck from time to time when he moved in close to help her turn the pages of the scrapbook, or take a closer look at a faded photograph. His pants were pressed and his shoes, shined to perfection. That was Henry—perfect to the nines. She liked that. She liked that he cared about the little things.

He looked exactly the same as she had remembered, except maybe for various improvements painted by time. His were the eyes of a compassionate man who had seen some things in his life; done some unforgettable things, no doubt. She liked knowing that this, too, was something that they had in common. Henry managed to blur all the lines.

And when they finally kissed, it was a sweet, stolen kiss, catching her off guard. She reciprocated in kind with a soft peck to his cheek, and when he pulled her close again, their mouths and bodies merged in a deep, soulful fusion that left her breathless.

Henry stayed the night, and he and La Costa made love—it was more heartfelt and honest than she had ever known. La Costa abandoned her fears, if only for the few fleeting hours of nighttime that remained. She did not want the coming dawn to disrupt the sweet and dreamy state into which she had fallen—let herself fall—for once. She lay awake and listened to the soft, rhythmic breaths, watching as Henry's chest rose and fell with each one, allowing herself to believe that with the coming dawn, that maybe they were destined to be something more than old friends. Perhaps, for the very first time in her entire life, La Costa thought, she could let another person in without the fear of compromising her dignity or her heart. *This must be what they mean by kindred spirits,* she thought. She gazed out through the glass windows, at the starry sky that bathed the room in a soft, warm glow. But was she truly *worthy?* All she could do was to try to believe, and to hope that what she was feeling deep inside, was real.

CHAPTER THIRTY-FOUR

FROM THAT POINT FORWARD, LA Costa and Henry never spent more than three days in a row separated from one another. Business trips to the East Coast meant lingering airport goodbyes and long, late-night phone calls, when, at the end of the day, one would call the other on their cell phone and talk or text as long as the batteries would last. La Costa would often drive to La Jolla to Henry's bistro to find him picking up a shift in the kitchen or unloading crates of wine through the service entrance. She just wanted to be close to him. Some days, she would sit, sipping a cappuccino, at a corner table with a fickle Wi-Fi connection, tapping away at her laptop, working on her daily word count or writing her blog as Henry worked managing the restaurant. Occasionally, the two would meet for dinner in the city, steal away an evening or two at the LA condo, or plan an impromptu fun escape weekend at the beach house.

It was two months in before La Costa introduced Louis to Henry, and it was not without much trepidation. La Costa thought it would be less intimidating for Louis to meet Henry on his own playing field—or, court as it were. She had arranged for Henry to join her for one of Louis's Friday night games at the high school, and then for the three of them to enjoy a casual meal at Louis's favorite pizza joint. Much to La Costa's delight and relief, Louis was on board.

"Mom, it's not like I haven't known about this Henry dude for all this time. I have eyes and ears, you know," Louis said, kicking off his high-tops and sliding across the shiny marble floor over to the fridge. "Do we have any Fresca?"

"Well, I just wanted to prepare you, that's all. Henry Paige is a great guy, and I've actually known him for many years now. It's just recently that we started getting to know one another better," Las Costa said.

"Uh-huh." Louis was half-listening, riffling through the freezer for the Hot Pockets.

"So, is Friday good, after your game?"

"Yeah, that's okay with me, Mom. Really, it's not a big deal. Chill." He kissed her on the cheek, and then reached for his earbuds. "Oh, can you nuke these for me, please?"

It was as simple as that. They all had a date.

As expected, Louis and Henry hit it off, and La Costa could not have been happier. Louis had played one of his best games ever. As a power forward at nearly six foot two, Louis had inside game, for sure. He could shoot, get to the hoop, and rebound like the pros. He was all-star varsity and it showed, making thirty out of fifty shots, sinking every free throw, and breaking the tie score with the win at the buzzer.

"Dude, that was some game!" Henry said, leaning in for a handshake, and then slapping Louis firmly on the back. "I'm your mother's friend, Henry Paige. So nice to meet you. Call me Henry, all right, Champ?"

Louis, fresh out of the shower and wearing his finest

street clothes—athletic pants, a Clippers T-shirt, and Jordans—grinned and hoisted his gym bag over his shoulder. "It was a good game for you guys to see. Nice to meet you too."

"Are you kidding me? You were amazing!" La Costa proceeded to cover Louis unabashedly with kisses all over his cheeks and forehead—red lipstick marks, be damned! She was a proud mama!

"Aw, okay. Now I have to go back in and wash my face." Louis dropped the gym bag and turned back in the direction of the locker room. "Love you too, Mom!"

"Be quick, baby! We'll meet you at the car."

La Costa smiled. "He's my superstar, you know."

"I do think I know that, yes," Henry said, grabbing Louis's gym bag. "La Costa, he's a winner, I can tell. Just like you." Then he took her hand and kissed it sweetly. "Let's go."

Life, it seemed, had begun for La Costa the moment Henry walked back into her life. Not three months into the courtship, he professed his feelings and promised to love her and to take care of her forever. When the prospect of making a lifetime of it, however, they had both shared a mutual belief that getting married was not the goal. Such institutions were for "other people." It was not necessary for them, they believed, to compartmentalize their love with contracts and clauses of betrothal. This made the relationship flourish and enabled La Costa to relax into it, knowing that her life was still her own. That she and Louis were still a team of two. She and Henry had a commitment bonded in trust and free will, something far more sacred to them than any ceremony or contract could offer.

She was, to him, the promise of a lifetime dream fulfilled.

And he was to her, the dream she had long given up on believing in. Every day forward, she had to pinch herself to see if she was living her real life, or a dream.

CHAPTER THIRTY-FIVE

NOVEMBER 2014

L A COSTA LOVED LITTLE ELSE more than the
holidays. Thanksgiving was never an occasion for
celebration when she was growing up, but ever since Louis
had been able to chew solid foods, she was on board with
making every holiday one for the record books. Especially
the years that they had lived with Georgia, plates were ever
filled with delightful, scrumptious meals and baked goods
suitable for a patisserie.

"So, you learned how to do all of this from Georgia?"
Tess asked, holding a glass of mimosa and parking herself
on a high kitchen stool at the imported stone counter.
"This is *gorge*, my *Ketzel*. What is it, Italian?" Tess said,
running her hand over a stretch of the gleaming marble.

"It's actually enameled lava. And *shhh*, don't tell anyone.
I Googled the turkey and Pinterested the dessert parfaits.
The pies and the casseroles are all Georgia all the way. Of
course, I had to Facetime with her two weeks ago for a
run-down on how to get the squash casserole going. It's a
southern delight, right out of her recipe vault," La Costa
said, elbow-deep into the oven to check on things. "I'm

so glad that you guys could join us for this little family gathering—and what a family we all are! Right?"

"What? The pleasure is ours. It's an honor to be invited to this stunning palace in the sky. As for me, I don't cook. Demitri knows that he didn't marry Martha Stewart. We usually just make reservations somewhere, and then head over to the folks' for dessert. Which reminds me, can I have one of those pumpkin pies to go? We're driving to San Diego in the morning to see Demitri's parents before we fly back to Jersey on Sunday."

"Of course, Tess. I'll box two of them up for you to take to your in-laws before you have to head out. Have I told you how glad we are that you and your family are here? That you came all this way to spend Thanksgiving with us?"

"So sweet of you, *Bubbi*. My little Ella just loves Louis. So, too, do the demon twins, but they'll never show it. In fact, I think that Sienna has a little crush."

"You think? I can never tell. They all just always look so bored in our presence, or just completely absorbed with their iPods and gaming consoles. I swear, I can't get Louis to actually pick up a book."

"That's actually ironic, don't ya think?" Tess said.

"Well, he certainly doesn't need to be reading what I write! I promise you, no interest there, except for the lifestyle it brings." La Costa wiped her hands on a dishtowel and said, "Looks like dinner will be ready in about an hour. Where's that pitcher of mimosas that Henry whipped up?"

Tess smiled, feeling quite proud of herself and the great team that she and La Costa had become. Things were running on all cylinders, and there was no end in sight. La Costa Reed was holding her own in the rankings, and the new year would only promise more good things to come.

"Oh, and speaking of which, what is it with that new

man of yours? I tell you, he's a prince! He took all of the kids down to the spa to wear them out in the saltwater pool with a marathon run of Marco Polo, and then officiated a quick pickup game on the basketball court. He's a keeper, that one, for sure!"

"That he is, Tess. He has two boys of his own, both superstars at their colleges out east. He just got back from having an early holiday with them in DC. I don't think I have ever been happier about so many things. I am often afraid to say that out loud, fearing I might jinx something."

"Not a chance. If he makes you happy, that's all you need to know. You're simply beaming, *Bubbi*." Tess grabbed the pitcher and poured a flute for La Costa. After refilling her own, she raised her glass and proclaimed, "I glow, too, from time to time, but now it's just hot flashes. Here's to more magic, manuscripts, and memories to come! *Salute*, my friend!"

The two clicked glasses and fell into a fit of giggles.

The woman in the blue bandanna sat calmly in the waiting area. The paperwork had been completed weeks ago for her release. A bundle of clothing, all she had been wearing on the day of her arrest, was returned to her, along with a manila envelope containing some personal effects and sixty-six dollars in small bills. She ripped open the envelope upon receiving it and dumped the contents into her lap, her skittish fingers touching every piece of paper, searching manically for the glossy photo. It was there. Crumpled and faded, but it was there.

She leaned over to the woman sitting on her left, holding a similar stack of clothing and a discharge envelope, and said, "Is someone picking you up?"

"My sister," the woman said. Panther had known her

from the exercise yard and from a work assignment the past summer. "Need a ride?"

"Yeah," Panther said, handing the woman the crumpled cash.

"Keep it, babe," the woman said. "You're going to need it. We can take you as far as Baton Rouge. Cool?"

Panther nodded. It would be a start.

CHAPTER THIRTY-SIX

L A COSTA WAS TWENTY-FIVE HUNDRED words into the first draft of her next romance trilogy, with the working title: *The Jess Trader Chronicles*, when Henry emerged from the bedroom, dressed and ready for the day. He leaned in behind her at the keyboard and nuzzled her neck with a chin full of prickly stubble.

"I know you don't think that you can come up in here without a clean-shaven face and kiss me," La Costa teased.

He knew how much she hated his scratchy post-dawn beard, but it was already past eight, and he had to get to the bistro.

"I'm sorry, babe. I have to run. I wouldn't be so grizzled if you would have let me get any sleep last night," he said, pulling her hands from the keyboard and wrapping them around his neck. "My staff doesn't mind the new look. Everyone knows that I've gone to seed since you stole my heart."

"Is that so? Seems to me that someone passed out last night after too much wine and turkey. Once our guests were gone, so were you. As soon as you hit the pillow!" La Costa said, straightening his collar. He looked adorable in his button-down shirt and starched chinos. Who would have ever thought that her type was this delicious-smelling, intoxicating, clean-cut white man, Henry Paige? Certainly not her.

"Where's Louis?" Henry asked, reaching for his car keys and slipping the Tumi satchel strap over his shoulder.

"He went back to the hotel with Tess and her family. They are taking him with them on the road trip to San Diego. He and Reyce are like brothers. Said he wanted to go."

"So that means . . . ?" Henry smiled.

"We are going to be blissfully alone for the next couple of days. They will drop Louis off when they make their way back to LAX on Sunday to fly back to New York."

"Oh," Henry said with a sly smile. "We will definitely have to take advantage of that."

"You read my mind," La Costa said. "But not before I get this word count done for the day. Till then, I can't even think about that, so go on and get. I have work to do."

Henry gave her another kiss and squeezed her waist. "Don't work too hard. Dinner tonight at my place?"

"It's a date. Now, go!" La Costa said.

Not two minutes after he had left, La Costa's phone buzzed. It was a call from South Carolina.

"Ms. Jackson?" The voice on the other end of the line was terse and formal. "I am attorney Anderson T. Wade. I have some unpleasant news to tell you about a Ms. Georgia Byrne. I am sorry to say that she passed away ten days ago."

La Costa sat, stunned and silent, in the chair, staring at the blinking cursor on the screen. She barely heard the lawyer's voice droning on the other end of the line as tears welled up in her eyes and her body started to tremble.

"I am handling the details concerning the terms of the will, which has been presented to court for probate on behalf of her executor. You have been named in the terms of Ms. Byrnes's will as a person of interest in the estate. Her great-niece is requesting that I contact you. When can you be here?"

CHAPTER THIRTY-SEVEN

THREE DAYS LATER, LA COSTA received a copy of the will, which had been overnighted to her Los Angeles residence. La Costa couldn't believe it. She had just spoken to Georgia two weeks prior, and she had looked fine. Quick and sharp as ever. The attorney, Mr. Wade, had not given her any information about what had happened. She would just have to wait until she could get to South Carolina and was able to meet with Georgia's great-niece to find out.

La Costa had managed to rearrange her scheduled appearances for the next week, much to her publicist's dismay, in order to fly to Hilton Head Island to sort out the details. From the preliminary and pedestrian reading of the documents, it appeared as if La Costa had been named as one of the beneficiaries of the estate.

"How long do you think you will be gone?" Louis asked, as he watched La Costa pack a sensible overnight bag that would qualify as a carry-on.

"Not long, sweetie. It's just to settle some paperwork and to pay our respects. I would take you with me if it didn't mean you would miss any more school."

"I know," Louis said somberly.

La Costa stopped packing and sat down next to him on the bed and pulled him close. "I know that you loved her, baby. I did too. We are really going to miss Ms. Georgia, aren't we?"

He let a tear slip from his eye. It was a shock to them both, and it would be the first time that Louis had ever lost a loved one. La Costa wondered if she was doing the right thing having him stay behind. He would be in Henry's care, which made the most sense. By now, Louis was much too old for a formal sitter.

"I'm going to need you to look out for things while I'm gone and listen to what Henry says. He will be staying here at the condo evenings, but you are on your own during the school day. I've spoken to the doorman, and he is aware that I'm not going to be here, and that Henry will."

He nodded and wiped his nose with the back of his hand. "Yeah, okay. Oscar's cool. He lets me use the express service elevator and the basketball court after hours."

"You go to him if you need anything. You have my cell number, right? I'm going to check on you throughout the day, though, okay?"

"Okay."

"I love you, sweetie. More than you can ever know," La Costa said, giving him a firm, lingering kiss on the forehead.

"I love you too, Mom."

Four hours later, La Costa was on a plane for the nearly five-hour flight to Hilton Head. When she had arrived, she checked her messages while hailing a cab to the hotel. She had several texts from Henry: CALL ME WHEN YOU LAND. . . BE STRONG! WE MISS YOU! And one from the lawyer, with directions to his office for the next morning's meeting.

La Costa stepped out onto the pavement and was hit with the warm, beach-tinged humid air of Carolina. A feeling of sadness mixed with fond memories followed. In a strange way, she felt like she had come "home" to a place that, like no other, filled her soul with peace and gladness. She could not imagine never seeing Georgia, or her bright, all-knowing eyes ever again.

She slipped into the back seat of the cab and texted her two men confirmation that she had arrived safely and punctuated each message with a series of x's and o's and emoji hearts.

Still, there had been at least twenty texts from Tess and the publisher needing her attention. La Costa sighed. It was going to be a long night after a long day.

The next morning, La Costa arrived at the lawyer's office and was introduced to a roomful of people, one of whom was Georgia's fresh-faced great-niece, Desi Byrne, a millennial with ivory skin, a Brazilian blowout, and Georgia's jewel-toned eyes. She was accompanied by her personal lawyer and seemed more bored than sorrowful when La Costa offered her hand to relay her condolences. "I am so sorry for your loss. She was such a vibrant and strong woman. Do they know what took her?"

Desi gave a limp handshake, her hand barely grazing La Costa's and mouthed, *cancer*, followed by a rude, full yawn.

Being in her frosty presence made La Costa's famed "ice queen" publisher look like a fairy princess.

The meeting was long and exhaustive, as Georgia's assets were many, including the business holdings, royalties on her book and movie rights, which would continue paying out for some seventy years into the future, assorted stocks, CDs, and two sizable savings accounts. But the outcome for La Costa was swift and conclusive. Less than one hour into the meeting, La Costa was made aware of the reason she had been summoned.

She phoned Henry from the lobby of the lawyer's modest office on Chamber of Commerce Drive to let him know the startling news. "Are you sitting down?" La Costa asked him.

"I'm having a bit of lunch, babe. How did it go?"

"Well, put down the roast beef, honey, because Louis and I just inherited Splendor Bay!"

CHAPTER THIRTY-EIGHT

DECEMBER 2014

L A COSTA AWOKE TO THE glorious sound of Henry snoring beside her. She reached out for the now-familiar warmth beneath the bed sheets that formed a sort of cocoon around them both. Henry was her man. She felt sheltered by his strong frame as he lay near to her on a shared pillow. Her nightgown was still folded neatly on the edge of the bed, evidence of the need not to wear it after all, as they inadvertently had tumbled into bed and made love well after midnight. A pleasure, like this morning, celebrating the luxury of an empty house reclaimed. With Louis away overnight at his friend Kayden's condo twelve floors down, she and Henry were wonderfully alone.

They had spent the night prior discussing their lives and plans for the future. It was nearly Christmas, and soon, would be the new year. In just three years' time, Henry would be handing the reins of the bar and restaurant over into the competent hands of his eldest, Zachary, who would then begin on as full-time manager of the bistro in the spring after graduation. Then, his second born, Grayson, the marketing genius, would join on the following fall, at which time, Henry would embrace early retirement in all its glory and forms. In short, he would have more time to mentor his sons with the business as well as have more free time for her and Louis.

The acquiring of Splendor Bay could not have come at a better time. It would be something that they could share together, putting them further on common ground. It was a place where La Costa had come into her own, and now, much like Georgia and her beloved Macklin, she and Henry could do the same. Couldn't they? The house came with the business of running the B&B, and nobody knew better how to run a successful business than Henry. At worst, they could hire out a management firm to keep the historical inn up and running in the short term, keeping it the unique and special treasure that it was.

And seeing as how knights in shining armor were so very hard to come by these days, La Costa could not have been more grateful to have been rescued by the king of all Prince Charmings, Henry Paige. She couldn't wait to show Henry what she and Georgia had made of the historical house. They had plans to fly to Hilton Head Island just after the holiday over Louis's winter break. She had the keys, the deed, and big hopes for the future.

Henry was more than La Costa's prince. He was her inspiration, encouraging her that she could indeed do anything she set her mind to, including, and not least of all, letting him love her.

CHAPTER THIRTY-NINE

LAS VEGAS, NV

AJ BENT OVER THE POOL table with a Winston bobbing from his copious lips, taking a few practice shots. He was a tower with tree-trunk legs and rock-hard limbs. He had eyes the color of strong coffee, a cue-ball head, and a jagged scar on his forehead near his left ear, courtesy of a prison fight. He was a slow talker with a booming voice, who preferred to speak with his fists. He was mean, vengeful, and jealous, and more than anything, he didn't like to lose.

He studied the rack and chalked his cue, waiting for his mark, a former frat-boy wannabe poser from some flyover state, thinking he could score some action in a two-bit pool house on the Strip. There was always action to be had. AJ's accomplice, Gunner, was a con from Detroit who knew how to spot the suckers. He had the hustle down to an art form. He first would befriend the mark at a different bar, play a few rounds with him, letting him win, and then suggest that they find some bigger thrills. "I know a place where there's action twenty-four-seven. With game like yours, you could really clean up. Any rail bird can tell you how easy it is to make an easy score, ya just gotta know where to go."

First, they would start the mark at ten barrels at twenty-five dollars a game. AJ would play below his speed, eventually driving the mark "on the hill," where the only thing needed was one more win to land the set. This was when they would up the ante to a dime set—one thousand dollars a game. AJ was calculating and patient. Rarely did he fail to take the mark in the end for all he had.

AJ was cold and mean. He fought dirty, conned, and used others for his own gain, and most of all, he despised women. They were all bitches and whores to him, just the same. He had served his first eighteen months in prison when he was nineteen. It was a woman who had fingered him for stealing her identity in a sweetheart scam and assaulting her, a woman who had prosecuted him, and it ultimately was a female judge who put him in that hell hole. When he finally got out, he dabbled in petty crime, drug possession, and illegal possession of firearms, but was never caught. He was too slick and too smart for that. He played the odds and would bet on just about anything, especially himself. He was fearless.

Raised in South Compton from age six, life for AJ and his little brother, Tavon, in the mid-seventies was a nightmare of abuse and neglect from the start. Their father, Lionel, was a custodian who cleaned toilets in the rat-hole project that they lived in, and who spent his free time drinking, betting on fast dogs, and taking turns beating on his two sons. Their mother, Opal, prostituted herself to support a raging crack habit and spent her sober hours of the day plotting her husband's death. The brothers were malnourished, unclean, and unloved most of the time. The day that AJ came home to find Lionel had bought it with a single shot to the head, Opal was nowhere in sight. That changed everything for him. His mother had taken what little there was left, along with little Tavon, and vanished. Not wanted in the bargain, AJ was on the streets at just fifteen. In spite of his age and only having an eighth-grade education, he learned to fend for himself. His motto becoming: *Take first, or be taken.*

Damaged goods, he eventually sought validation in the strip clubs and bars in and around LA in his twenties. He was consumed with the lure of sex, power, and making a quick buck however he could. When the prospect of making it big in the sex trade went cold, he turned back to the only other reliable asset he had, organizing a sequence of armed robberies at a number of local gas stations and quick marts for fast cash. That is, until 2003 when his sometimes-on, sometimes-off, ex-girlfriend, Panther St. James had resurfaced, assuring him that she had "done away" with the baby after their breakup and was now willing to be an accomplice in his life of crime. Regrettably, however, she ratted on him in an attempt to lessen her own sentence in connection with a botched burglary in Watts one sweltering summer day.

She got a cakewalk sentence in a women's correctional facility, and he did seven hard years in California State Prison for being in her phone contacts. Needless to say, he was not inclined to forgive her. His street smarts and lust for payback would not allow it.

It had been a long night, and the pool hall had thinned out. AJ took a swig of his Rémy Martin, settled with Gunner, and headed home to his fleabag apartment on Donna Street in North Las Vegas. It was there that he would continue to hole up, biding his time and counting the days until redemption.

CHAPTER FORTY

DECEMBER 2014

L A COSTA AND LOUIS PACKED up for a two-week respite that would have them returning to the shores of Hilton Head Island and the magnificent shuttered haven of Splendor Bay in time for the holiday. It was just before Christmas, and the inn's décor, which would normally be teeming with green and gold garland and flocked Christmas trees in the living room lobby, was strangely barren and empty. Every sleeping room and suite appeared abandoned and small details everywhere seemed to have been overlooked, bordering on neglect. "I can't believe that Georgia would have left things like this, La Costa said, smoothing a furrowed brow.

The plan was laid out. Henry would be arriving the next day, Christmas Eve, and joining them for the weekend. Then, Louis would fly to Newark to spend the New Year with Tess and her family in the Catskills, which was La Costa's gift to him, along with a stunning new set of snow skis and winter gear, which she had shipped to New Jersey. Henry would stay on with La Costa in Hilton Head through the first weekend of the new year, until he had to return to La Jolla and the bistro. La Costa would remain to sort out the details of the newly acquired property and business. It was in theory, going to be like a dream. The thought of being all together like a family was all that La Costa could see in her near future, not this.

Further, upon settling in, La Costa noticed that strangely, there were no guests on the registry, or bookings for the new year. There was no day manager on the site. The house staff was gone, and although the inn looked generally ready for business, it was vacant.

A phone call to the lawyer handling the transaction filled in the blanks. "I'm afraid that all the books had been cleared months ago. Georgia Byrne was not doing a booming business for at least a year. Procedures will need to be in place to make repairs and bring many of the violations currently on record up to code, before you can run the inn as the new proprietor," he had said. "Everything has been shut down. Oh, and I do have some utility bills that you will need to take care of right away. They appear to be past due."

"I see," La Costa said. "Thanks, Abe. I will definitely be in touch."

"We'll talk after the start of the new year. You can let me know how you want to proceed then. Merry Christmas," he said, and hung up.

It definitely was a wrinkle in the plan, as far as La Costa was concerned, for what she otherwise was hoping would be a smooth transition. She had no idea that Georgia might have been struggling and let the inn slip through the cracks.

"What in the world are we going to do here? It's like an abandoned old mansion," Louis said. "A lot of the light switches don't work."

"We are going fill it with love and let the spirit of Christmas and Georgia's memory bring it to life. We'll stay on the main floor and keep the east and west wings dark." *One can only imagine what it would cost to keep them operational,* she thought. "There are at least three bedrooms off the parlor."

"It's strange being back here, but I'm glad we are," Louis said. "I'm going to put my stuff in my room."

"Okay, baby," La Costa said.

She walked into the kitchen and turned on the light. It, too, was quiet and desolate. The counters and shelves once filled with canisters and pie plates and casserole dishes were empty. There were no plants in the windowsill, and the curtains above the sink were faded. A roach scurried across the ceramic flooring and disappeared into a cabinet.

"Oh, *hell* no," La Costa said aloud. Then, calling to Louis in the other room, "Sweetheart! Grab your jacket. We're eating out tonight!"

CHAPTER FORTY-ONE

CHRISTMAS DAY

DESPITE THE SHOCK AND DISAPPOINTMENT of Splendor Bay's fall from grace, the sentiment of the holiday and La Costa's outlook remained untarnished. She prepared a lovely meal for Louis and Henry by ordering in a feast of ham, candied yams with marshmallows, three-bean casserole, and cranberry sauce from a local Southern-style restaurant. La Costa prepared the living room with lighted candles and piped in soft holiday music from her iPod onto a portable speaker. Georgia's china had been uncrated, washed, and placed atop the heirloom lace tablecloth that La Costa had fond memories of folding and unfolding with each formal holiday and celebration in the wonderful years past that she and Louis had spent with Georgia.

Together, the three enjoyed the festive meal, feeling very much like a family of a different kind, but a family, nonetheless. La Costa suggested that they should go around the dinner table and take turns announcing what each of them was most grateful for in the past and what each hoped for in the future year ahead.

"I'll go first," La Costa said, dabbing the edges of her

mouth with a stiff linen napkin. "I am most grateful for you two wonderful men, my incredible, smart, and funny son, and my loving soul-mate companion, Henry. I love you both more than I can express, and I am hopeful that the new year, although sure to be wrought with some surprises and twists, will be one that we can all embrace together."

Henry squeezed La Costa's hand with pride, and had a similar hope in his eyes to match hers.

Louis fidgeted a bit and struggled to find a place to rest his glance. Then he nodded and said, "Me next. I am grateful too, for you, Mom, and to you, Henry," he said, still looking down at his plate. "I guess you make my mom happy, and that is what it's all about. For the future, I want to kill it on Hunter Mountain with my new bad-ass snowboard this weekend. Oh, and to not break anything!"

La Costa and Henry laughed.

"You and me both!" La Costa said.

"What about you, Henry?" Louis said, returning a high-five that Henry had served up over the platter of mashed potatoes.

"I am most grateful for you both, of course. Reconnecting with this beautiful woman after all of these years, and for my family—my boys, who also continue to make me proud. I am looking forward to the coming year with gratitude and trust that if I stay on long enough, I can continue to score some of your mother's delicious peach pie because I know this store-bought one is not going to even come close!"

"Oh, snap! Flattery like that will get you seconds every time, for sure!" La Costa said, smiling. "I am going to warm that pie up in the microwave. I am sure you two can find a way to choke it down with some vanilla bean ice cream on top."

The remainder of the evening was a perfect blend of time-old traditions celebrated, and some new ones in the making. Henry lit a fire in the parlor fireplace, above which, they hung three felt stockings that La Costa had purchased from a local dollar store and wrote their names in glue and glitter on each one. Together, they watched two holiday classic DVDs, strung microwave popcorn as garland for the artificial Christmas tree on display off the lobby entrance, and played a marathon game of Yahtzee until well past midnight. It was a bit unconventional, but nonetheless, La Costa couldn't have possibly been happier.

Louis slipped off to bed soon after, leaving La Costa and Henry cuddling on the couch beneath a colorful patchwork quilt that Georgia had sewn. A bottle of wine and two more slices of pie made for a midnight snack. The blanket had a pattern of seashells and starfish on it. "I used to slip under this blanket with Louis when he was little, and we would wiggle our feet under the little starfish guy here and make it look like he was dancing," La Costa said, laughing.

Suddenly, a sober reality came over her, and she looked around with a growing frown. "What am I going to do, Henry? This place is a mess, a far cry from what it once was."

"Or, *could* be?" Henry said, stroking her hair, which lightly grazed her shoulder.

"I'm just not sure what to think. Frankly, running a full-scale bed and breakfast operation is very much a full-time job. This has all happened so fast—I just don't know what I am supposed to do."

Henry listened, caressing her arm with a calming reassurance.

"I have deadlines to meet with my publisher for this newest book series, and I'm still in the midst of promotion of this current launch. Really, how is this going to work? I can't be in two places at one time. To give the commitment this is going to demand."

"Let me ask you something, babe. Does it have to be an operation that runs year-round, twenty-four-seven, around the clock?"

"What do you mean?"

"What if Splendor Bay was a designation with a purpose or cause that only opened its doors a few times throughout the year, like for a retreat, or as a fundraising venue?"

La Costa's face brightened as she saw a similar vision come into view. "There's an area on the east side of the property that can be zoned for a social center or dining hall."

"And the property in back, where the pickle ball courts are, that could be repurposed into regulation basketball and tennis courts," Henry said.

"And the town is filled with beach vendors and excursion outfits that might want to partner with us to offer package deals for boat rides, snorkeling, or other activities."

"You can simplify the configuration of the sleeping rooms and suites to make them accommodate more beds, with dorm-style rooms, like for an—"

"Overnight camp!" La Costa shouted.

"Exactly!" Henry said, mirroring her excitement. "You can make this a kids' camp, for instance, that runs several weeks in the summer, and maintain the building in the off-season with minimal upkeep. You can rent it out for private corporate functions or special events on a selective basis, in order to continue bringing in revenue at off-peak times. Right?"

La Costa was reeling. "Wow—that's exactly what this needs to become. What better tribute to Georgia and Macklin's memory could there be? But, Henry, how in the world am I going to make all that happen?"

"I am going to help you, of course. Have you forgotten what I do for a living? This will be a piece of cake. A labor of love. *We* can do this."

La Costa needed no further assurance. The fact that Henry was so willing to take on this project with her, was all that she needed to know. Together, they could bring back Splendor Bay's vigor and magic—but with a *real* purpose.

"Think of all the good it could do for so many kids." La Costa sighed. Then said, "But your own life and plans, Henry. I don't want to saddle you with any more work or worry than you already have."

He kissed her sweetly on the nose and chuckled. "*You* are my life and plans, if you haven't noticed. Let's do this, together."

The next night, after seeing Louis safely off to the airport, La Costa and Henry spent the evening drawing out plans for the inn's concept renovations that would transform the house and sprawling property into a haven for kids to play, learn, lodge, and explore the stunning island with its myriad of activities and recreational possibilities. They would need to attract only the best camp leaders and youth management programs and be discerning about whom they would take on with their unique offering. "I want this venue to be something that serves kids who would not otherwise have an opportunity to experience something like this, something as special as Splendor Bay."

"You mean, like at-risk youth?" Henry asked, sifting

through a stack of drawings and spreadsheets he had compiled as they powered through the night fueled on take-out pizza and a third bottle of Chianti.

"Exactly! I want us to reach out to organizations that cater to special needs kids too. We will be required, of course, to meet code on all of the compliance accommodations, and—"

Henry grabbed La Costa, who was pacing excitedly, with her reading glasses perched on the tip of her nose, and pulled her down onto his lap. "Whoa there, girl! You are going a mile a minute. Let's agree that whatever this thing becomes, it's going to be great because *you* and your loving heart are behind it one hundred percent."

She smiled and stroked the silver streaks in his hair tenderly. "Who are you, Henry Paige? How did I get so lucky to find you?"

Henry pulled her in close and kissed her softly at first, and then, with mounting intensity, enfolded her with his sturdy arms, pulling her into him, delivering breathless, hungry kisses as he traced her back and shoulders with his nimble fingers. Then, planting soft, gentle kisses up and down her neck, he lingered until she purred his name. *"Oh, Mr. Paige."*

They stumbled to the bedroom, and soon found themselves atop the antique feather bed that squeaked and creaked so much that it made them giggle at their own exuberance as they struggled to free themselves from their clothes. "Careful, or we'll wake the dead," La Costa said, straddling Henry and pulling her T-shirt seductively over her head, slow and easy, letting him wait for it. She still had some moves, for certain.

"No matter," he said, grinning, "because I'm already in heaven, baby!"

Exhausted, the two fell asleep in each other's arms, with the window left open and the smell of the ocean permeating throughout the room alight with silver moonbeams. The gauzy curtains moved in concert with the night air, and the sound of Henry's staccato breathing. Suddenly, La Costa yelled out, "No!"

She sat up abruptly, gasping for air, with the tatters of a bad dream trailing in her fuzzy brain.

Henry awoke, reaching for her. "Babe, what happened?"

La Costa, who was now trembling, struggled to take hold of herself, crying. In the moment, she suddenly remembered what had struck her with terror. "It . . . it was. Oh, Henry!" she sobbed in great gasps, huddled in his arms.

"Sweetie, I'm here. It's okay. I've got you. What was it? A bad dream?"

She sniffled and pulled the covers up beneath her chin like a child.

Henry waited as she breathed and swallowed hard to calm her nerves.

"I'll get you a drink of water," Henry said, swinging his legs over the side of the bed.

"No! Don't leave," La Costa said, reaching for his arm. "Please just stay here. Just hold me."

Panther St. James stared at the flimsy silver dime store tree that was propped up on a card table in the sparsely furnished studio apartment. The television was playing a holiday Hallmark movie, but the sound was off. The whir of cars and foot traffic could be heard on the street outside due to a broken window that didn't close right. That was one of the reasons that she slept with a knife beneath her pillow and her eye on the door at all times. A single tree ornament that had been strung on one of the doleful boughs, flickered from the refracted glow from the television. It was a clear globe with multi-colored Mardi Gras confetti snow.

It was nearly time for her to start the evening shift at the diner. It was the first Christmas that she had a tree in more years than she could remember. It would, however, be her last spent here, in this two-bit going-nowhere town. It was the first of many she would have to move to in the coming months in order to disappear, to blend in, to go unnoticed. At least it offered some solace, as nobody would ever think to find her in Baton Rouge. But it was only temporary. Like so many things. A new year was coming, and even though uncertain as to where exactly she would be heading next, she knew one thing for sure. She had to keep moving.

CHAPTER FORTY-TWO

"GOOD MORNING, BEAUTIFUL," HENRY SAID, greeting La Costa with a kiss. He was holding a tray of fresh-brewed coffee, cut-up bananas with berries, and two toasted bagels when she emerged from the bathroom in her bathrobe.

The hot shower had done her good. She did feel better, but she was still a bit embarrassed. "Was I bad last night?" she asked.

"Bad? No. Just scared," Henry said. "Let's have this here," he said, placing the tray on the antique writing desk and pulling up another chair facing the window. "Has this happened before, sweetheart? Do you want to talk about it?"

La Costa nodded and folded herself into the upholstered chair, looking out at the ocean. The Atlantic was a much different entity than the Pacific back home. It was greener in color, and had stronger currents, and it seemed as opposed to the beaches of California to be bluer and calmer most months of the year. Either way, both oceans spoke to her like nothing else. She felt an affinity for the vast, endless horizons of either shore that always seemed to make her feel comforted.

She didn't touch the food, and she took the coffee black. "You read my memoir, Henry, right?"

"Yes, twice."

Her eyes were large and sorrowful, as if she was seeing something he could not see, pulling at her heart. "I put it all out there in my biography. Well, most of it," she said, turning to face him dead-on. "It's just that, there are some things that I've never shared with anyone. Some things that you need to know. If you want to know."

Henry took a settling breath.

She went on, "I was fully aware that reliving it all could bring up bad memories, and for the most part, I was fine. Until . . ."

"You met me?" Henry said. He could see through her, it seemed, and that was exactly why she had to come clean about it all—her childhood abuse at the hands of her father, Crete, the miscarriage, and most importantly, the truth about Louis. If ever there was going to be a future with Henry, he would have to know the whole truth, every detail. Seemingly, it was torturing her in her dreams, and threatened to consume her with guilt now more than ever. In the past, she was able to tamp it down, stow it away. Put it in a box. But now, it was all coming to the surface with the release of her biography, the unearthing of her past, the amped-up publicity that was putting her front and center. What mattered most was how it might affect a life with someone like him—a man as wonderful as Henry.

Henry leaned in and assured her, "Nothing you could tell me would ever change how I feel about you. La Costa, I love you, and I'm not going anywhere." His blue eyes reached through to her very soul.

La Costa proceeded to lay her heart bare. She recounted

the myriad of childhood abuses and neglect. How she had only come to know shame and brutality from the hands of men in her life that allowed her to seek solace and acceptance on the streets and in the strip clubs, where she sold a broken soul for rent money. "I am not proud of what I did, but I have no regrets as to how I was able to come out of it on the other side."

Henry listened, his head bowed in silence, wiping large tears that spilled from his eyes, letting her speak and unburden her heart in the way that she needed to. She spoke about Crete; that, and the anger and rage that she left on the shore the day that she set her own stillborn child adrift in the ocean, a result of her reckless choices. She spoke about trying to break out of the cycle, meeting Panther, and being brought back into a world that valued fast and easy money. "I wanted to put it all behind me for good when I moved to Nevada. Then, Panther just walked back into my life, and that time, changed my life forever when she left Louis with me. He was my greatest test—my purpose." La Costa brought forth the note that Panther had left her on the night that she had left Louis in her care. "I carry it in my wallet so that he would never find out. He knows that he is *adopted* but not that Panther, and I suspect AJ, her degenerate boyfriend at the time, are his birth parents. I told him that I chose him, and that our bond was sanctioned by the angels. What else could I do? He's my life, just as sure as if I had given birth to him. I swear to God, I—"

She broke down in a fit of sobs. Henry slid from the chair, caught her in his embrace, and held her close. "I got you, baby. I got both of you. I promise. No more secrets. It's going to be all right. This just means that you know that you can't turn your back on your past. You've proven that. It makes you who you are, and I love all of you."

She sniffed and blew her nose. Then, touching his forehead with hers, she drew a sigh of relief. "We're going to be okay, right?"

"We're going to be more than okay, Ms. Reed. We've got this."

CHAPTER FORTY-THREE

NEW YORK
EARLY MARCH 2015

GLOBAL NETWORK PRODUCER, BUMPY FRIEDMAN, woke up early to hit the treadmill. It was positioned in the far corner of the den, across from the large-screen TV he had mounted on the wall. He could only set the machine to a slow-walk setting, as his physical therapy regimen was tame, to say the least. Bypass surgery was a bitch to get on the other side of, and he'd had a triple doozy to nurse. As long as he kept his feet moving on the cushioned belt surface for twenty to thirty minutes at a stretch, and his ticker going, he was good.

Just as he got ready to start up, he realized that he had left his earbuds on the nightstand. He quickly circled back to the bedroom and shifted through the papers and stack of books on the nightstand next to the lamp, to find them. This caused a book to slide onto the floor. It was one of many that his wife, Hylda, loved to read before bed and throughout the day when she had what she called, "book time," her highly guarded private respite on the patio, or in the sun room, where she liked to read. It was a romance tome with an attractive cover and large, raised lettering and fancy font: *Rebellion—Book Two in the Rebecca Steele Series.* The author's name, LA COSTA REED was prominently displayed across the top. Bumpy flipped open the jacket and perused the author's bio. La Costa Reed was an attractive, full-figured black woman with soulful eyes and a money-shot smile.

Quickly, he grabbed the earbuds and tucked the novel beneath his arm. Hylda wouldn't miss it. She had every book the woman wrote, including her memoir, which Hylda had read last summer. On second thought, he searched for it too, on the bookshelf in the living room, and upon finding it, he tossed it, along with the hardback, into his open briefcase on his desk.

He walked back to the den, thinking he would ask Hylda for her thoughts about maybe taking a look at La Costa Reed for consideration to co-host his new daytime pilot he was currently about to pitch to the network. He was full of great ideas these days, it seemed, and the universe was not shy on delivering. Good thing, because time was running out, and his ass was on the line.

Then he jumped on the treadmill and started with a slow, steady incline, and with high hopes for the vision that would take the network to number one.

Tess got the call the very next day. Bumpy Friedman had wasted no time in hunting down La Costa Reed's eager agent, who phoned him back not twenty minutes after he had left a voice mail on her mobile.

"Mr. Friedman, thank you for calling. How might I help you?" She was well aware of his standing in the industry as a grizzled but seasoned producer of some very iconic and well-awarded daytime programming.

"My wife is a huge fan of La Costa Reed. I see that she

has a very impressive backlist, and my people tell me that she has a strong fan base with the female demographic in the age range that we are targeting for our newest project. I'd like to speak with you about it, if you think that Ms. Reed would be interested."

"Would this be for her writing? A script perhaps, for a drama?" Tess asked, fanning herself with the grocery list she had in her hand, as he had caught her in the middle of her Monday shopping excursion at the deli counter, as well as an ill-timed hot flash.

"Oh, no. We're looking to fill a seat, so to speak, that presents drama, only a lot less *scripted*," he said, chuckling. "We'd like to audition her for a position as a co-host of a woman's live talk show."

"It might be something we would be interested in," Tess said, trying to sound noncommittal. "Of course, we would need to know more about what would be involved. La Costa is quite in demand as of late, what with the buzz still swirling around about her provocative memoir, the launch of the new series, and—"

"Understood. I'd like to have a meeting to discuss the opportunity as soon as possible," Bumpy said. "I'm on a deadline here myself."

"Oh, well, I'm afraid that La Costa is with her son on spring break in the Carolinas for another week, but I can meet with you," Tess said. "How about Market Diner on Eleventh Street in the city? Say, tomorrow at one o'clock? Is this your cell? I'll text you when I arrive."

"See you tomorrow, then," Bumpy said.

Tess jumped off the call. What luck! She knew that juggling TV producer-types was the easy part. The challenge was going to be getting La Costa on board. *Live television!* How would she ever be able to convince La Costa to audition? If this was the real deal, a break like this could do more than launch another book series—it could clinch a career.

CHAPTER FORTY-FOUR

"WHAT? ARE YOU KIDDING?" LA Costa said into the tiny camera at the top of her computer screen. "Global Network might want *me* to anchor a talk show?"

"You and three others—it's a co-anchor gig, and if you do this, La Costa, it will be a game-changer," Tess said on the other end of the video call from her she-cave office.

"You are forgetting one little thing," La Costa said, wincing from the cacophony of construction noises emanating from behind her. "I do not do well in front of television cameras—especially *live* broadcasts."

"Are you telling me that you would pass on a deal of a lifetime, because of a little stage fright?" Tess said, giving the desk a firm bang of her fist that caused her screen to jump.

"Look, Tess. We are up to our eyeballs here with this renovation. The kids' camp plan is well underway, and even though Henry is here to oversee it most weekends, it's still looking like a miss for a summer opening. I'm now deep into the revisions of book two in the new trilogy, about to finish the last round of the memoir book signings, and planning for the fall release book tour. If you can figure out a way to clone me, go ahead!"

I'll take that as a yes, Tess concluded, and promptly changed the subject.

"How are those edits coming?" she asked. "Patty is holding our feet to the fire on the first pub date."

"I'm managing to make progress daily, but I really do much better in a quieter atmosphere. There's a café I steal away to from time to time, but it's hard to work there as well. I could go back to my writing office in LA, but I don't want to miss any more time with Louis."

"He's helping Henry with the renovations, right? You don't need to be there, La Costa. Why don't you come here for a few days? I can offer you my she-cave. I promise, no hammering, sawing, or demolition going on here—and no butt crack in sight!"

"That's tempting," La Costa said. "I could swing back through after the weekend and meet up with Louis and Henry mid-week, and we could all fly back home to LA together. Are you sure that's okay with you?"

"It's my pleasure," Tess said. "I'll get you a flight out for tomorrow, and the guest room ready."

Tess smiled. *And that is how it is done.* Part one of her plan was in place. What luck that the acclaimed television show host Kristen Michaels of the *Kristen Michaels Show* was on hiatus having some "rehab" of her own, with a little nip and tuck overhaul that would have her out of commission for weeks. As a fortunate result, the local network was in need of a series of hosts to fill in during her absence. Tess had the scoop on everything going on in her town, and this was no exception. She would pull a few strings and get La Costa in, front and center. Part two of her plan would involve, of course, actually getting La Costa to do it.

Tess reached for her cell phone and contacted Bumpy Friedman as fast as her thumbs could navigate the tiny keyboard with an exuberant text: IT's A GO FOR MONDAY, MR. FRIEDMAN. LA COSTA WILL BE THERE!

CHAPTER FORTY-FIVE

NEW JERSEY

"I'VE GOT AN OPPORTUNITY FOR you while you're here," Tess said as she helped La Costa with her bags, sliding them into the back of her well-traveled SUV.

"What kind of opportunity?" La Costa was happy to be in the big city. She had missed the rhythm of its chaos and never-ending spectacle of lights and sounds.

"You'll see. I have you booked for another appearance at the local network on Kristen Michael's show on Monday. Don't worry, I've cleared it with your publicist. You can spare a bit of time away from your manuscript, right? We should do this. It will keep you relevant."

"Fine. As long as it is the only one during this visit. It was to be a working break, right?"

"Right," Tess said, smiling.

La Costa spent most of the weekend holed up in the she-cave, pounding away at her laptop, or poring over edits that she shared with her editor via email. Tess laid low, surfacing only to rescue La Costa from malnourishment with a scrumptious meal ordered in, or to distract her with a bottle of wine when the day was over. Then, the two would sit on the floor in Tess's enormous closet, where La Costa would marvel at her impressive shoe collection.

"It's really insane how many pairs of shoes you have, girl. I thought I was bad, but you got me beat." La Costa's fetish was for leopard-print pumps. "I have forty-eight pairs at last count, but that includes all of my stilettos!"

"Oh, I don't count them. There's more stashed away in the garage, if you can believe it. Demitri would *plotz* if he knew! Hey, what can I say? We all have our vices. Secrets *are* the secret to a happy marriage." Tess smiled, only half kidding. "Speaking of vices, how are things going with you and Henry? It seems pretty hot and heavy, if you ask me."

"I'm happy, Tess. I'm really happy. It's like I have to pinch myself some days, just trying to believe that this wonderful man has walked into my life."

"Back into your life, right?"

La Costa nodded, smiling.

"Well, it's obvious that he is a good man, and that he loves Louis, so . . . ?"

La Costa shrank from the question. "So what?"

"So, when are you guys going to make it legal? I mean, why not?"

"We'll see," La Costa said. "I would have a whole lot to think about before doing that. It's been really nice with it just being me and Louis all these years."

"Seems to me that you have all become quite the little family."

"I do trust him, Tess. More than I have ever trusted any man. Do you really see us that way?"

"I do, *Bubbi*. My mother always says, 'Falling in love is like falling in water. We can fall in it. We can drown in it, but we can't live without it.' No reason why you should."

"I never thought of it that way. That's really beautiful," Las Costa said, stifling a yawn.

"And I think that you, my dear heart, need to get some sleep. We have the television appearance tomorrow. They want you there early—with clean hair and no makeup. They will fix you up."

"Thanks, Tess. I really appreciate how you always have my back," La Costa said, reaching in for a hug.

"It's all you," Tess said. "Plus, let's be real. Your success keeps me in new shoes."

CHAPTER FORTY-SIX

NEW YORK CITY

L A COSTA ARRIVED ON SET prepared for the interview. She wore a beautiful crème silk blouse, a black leather skirt, and her signature leopard-print peep-toe pumps. Luckily, she never traveled without a change of wardrobe and was usually at the ready for just about any occasion. Tess had been unusually quiet on the car ride to the studio.

"Let's get you into hair and makeup right away. I'll go over the show notes with the producer, and meet with you back at the stylist's chair," Tess said, when they arrived. The studio was pulsing with a well-choreographed dance of technicians; show runners, and production crew running about tending to the pre-show details.

La Costa remained blissfully unaware that her "appearance" on the set would be more than a four-minute interview. She had been informed by Tess that the segment was going live, and that this time, it would not be taped. That alone was enough to give La Costa sweaty palms, and she was working hard to keep her breakfast down, while psyching herself up in the mirror, just twenty minutes prior to show-time.

"You will be doing one segment—the opening segment—and there is one thing I need to tell you regarding the show rundown," Tess said, closing in on La Costa with several large blue note cards and an Evian water.

La Costa knew that the rundown was a timed outline for the elements that went into the program. "So, I'm the first guest?"

"Not exactly." Tess swallowed hard and motioned for the stylist to give them the room. Tess's phone buzzed in her pocket. She glanced at the tiny screen and smiled. Bumpy Friedman had just arrived and was heading to the control room to watch the segment.

"You're scaring me, Tess. What is going on?" La Costa shuffled through the note cards. "These are for Kristen, the host."

"Not today. Please don't hate me, but you are going on as a fill-in show host for the first segment. Kristen is not here."

"Not here?" La Costa was incredulous.

"She's on nip-and-tuck leave. The show is running guest hosts in her place the remainder of this week. It's just for the opening segment," Tess said, handing her the script. "It's very basic, off-the-cuff stuff. You're on until the second commercial break. There will be a producer on the sidelines feeding cues into your ear monitor."

La Costa's mouth dropped. "What? Tess, how could you have agreed to this?"

Tess continued, "Trust me, La Costa. I would not have taken this chance if I didn't believe in you. You've got this. You will be bringing on a local housewife who makes cat toys out of recycled household items. All you have to do is give her the spotlight. Just follow the note cards and ask her the interview questions."

La Costa hesitantly re-examined the note cards. "Just ask her the questions, right? I can do this."

"You definitely can do this. I know you can. Just go out there and be yourself. Talk to the woman as you would one of your fans. That's all that you have to do."

"I can do this." La Costa touched her forehead tentatively. She was beginning to sweat. "I can do this," she said again, in an effort to convince herself.

"That is the spirit! Of course you can!" Tess rallied. "This is the La Costa who writes best-selling books and makes readers laugh and cry, and sometimes crap their pants!"

La Costa shot her a stern look. "Oh, you're going to cry later, Tess. I *promise* you that."

A knock at the door ushered in a skinny man in tight jeans wearing a headset. "They're ready for you, Ms. Reed. Right this way."

Tess held her breath. "Are you ready?"

"Ready as I'll ever be," La Costa said with conviction. "Let's do this thing!"

Tess collapsed into the stylist's chair and made the sign of the cross. It couldn't hurt.

From the production room, Bumpy Friedman, along with the producer, vision mixer, and script supervisor, looked on as the director barked commands to adjust the cameras, lighting, and graphics run-through prior to the live broadcast. In an industry where it is paramount to be able to think on one's feet, everyone was pulling for another successful show and performing their tasks with precision.

"Camera one, pan left and up a little," the director volleyed into the studio microphone, directing the camera to zoom in on La Costa's striking and strong profile in camera position two. The technical director made adjustments for the light bouncing off of her wide hoop earrings. La Costa sat on a gleaming chrome stool, scanning the note cards beneath the bright studio lights, struggling to keep calm and focused. *You've got this. You've got this.* She played the mantra in her mind on a continuous loop, oblivious to the eyes that were on her from the control room and the flurry of activity on the radios, intercoms, and PA system on the set.

Bumpy had fifteen precious minutes to take in the show before he had to leave for his ten forty-five appointment back at his network office. It would be all that he would need.

Tess took her place in the viewing room off to the side, from which she could see all of the action on the stage. She stood the entire time, unable to sit due to the butterflies doing cartwheels in her gut.

The show's theme music was cued and at the ready. The clock ticked away the seconds to the live broadcast. La Costa took a deep breath and gave her best smile into the blinding white lights. She would find the spark inside of her that was fearless and brave and capable.

In the control room, the director sprang into action. "Fifteen seconds. Stand by in studio.

Ready ONE on your wide shot; ready TWO on a close-up of Reed. Stand by to key in title. Take ONE; hit music—key title."

Once the music faded, the unseen announcer delivered the show opening: *"It's a good day* on The Kristen Michael's Show *with today's first guest host, best-selling romance author, La Costa Reed!"*

La Costa smiled widely and beamed. "Good morning, New York! I'm so happy to be here today to help put a little sunshine into your morning."

At the end of the segment, the camera trucked right to the mid-position and zoomed back for a wide shot. Then, the studio lights dimmed, and it was over. La Costa thanked the cat-toy lady and unhooked her own lavalier mic.

Tess ran toward the control room, disappointed to find that Bumpy Friedman had already left. She searched the studio floor for La Costa, who was nowhere in sight.

La Costa hadn't a second to spare. She high-tailed it straight to the dressing room, where she hit the restroom, just in time—and puked.

Three hours later, Tess and La Costa had a good laugh over a light lunch about the debacle that had La Costa's head still spinning. Tess showered her star author with accolades and praise from the show producers. "They loved you, *Bubbi*. Said you were a natural."

"A natural wreck," La Costa said, hoisting her suitcase into the SUV herself and sliding into the passenger seat. She could not wait to touch down at Hilton Head airport that evening, and to reunite with Louis and Henry. It had been a whirlwind few days.

They pulled up to the curbside drop-off. "Say hi to those two handsome men of yours. Thank them for letting me steal you," Tess said. "I mean it. You did great."

La Costa smiled. "And no lie, I'm definitely going to get you back for this. I promise. I think I left two years of my life back there on that studio set."

Tess laughed nervously, and La Costa felt compelled to ask, "Is everything all right?"

"Of course, *Bubbi*," Tess said. "You know, I just want you to have every opportunity to share your incredible light with the world. That's really what I want for you."

"I know," La Costa said, squeezing Tess's hand. "You push me in all the good ways. And I am grateful."

Tess nodded and swiped at a tear that threatened to belie her hard-ass demeanor. "Yeah, I got nothing. It's just that the goddamn change has me going all weepy sometimes. It's a pain in the ass."

La Costa smiled and gave Tess a warm hug that forgave all. Then, she disappeared with her suitcase through the sliding glass doors.

Back in the car, Tess blew her nose, and then checked her phone that had been buzzing for the past half hour. There she saw it—the first of several texts from Global Network and Bumpy Friedman that simply read: LA COSTA WAS PERFECTION. WE WOULD LOVE TO SIGN HER. WILL BE IN TOUCH.

CHAPTER FORTY-SEVEN

THE NEXT NIGHT, LA COSTA laid against Henry's chest, which was wet with sweat; their hearts were pounding wildly from the joyous ride they had taken just moments earlier in loving ecstasy. La Costa breathed a sigh of relief, knowing that she was back on familiar ground and in the comfort of her routine and Henry's loving arms. With the recent impromptu talk show appearance, she had experienced enough adventure to last her for a while.

The two were blissfully alone, stealing an evening away at Henry's townhome, where La Costa had surprised Henry with a home-cooked meal. Louis was at a campsite at Cali Lake with his buddy Kayden and his family, stretching the remaining days of spring break as far as possible before the start of the new semester that next week.

The two had lit a fire of their own beneath the cedar-beamed walls of Henry's birch wood living room. They lay naked and satisfied atop a cushion of quilts, basking in the afterglow of desire, lost in their perfect love.

The roast remained on the kitchen counter in a pan, uneaten, just where La Costa had left it two hours earlier. Right before Henry decided to role-play one of La Costa's heartthrob protagonists from one of her novels.

He had scurried outside to the patio and knocked at the door, then disguised as a burly stranger, feigning distress. *"Excuse me, madam. May I use your phone? You see, my car broke down, down the road a piece, and I should really call my wife to let her know that I'll be running late."*

The beans were boiling on the range, and she was just about to start the biscuits.

He had gestured gallantly, pretending to remove his hat when she beckoned him in from the night. *"Well, of course, kind sir. Come right in now, and get yourself out of that cold. It's not every day that a handsome stranger such as yourself shows up on my doorstep."*

"Why, thank you, kind woman," he said, with a stoic face. Then, following her through the den into the kitchen with his eyes, he broke into a Cheshire grin.

"Not at all. There you are. The telephone's in there." She turned, leaving him helpless to do anything but stare at the vision of visions as her ample hips moved in an easy glide across the wooden floor, back toward the kitchen. She was barefoot, and the hem of her long skirt just grazed her ankles when she walked.

She stood at the stove, stunning and beautiful, pulling at his heart. She was stirring something in a saucepan, the sight of which simply did him in. There was something about La Costa that could even make stirring brown gravy, bring him to his knees. It was the call of the wild that commanded him to abandon the charade of their little game and claim his old identity back. He bear-hugged her from behind, wrapping his arms around her large, beautiful body.

"Gotcha!"

La Costa startled playfully, annoyed by his sudden change in demeanor, mid-script. "Hey!" she protested. "You're supposed to play the handsome stranger. Don't break character!"

He shrugged. "I can't help myself, Ms. Reed. I just love to watch you stir that gravy!" She shrieked and giggled as he gathered back her hair and kissed her neck. Softly stroking her back, he nuzzled her ears and cheeks until she rescinded and turned off the stove. They carried the wineglasses into the living room, spread the blankets on the floor, and then Henry lit two raging fires: one in the hearth and the other, in La Costa's soul.

Tess could wait no longer. She had to call with the news. She had to tell La Costa about Global Network's offer and risk putting her into a full-blown panic attack. Would La Costa be as forgiving when she learned that Tess had duped her into auditioning for Bumpy Friedman during her guest host appearance on the *Kristen Michael's Show*? As La Costa's agent, she *had* to present the offer.

From her desk, Tess had spent the night reviewing the voluminous contract for Global Network's offer that had been couriered to her earlier. La Costa would be the third of four high-profile women hired for Bumpy Friedman's new talk show juggernaut, *The Gab*. The details of the formal signing would be forthcoming, pending acceptance of the terms therein, etcetera. She took a deep breath and phoned La Costa.

It was nearly nine p.m. in California, but Tess rationalized that time was money.

"Are you sitting down?" she asked when La Costa sheepishly answered the phone.

"I'm about to resurrect an interrupted meal for my man," La Costa said, slamming shut the door to the microwave. "I love you, girl, but can this wait?"

Tess shrugged. "It depends on how much you want this deal."

"What deal?"

"The deal that you cinched with Global Network to be the third hire as co-host of their debut talk show, *The Gab*." She paused for effect and let the news sink in.

The connection went silent. "What?" La Costa said as she stepped with bare feet out onto the patio with her cell phone glowing against her cheek. "Come again?"

"You are who they want. Bumpy Friedman loved you on the Kristen Michael's gig. How great is that?"

"I don't understand."

"The show's producer, Bumpy Friedman, saw your live guest host spot. His wife is a huge fan. She gave you the nod, and he agreed to see you in action, La Costa. He was there at the studio, and he loved you!"

"But how—?"

"I might have had a little to do with that as well, *Bubbi*, but that is not important. The thing is—you got the offer!"

La Costa could not believe what she was hearing.

"All we have to do is say yes."

"Tess, I have to think about it. This is so sudden. You haven't committed to anything yet, have you?"

"No, but you have to know that they are desperate for your answer. Friedman is on a tight deadline. You cinched it with your performance. It's yours if you want it."

"Give me some time. That's all I ask."

"Think it over. This is a life-changing offer. Call me back, girl."

Tess was off the line, and Henry was standing in the doorway, frowning. "Everything okay?" he asked, looking like her past, present, and future rolled all into one dream come true.

La Costa smiled and hugged his neck. "It's just Tess being Tess," she said. "Let's dig into that roast I made earlier, and I'll fill you in."

CHAPTER FORTY-EIGHT

RIVERSIDE. CA

PANTHER ST. JAMES SPENT HER shift breaks at the campus diner slumped in her nineties Nissan Sentra smoking filtered menthols. The car had ripped floorboards, a leaky clutch, and a missing gas cap. It was, however, a steal for the eight hundred dollars she was able to squirrel away in tips from a stint as a cocktail waitress in west Texas, where she had laid low for several weeks. She bought the beater in Nogales after a bus ticket brought her all the way across New Mexico to Arizona. The tin can with one working headlight then brought her, miraculously, to the California border, where she settled on Riverside, fifty-some-odd miles outside of LA, when the engine overheated in front of a walk-up studio with a rental sign in the window.

It seemed like as good a place as any, as four months and five cities managed to keep her decidedly hidden from the trouble that was sure to find her when she would not be looking. To keep her one step ahead of AJ and his rage. Just long enough to reclaim what was hers.

She checked her watch and stretched the remaining seventeen minutes flipping through the dog-eared paperback that was wedged between the parking brake and the passenger seat. It was a La Costa Reed novel, and something in the prose made her flinch. The glossy photo of La Costa on the book's back cover seemed to further irritate her, when she flipped it over, to study it for the one thousandth time. She flicked an ash out of the window and continued to read the pages with a stern but measured countenance.

She slid her finger across a piece of paper torn from her ordering pad, which she used as a bookmark and kept for safekeeping. On it was scrawled the phone number of a social worker at the women's shelter downtown. Another waitress from the diner had fronted her the name of an Amelia Rhineholt, who was supposedly well versed in child custody law in California, and who worked pro bono. "Give her a call," the co-worker had said. "She'll help you out."

Panther was tapped of resources for sure, but rich in the need to set things straight. To make things right. And she would, she vowed, do whatever it might take.

CHAPTER FORTY-NINE

THE NEXT MORNING, LA COSTA kissed Henry sweetly before heading back to her apartment to pack for a book signing tour in the Northwest.

"I hate to leave you guys, but duty calls. I'll be in three states over the next five days. Do you think you and Louis can survive?"

Henry chuckled. "Oh, I think we can manage. I'll swing by practice tomorrow evening and pick him up with a mega meat lover's pizza and a boatload of bread sticks. We'll have a feast for a king at your place. I can't wait. Netflix and toilet seats left up all the way!"

La Costa snickered. "Just clean up any mess you two make before I get back. What I don't see, didn't happen."

"I'll be heading back here to La Jolla tomorrow. Way too much going on with our spring wine tasting. Are you sure Louis will be fine staying on with Kayden and his family the rest of the week?" Henry asked.

"Be fine? I can hardly convince him that he is *not* related to those people! No, he and Kayden share everything—the same clothes, the same gym shoes, the same schedule at school. I don't even think that Dorleen and D'Juan notice whenever Louis is there, or Kayden is here with us. I'd say, there will be no objections there. I'll continue to check up on him like a hawk, though. I got GPS on his phone, so he's on a short leash, for sure."

Henry poured her a coffee in a to-go cup with a lid for the road. "What are you going to do about the Global Network offer?" he asked expectantly.

They had spent the better part of the late-night hours into the early dawn devouring the peach pie and discussing every angle of the gigantic gearshift that signing on to the TV host gig would cause to La Costa's career, her and Louis's life—their life together.

"Truly, I haven't decided yet," La Costa said.

"I just want you to know that whatever you decide, babe, is what I truly want. Moving to New York would be a huge change, but it would put you closer to Splendor Bay, not to mention your publisher, your agent, and—"

"Farther away from here," La Costa interjected. "Farther away from this home, Louis's dream university. I just don't know. I'm going to speak with Louis when he comes home from school today. I need to have his input before I give Tess my answer."

"I told you this morning, my love, and I'll tell you again. I am behind you one hundred percent. It's not every day that an opportunity like this falls into your lap." Henry smiled and kissed her sweetly on the lips.

His beard, which was beginning to grow in, felt like sandpaper, but she did like the way that it made him look even sexier.

"Thank you for our beautiful dinner last night, and *everything*," he said, squeezing her bottom playfully. The dog, Merlot, bounded across the tile and bumped into their legs, nearly knocking them off of their feet.

"I guess someone's ready for his walk," La Costa said, laughing.

"Oh, before I forget, I slipped something in your overnight bag for you to look at on the flight to Portland," Henry said. "It's just something that I wanted to show you." He grabbed the dog leash and bounded out onto the patio, with Merlot's tail thumping against his calves. "Have a safe flight! Talk tonight."

La Costa blew him a kiss, grabbed her car keys and her overnight bag, and headed out the door.

Later that afternoon, back in LA, La Costa heard the front door slam.

"Hey, sweetie, how was school?" La Costa asked, still focused on the computer screen, putting the finishing touches on a chapter for her current work in progress. Book tour or no book tour, Patty, her publisher, expected deadlines to be met, God help her.

"It was good," Louis quipped, tossing his gym bag in the hall. "Can I go down to Kayden's for dinner tonight?"

La Costa stopped typing and swung around in the chair. "I'm sorry, honey, but I really wanted it to be just us two for dinner tonight. You know, I'm leaving for a few days for the signing tour, and I really need to talk to you about something."

"Okay, but can I pick the place?"

"Sure."

An hour later the two were seated at a bright Costco picnic bench beneath high florescent lights in the food court of the bustling box store.

"Really? Sushi *at Costco*?" La Costa was baffled. "This is your idea of dinner?"

"It's rad, Mom. They have the best wasabi, I'm telling

you. Try some! Plus, I like to people watch here. It's dope."

"I think you like to girl-watch, but that's another talk." La Costa rolled with it, as she had long since learned that her Louis was full of surprises and extremely avant-garde when it came to music and cuisine. It had to be a teenager thing, she reasoned. "Listen, I have something very important to run by you. I received an offer through Tess from a network television company to be a part of a pilot talk show."

"Like as a guest? No big deal, you do that all the time—except for this last one you did, where they put you on as the guest host and you hurled."

La Costa's voice dropped. "Little did I know that I was auditioning for a co-host position." She paused and let it sink in.

"Oh! Did Miss Tess punk you?"

La Costa nodded. "Yep. She wasn't exactly forthcoming with the details of my appearance on the show until after it was over. Apparently, the network's producer was there." The very thought of reliving the experience, along with the smell of the fishy globs that Louis was wolfing down, was beginning to turn her stomach. She fought the mounting nausea. It was a good thing that she opted for a simple salad instead.

"So, they want you to be a talk show host?"

"Global Network wants me to be one of four women co-hosts of their debut talk show in New York. If it goes well and the show is picked up, it would be a huge commitment, baby. It would mean moving to New York."

She paused and let the second point sink in.

Louis stopped chewing. "Wait, what?"

"If I take this job, I would be expected to be there daily to do the live shows. There would be no way to commute from coast to coast five days a week. It would mean some changes for us, for sure. Starting with your choice of school."

"*Choice?*"

"Well, you could stay here and attend UCLA, but it would have to be in a dorm on campus. We would keep the apartment and the Newport Beach house for weekend visits."

"Or . . . ?"

"You could look at being a little closer and opt to go to a university in New York, or North Carolina."

Louis lit up like a Christmas tree. "Michael Jordan went to the University of North Carolina, right?"

"Yes, I believe that he did, but that would be a dorm situation as well. How do you feel about that?"

Louis kept chewing and shrugged.

"We can put in applications for several options and see what happens," La Costa went on. "Regardless of what you choose, I promise that our home here will remain. We would just need to work out how to juggle between the coast lines."

"What about Henry? What does he say about all of this?"

"He supports us, whatever we decide. I will tell you that I love and care for him very much. I am hoping that there is a way we can make this work for all of us."

Louis nodded. "Yeah, Mom. I think that if it's something that you want to do, I say—do it."

La Costa's heart leaped. Could she love this boy any more? "You know, all I really want is to continue to take care of you and keep you close if I can help it. That's my number one job."

Louis smiled. The slight gap in his front row of teeth melted her heart every time; probably a gift from his biological father, further confirming that AJ's blood most likely flowed in Louis's veins. She was somewhat glad, though that he never wanted to have it fixed. It was as unique unto him as his precious heart.

"Yeah, you should definitely take the job," he said.

"Are you sure? I mean, about your school?"

"Can I think about it? I don't know right now," he said, slurping his coke. "I'm down anywhere that I can play ball—and kill it with the academics."

La Costa sighed. What she thought would be the toughest obstacle, just volleyed her a lay up. "You know, I think that Tess's son Reyce is going to UNC, so how cool would that be?"

"Really? I'm going to text him right now and see," Louis said, excitedly. "How awesome is it that you are going to be a TV star? Oh, swag money—does this mean we are going to be like, really *rich*?"

"Well, rich enough to enable us to bridge that distance coast to coast and to keep you in sushi and sneakers, I guess."

"Cool."

CHAPTER FIFTY

PORTLAND, OR

L A COSTA ARRIVED IN THE city early enough to take advantage of the local sights. The stunning Portland Art Museum, Providence Park, and Pioneer Place shopping mall were all within walking distance of the boutique hotel, with its gleaming art collection and luxury amenity-filled lobby and restaurants. Her invaluable personal assistant, Florian, had plotted a points-of-interest map for her, which he had printed out and included with her itinerary. The bookstore's headquarters, Powel's City of Books, occupied a full city block, and would be the location for her book signing the next morning.

When she returned after dark, she took a quick shower in the enormous bath suite, indulged in designer toiletries, and then wrapped herself in a fluffy bath robe. She ordered room service and began to unpack her clothes for the next day's event. There, nestled beneath her floral A-line dress with the sassy leather belt, was a pristine manuscript secured with a giant rubber band and a post-it that had the words: READ ME! written with a black Sharpie on it, punctuated with a smiley face.

La Costa raised one perfectly arched brow when she

read the author's name: Henry T. Paige. *Henry, what have you done here?* she mused, as she flipped through the unassuming pages with a quick, cursory check—double spaced, twelve-point Times New Roman font, one-inch margins on all sides. Each page's header included the author name, page number, and title: ISLAND OF SWALLOWS all in caps. It was clean, tidy, and a respectable and ambitious word count at ninety thousand words.

"Goodness, my Henry has written a book!" she blurted aloud and fell, laughing gleefully, onto the bed. She reached for her phone to text him that she had found his manuscript but then stopped herself. Instead, she retrieved her reading glasses, leaned back against the headboard, and began to read the prologue with a mix of dread and hopeful anticipation. *Would it even be any good?*

Fourteen pages in, she was well on her way on a journey that would take her on a thrilling ride that began with a Mardi Gras festival in the late nineteenth century at *the Carnaval de Cozumel*, where a dark and dangerous marauder, posing as a *Comparsas*, kills two carnival-goers in the dark cobblestone streets after a day of festive celebration. The killer flees into the night with a ring wrenched from one of the victim's severed fingers. Then, dizzily depositing the reader into modern day, the action shifted onto a chartered fishing boat off of a tourist island in Mexico, filled with restaurants, hotels, and a flurry of bustling bars and plazas. It is here the reader meets the unassuming protagonist, Alec Slater, about to pitch a diamond engagement ring over the railing into the Caribbean. It is at this point that he witnesses a shocking crime in broad daylight.

Six and a half hours later, and blurry-eyed, La Costa finished the last page, still in her bathrobe amid a stack of dirty room service dishes and sundry snack wrappers from the honor bar. She yawned and checked her phone, shaking her head disbelievingly. It was well past one a.m., and she had not even noticed the multiple text messages that had stacked up in her queue since she had first informed Henry that she had touched down. Henry had texted earlier that he and Louis were having a guys-only night, and that they hoped she was enjoying the sights in Portland.

The manuscript was a marvel. If it was Henry's first foray into writing fiction, it was impressive, to say the least. She had taken early on to getting her own notepad and making edits and suggestions as she read along, but resisted the temptation to do so as she read further. She had been so caught up in the story that she didn't want to stop the momentum of giving it one full read. Overall, it had great promise, and the idea of Henry possessing such talent and trusting her with his work, only made her love him more.

She had decided not to wake him. Instead, she would wait to talk to him about it later. If he was interested in trying to land a publishing deal, she would be more than happy to help him in any way that she could. She was certain that Tess knew someone who represented thriller authors.

La Costa settled in for a good night's sleep in the luxurious hotel sheets, as thoughts of a bright and unknown future tugged at her whirring mind. *How blessed are we?* she thought, quickly drifting into a cloud of hazy dreams.

CHAPTER FIFTY-ONE

THE NEXT MORNING, HENRY AWOKE to an apartment littered with pizza boxes and half-drunk cans of soda. He had invited Louis's friend Kayden to join them for a marathon Xbox gambol the night before. "We better get this mess cleaned up before your mom gets back," he said to Louis, who had sleepily wandered over to the refrigerator for a swig of orange juice.

"Is Kayden still here? It looks like he crashed on the couch," Henry asked.

"No, he went back down to his apartment around midnight," Louis said.

"Okay, well, you hop in the shower. I'll get rid of this mess, and then I'll drive you to school."

Within the hour they were down in the parking garage and in Henry's jeep. They turned onto Club View Drive, and Henry knew that he only had a short window of time to have the chat with Louis that he had wanted to have the night before. "So, has your mom told you about the talk show offer?" he asked, hoping to be heard over Louis's playlist that was streaming in his earbuds.

"Yeah, I know it's in New York and all."

"So, what do you think?" Henry asked.

"I think it would be okay for her to take it. I have been looking up some of the schools on the East Coast, so I wouldn't be far away."

Henry smiled. This boy was definitely protective of his mother, as he should be. "Can I ask you something a bit more personal? How you would feel if your mom and I were to make things between us more *permanent*?"

Louis removed his earbuds and turned toward Henry. "You mean, like—?"

"Yeah, I am thinking about asking her to marry me."

Louis paused and then stared straight ahead.

Henry's heart sank in the moment it took for Louis to crack a smile.

"Took you long enough, man!" Louis quipped as he shoved the earbuds back into his bobbing head, returning to his music.

Henry threw him a soft jab to the bicep, and the deal was sealed. Permission granted.

"Good talk," Henry said, smiling.

Later that afternoon, when Henry got back to La Jolla, he phoned La Costa from the bistro.

"Good day, Ms. Reed. How are things going in beautiful Portland?"

"Hey, baby—just fine. However, we need to talk about that little package that you smuggled into my luggage. Henry, why didn't you tell me that you wrote a whole manuscript!"

Henry balked, feeling a bit apprehensive. "I just wanted to give it to you for your thoughts. It's just a first draft, and—"

"And it is really good, Henry, it's more than good. It's *very* good."

The accolade came as a surprise. He didn't think that La Costa would bash his work, but to gush about it, that was something else. "Can we talk about it when you get back?"

"Oh, you bet we will. You can count on that, baby. I had no idea that you were working on this. You are just full of surprises, aren't you?"

Henry chuckled.

"Hey, how did it go with Louis last night? Is he getting his homework done and eating something other than pizza?" La Costa asked.

"Yes, he's fine. He's at Kayden's for the rest of the week. I told him to call or text me if he needs anything."

"Thank you for keeping an eye on him, sweetheart. I am heading to Vancouver next. I'm about to get on a flight. But listen, I'm also going to call Tess with my answer today. I've decided to accept the offer from Global Network. I'm going to do it!"

Henry beamed. "I'm giving you a high-five right now, but you can't see it. Sweetheart, that's great!

"Great? I'd say more like, crazy-scary. I'm terrified!"

"That means that you are doing it right," Henry said. "Congratulations, babe. You are on your way! You definitely deserve this. I love you."

"I love you too. I will call you when I get there. Don't sign any book deals until I get back," she said, laughing, and signed off.

Henry jumped back into his jeep with only one mission in mind.

CHAPTER FIFTY-TWO

THE JEWELRY DISTRICT ON BROADWAY in downtown Los Angeles was a far cry from the pristine, glittering, over-priced boutiques located in La Jolla's tourist row that was designed to separate amateurs from their money. Henry was aware that the diamond of La Costa's dreams did not reside on a padded pillow in the window of a high-dollar storefront. It was waiting deep in the vaults of the district's most guarded brick-front urban buildings; the most uniquely crafted gems and settings hewn right there in the heart of the city she loved. The city where they first met. Nothing less than the best would do for the love of his life.

Henry's jeweler's name was Amal. He was an eccentric little man with an Israeli accent and bright, dancing eyes. He had a store on Hill Street that patrons had to be buzzed into. An electronic surveillance system and an appointment were the gatekeepers that granted entry to Amal's treasures. The ancient office building had a myriad of cameras trained on one's every move from the transactions at the front counter to the workers in the back office. Amal had done a repair on a Rolex that Henry had purchased from him years ago, which was the only piece of jewelry that Henry ever wore as a rule. Of course, this would soon change, and he would be needing not only the most perfect of engagement rings, but wedding bands befitting his and La Costa's eternal love.

Amal greeted him with a jovial smile and a handshake. "Ah! Mr. Paige, so good to see you again. My friend, what is it you need? You come to me for engagement ring?" It was his standard joke with all his male customers.

Henry smiled widely.

Amal burst into a joyful little dance and bounded from behind the counter to deliver a zealous bear hug to Henry. "Yes? *L'chaim!* Come, Mr. Paige, let's find your bride the perfect ring!"

Two hours later, Henry merged onto I-5 toward Santa Ana and would continue on the interstate all the way toward San Diego. He couldn't stop grinning. The little felt-lined box in his shirt pocket filled him with an exhilaration and glee that he had not felt since he was a young man.

He checked his phone for messages from the restaurant. La Costa had called to say that she had arrived at her hotel in Vancouver and was checking in. He would text her when he reached the exit to let her know that he would call her later that evening. There would be so much to discuss about the television show deal, the move, the future. As for the proposal, he would wait a bit for the perfect moment to ask La Costa to marry him. It wouldn't be fair, he figured, to spring another thing on her right now.

Not two hundred thirty miles away, AJ Williams slithered into a pawn shop. "Dizzy G. sent me," he said to a large man with a goatee, who was perched on a stool near the door, eating his lunch from a white paper sack. The man escorted AJ to a room in the back of the shop and closed the door behind him when he left.

There was a single glass counter filled with sundry items, and another large man behind it who grunted when he stood up from a folding chair.

AJ slipped off the steel and leather Cartier Diver watch he was wearing from his massive wrist and placed it on the glass. Then, he pointed to the Smith & Wesson M&P45 that was front and center in the display case.

"That one."

The man behind the counter was short on answers and long on eye contact. He retrieved the metal carrier holding the medium-caliber revolver and set it down in front of him.

"Can I see it?" AJ said.

The man moved slowly and handled the piece with precision, presenting him with an open view of the barrel.

"Need to inspect it, dawg," AJ said.

The man handed over the disassembled gun. The cylinder locked up solid when AJ cocked it. Next, he examined the crane. There was no sign of pitting, cracks, or surface rust. It was a clean gun.

"It's good for concealed carry and self-defense?"

"Sure," the man said.

"Can I dry fire it?"

The man shook his thick head. "Naw. It works."

"Will this get it?" he asked, referring to the watch.

The man sniffed. "That and another bill."

AJ threw down a hundred and the deal was done.

CHAPTER FIFTY-THREE

THE NEXT SEVERAL WEEKS WERE a blur for La Costa. Just off the road, rounding off the last of her memoir tour signings, she now had a blissful window of uninterrupted time to complete the revisions on the second book in the new trilogy. With Henry working at the bistro weekdays and away on weekends to oversee the camp renovations in South Carolina, and with Louis busy at school and with daily basketball practice, schedules afforded La Costa long stretches of writing time, which she indulged in at the beach house, where she always felt the most productive.

There was just something wonderful about the rhythm of the ocean waves and the salt air that kicked her creative mind into high gear, ensuring that she would more than meet the deadline that she had set for the completion of all books in the trilogy, slated for release starting in late fall.

"How is it coming?" Tess asked from the jumping video image on La Costa's computer screen.

"What, are you Skyping me from a bouncy castle?" La Costa joked. "You're giving me sea sickness here."

"Sorry," Tess said. "I'm in a cab on my iPad. Manhattan traffic is a nightmare. I think this guy knows every twisty alley from here to Mid-Town. I feel like a crash dummy back here. How are the revisions coming?"

"Great. I will be ready to get started on book three very soon. I figured it would be good to finish them all before I start with the talk show. Less to try to do later on."

"Actually, the timing could not be more perfect. The trilogy will be hitting right as you move into this new role as co-anchor," Tess said. "I don't need to tell you how excellent it will be for publicity. I am so glad that you said yes. Girl, it's going to be amazing!"

"Speaking of which, have you heard any news about the signing? It's not a done deal until I sign on that dotted line, right?"

"Trust me. It's happening. I am in discussions with the network about every detail. There will be a preliminary acceptance of the terms, and then a group signing for all of the co-hosts. I will let you know as soon as a date has been selected for that. Then, about two weeks after the group signing, there will be a photo shoot for the entire cast. Everything, as far as we can tell, is tight and on schedule. By the way, how are Henry and Louis feeling about this new adventure of yours?"

"They are on board and couldn't be more supportive," La Costa said. "I can't say that I'm surprised, though. I am so grateful for those two. I just want to pinch myself sometimes. We just need to iron out the logistics between both coasts, and then I think we'll be fine. I haven't had time to hunt for a place yet."

"Don't worry about a thing. I have it covered. A former colleague of mine in real estate is on the lookout for the perfect East Coast apartment for you guys. You just keep those revisions coming, and I'll do the rest."

"Thanks, Tess. Truly, for everything" La Costa said, trying to navigate the unsteady image of her agent coming in and out of focus with every pothole. So much was starting to happen so quickly, and her brain felt like a whir of details, deadlines, and to-do lists to juggle. "Oh, have you had a chance to look at Henry's manuscript that I sent you?"

"The Cozumel vacation thriller? Yes, I did. I'm telling you, for real—it wasn't half bad. Is there anything that guy of yours can't do?"

"Right?" La Costa said smugly. "Do you know anyone who can take a serious look at it?"

"I am working on that too," Tess said, suddenly jolting forward as the cab came to an abrupt stop. "*Shit!* That was my coffee."

"Okay, I'm out," La Costa said, unable to take the bobbing motion on the screen any longer. It was time to jump off of Tess's crazy ride. "We will be up at Splendor Bay next weekend, so please be sure to text or call if you hear anything further from Bumpy Friedman's people."

"Will do, *girl*. Happy revising!"

La Costa was gone with a blip. Tess quickly reached for her cell phone as the cab slowed to a crawl, now in grid-lock traffic. She dialed Henry's mobile number, barely giving him a chance to say hello when he picked up.

"Hey, Henry—it's Tess. Is everything a go for this weekend?"

CHAPTER FIFTY-FOUR

TESS HAD CONTACTED HENRY A couple of weeks prior to suggest that they conspire to plan the perfect surprise party for La Costa. It would be a celebration in her honor for the new talk show signing, and Tess insisted that they host it at Splendor Bay.

"It's almost ready for bookings, right? It would also be a good test run of the facility's new banquet room, and overall, a great way to showcase the venue for similar events."

Who was Henry to argue? All but the upstairs dorm rooms were finished, and he was quite proud to show off the new face-lift in the entrance lobby and grounds.

Tess had deputized all of their tasks. "We can put out the word and invite as many people as possible to rally around La Costa as she takes on this bold new career move. I want her to walk in and be hit with the whole package—banners, balloons, the works!"

It would be Louis's job to get her there. Never in his life had he kept a secret from his mother, and it wasn't going to be easy. It had been murder on everyone, working so hard to not let La Costa in on their planning.

Henry was not only on board, but he couldn't be more

excited. He had arranged for a local photographer to shoot the venue beforehand, to get some marketing collateral of the décor, the event stage, and the beach-front gaming tables. It was going to be epic.

"Everything is set," Henry said. It was his hundredth call with Tess. "I will head up there on Thursday to meet with the event planner. Wait until you see it. La Costa is getting a full-scale Southern plantation and Hollywood premier theme party all in one. It will blow her away!"

"Perfect," Tess squealed. "I don't know who's more excited, Demitri and the family, or me. My Ella can't wait to watch *Gone with the Wind* in the new media room and later hang with the older kids at the bonfire. Oh—it's a go on the fireworks, right?"

"Check," Henry said assuredly. "It will be glitter, lights, and a red carpet reception for La Costa all the way. I'm telling you, it will be an evening she won't forget."

"Great. Text me if you think of anything else. Just make sure that Louis gets her there!"

When the weekend arrived, Henry could hardly contain his excitement. Mostly because he had a little surprise of his own planned to coincide with the festivities.

On Friday, at mid-afternoon, La Costa and Louis pulled onto the driveway in a Town car from the airport, as planned, entering through the ornate front doors to a chorus of cheers. La Costa nearly fainted when Tess and her family, a bevy of industry colleagues, and a handful of super fans, all yelled, "Surprise!" Louis had to catch La Costa's arm and steady her from the startling shock that nearly knocked her off of her Ferragamos.

"What?" La Costa was incredulous. "How in the world did you ever pull this off?" she said to Tess, who was jumping straight up and down across the room. La Costa had thought that her usually chatty assistant, Florian, had been especially tip-lipped the previous few days. Now, there he was, tossing a handful of confetti, and snapping photos with his phone, much to his and the crowd's collective delight. Never in her life had she ever been thrown a surprise party—let alone one as magnificent and audacious as this. The woman of many words was rendered speechless.

Every room on the main floor was transformed into another place and time with movie posters, spotlights, and roving actors and actresses dressed as Hollywood icons. "Rhett Butler" and "Scarlett O'Hara" ushered the guests into the brand-new movie theater on the main floor with popcorn and confections for the taking on pushcarts and buffet stations throughout the house. The banquet room entrance was flanked with eight-foot-tall golden Oscar statues and a sea of round tables topped with floral centerpieces and cascading rolls of film and cut-out stars on each tabletop. Lush fabric framed the stage, on which was featured a video montage of La Costa taken from a collection of her appearances and media reels. A disc jockey was set up near the dance floor, spinning a collection of high-energy tunes from past to present beneath a laser light show-infused ceiling.

The back of the property was a wonderland of carnival and casino games, face-painters, mimes, and fire-eaters. There even was a small petting zoo for the young children.

It would take La Costa hours to take it all in. Someone handed her a cool glass of iced tea.

"How did all these people get here?" La Costa asked Louis, who was beaming from ear to ear.

"They parked their cars a mile away at a hotel, and we bused them here."

"We didn't want to give anything away with all the cars!" Tess said, bounding forward and giving La Costa a bear hug that enveloped her in Chanel No. 5 and lasted two full minutes. "Hey, girl! Look who's in the spotlight!"

La Costa cried large, unstoppable tears that streaked her mascara and made her nose drip, but she didn't care. Not today. It was like a dream that she never knew she had wanted.

"Tess, did you invite the whole island?" La Costa mused, dabbing her swollen eyes with a wad of tissues that someone had handed her.

"Just about! There are a ton of event planners, florists, and hospitality folk here to check out Splendor Bay, so *you're welcome.*"

La Costa's head was spinning. "My word . . . where's Henry?"

She searched the crowd. Henry had waited for La Costa to catch his gaze, and in that moment, she knew that none of it would have been possible if not for him. He, no doubt, had been behind so much of what they had set out to do in bringing Splendor Bay back to life. And now *this?* It was just too much. She couldn't have loved him more.

The festivities ran all afternoon and into the night, when the entertainment moved onto the beach for a reenactment of an Old West shootout, and a large bonfire was only upstaged by the spectacle of bursting fireworks exploding in the sky, Disneyland-style. It was more than magical.

By ten p.m., the crowd had begun to thin out, and La Costa had grown hoarse from talking and visiting with her guests, feeling blissfully exhausted.

Tess and Demitri emerged with twelve-year-old Ella yawning widely and clinging to her father's arm. "The kids are exhausted. I think we broke their fun meters! Imagine that," Tess said. "We're going to head back to the hotel."

"No," La Costa said, rubbing her bare arms from the cool night air. "You all stay here with us. We'll make up some beds and—"

Tess shot Henry a knowing glance. "Well, we already checked in at the hotel in town with the large pool and the all-you-can-eat breakfast buffet in the morning, so we are all set. In fact, Louis said earlier that he wanted to head back over there with us, so he and the kids can have a sleepover."

La Costa smiled. Who was she to argue? Splendor Bay was a beautiful wreck from the party, and it was probably best that she and Henry have some time to themselves to decompress from it all. "Sure, no problem," La Costa said.

"We'll see you both in the morning, when we drop Louis back off on our way to the airport," Tess said, as she planted a kiss on La Costa's cheek. "It was a magnificent night, *Bubbi*. And in so many ways, I know, it's only the beginning."

La Costa embraced her tightly, and then reached up to hug Demitri's neck. "Thank you both, so much—for everything."

An hour later, Henry was still busy with the task of settling with caterers and prop company as they broke down the sets and hauled away the larger items back to their warehouses. He had been tending to something out back while La Costa took a soothing shower and changed into her comfy yoga pants and a simple T-shirt. She freshened her face and slipped into her favorite house slippers and

padded around the main house, in all its post-party dis-
order, wondering where Henry had disappeared to. She
couldn't wait to collapse with him on the couch, and to go
over every detail of the night, and especially to see some of
the photos he had taken with his new phone.

When she couldn't find him anywhere, she decided to
dial his cell number.

He picked up on the second ring. "Hello? Is this the
beautiful and amazing La Costa Reed calling me?"

"It is. Are you even still here? On this property? I am
beginning to worry that you might have ditched me like
everyone else, leaving me to clean up this mess! Where *are*
you?"

"I'm right here, in the back. Waiting for you."

"For me? You want me to come out there?"

"Yes, sweetheart. Come meet me outside," he said. And
then hung up.

La Costa puzzled. *What in the world?* She grabbed her
zippered hoodie and headed toward the front entrance. She
kicked off her house slippers and, in her bare feet, stepped
across the porch, down the wooden steps, and onto the
cool grass. It was dark, and the only light she could now see
was coming from the distance toward the beach. She could
make out a series of small, flickering lights glowing along
a stretch of the lawn leading to the water. The moon was
half-veiled by a slow-drifting night cloud that, every few
seconds, offered a bit more light as she ventured toward
the image of Henry standing several yards from her with
something in his arms.

"What is going on?" she asked, as she made her way
closer to him.

Henry said nothing and only smiled.

Finally, when she stood before him, she could see that
he was holding a bouquet of roses.

"These are for you, my love," he said.

"Thank you, babe, *but*—?" Suddenly, her heart began to quicken as he took her hand in his and led her toward the dock, which was also lined with small tea candles, leading a pathway to the edge of the pier, ending where a spattering of red rose petals were arranged in a heart at the edge of the slip. There, bobbing in the water, was a small utility boat that looked like a throwback in time. It had deep crimson teakwood edging that glistened in the moonlight. Henry motioned for her to take a look at the decal letters in script on the side of the hull, which read: SEXY INK.

La Costa raised a concerned brow. "You bought a boat?"

"Oh, this boat is not just any old boat," Henry said, pulling her in close for a kiss. "It's yours."

"Mine?"

"It belonged to Georgia and Macklin Byrne. It came with the house. It was here all along, in the shed under a tarp. I had remembered how you told me that Georgia once said that Macklin loved restoring it, and well, I have made it my little special project these many weeks that I have been coming here."

"You restored it for me?" La Costa could not imagine that she had ever been shown such an incredible kindness, nor had she received a more meaningful gift.

"Yep," Henry said. "Do you like it?"

La Costa simply threw her arms around him and squeezed. "I love it! And I love you, Henry Paige."

Henry held her close and drew in a steady breath, taking in the blissful cool and salty night air deep into his lungs. "One more thing," he said, slowly lowering himself onto one knee, his weathered hands trembling.

La Costa's beautiful face froze in disbelief.

Pulling a small ring box from his pocket, he lifted the hinged top and stared up into her eyes. They were the most beautiful eyes he had ever seen and would ever need to know for the rest of his life. "Will you marry me?"

La Costa's tears and shock cumulated into a resounding, "Yes! Yes, Henry Paige, I will marry you!"

She laughed and cried simultaneously as he slipped the ring onto her finger. It was the most beautiful thing she had ever seen, somehow managing to outshine every star in the night sky. They shared a kiss that would seal the promise of a lifetime.

La Costa's whirlwind day could only be topped by the prince of all men asking her to share her life with his. What this would mean for her and the future was yet to be known. And that uncertainty suited her just fine.

CHAPTER FIFTY-FIVE

PANTHER AWOKE TO THE SLIVER of sunlight that peeked from behind the broken slats in the blinds that barely covered the grimy window panel above the kitchen sink. Her futon, which passed as a couch by day, was a tangle of threadbare sheets, atop which was left a book broken open at the spine, from a late-night read. It was La Costa's memoir, *No Secrets*. The pages were tattered and dog-eared, some filled with endless sticky notes and highlights from a florescent marker.

It was finally the day. It was time.

Panther ran a hot shower, shaved her legs, and chose a floral sundress with spaghetti straps. She placed her hair in ringlet curls plastered close to her head, in order to slip on the snug silver-blonde wig that had blunt thick bangs and swept in an angle from the nape of her neck to her ebony shoulders. She went easy on the makeup and powdered her cheeks with a light blush and finished off the look with a sticky pink gloss.

She stuffed the memoir and some paperwork into a canvas tote bag, grabbed a bag of Doritos, and left the apartment.

CHAPTER FIFTY-SIX

L A COSTA'S FIRST LINE OF business when she got back to Los Angeles and to her desk was to Skype Tess and to relive the previous three days that had her head in the clouds, celebrating all the good news of late, not the least of which was Henry's beautiful proposal.

Tess had insisted on another live shot of the engagement ring, in spite of having seen it the morning after the party, when she and her family dropped Louis off.

"You know I still can hardly believe that it is happening, girl. It's stunning!"

"Isn't it?" La Costa beamed. "I guess I will have to keep up with the manicures again now that I'm hauling this thing around, right?"

"Well, we knew that Henry was working on something, but Demitri and I couldn't exactly figure out what. It was Henry who had asked us to take Louis for the night, and to say that it was *his* idea. Very crafty, that man of yours is!" Tess said, leaning in. "Hold it up closer to the camera. *Oy!* That's beautiful! I'm just so happy for you, *girl.*"

"Tess, the party was beyond anything I have ever seen. I just can't thank you enough for helping to put all that together for me. I am seriously still in shock," La Costa said.

"Well, you certainly deserved it. Now, there is still much to be done before the group signing, which, by the way, will be on August 21ˢᵗ. Put that date into your calendar and circle it in red."

"I'm doing it now," La Costa said.

"In the meantime, I will definitely try to keep you busy with summer signings and appearances. If it's up to me, you will be the queen of personal appearances—everything from podcasts to conference panels—anywhere we can gain visibility."

"Just leave me some time to write," La Costa said. "If I could ever stop staring at my ring!"

"Check *that*. Oh, I wanted to ask you. Have you decided on where you are going to have Louis's graduation party next month? Reyce wants *the works*, like you just had. I put the kibosh on that right away with that one. He's getting a backyard barbecue right here at Chez Kardamakis."

"Would you believe that Louis doesn't want a party?" La Costa said, her mouth bending into a frown. "Says that he just wants to go to Yellowstone with Kayden and his dad for seven days. But get this—he's asked Henry to go with him."

"That is really amazing," Tess said. "I mean, that he feels that close to Henry already."

"I suppose so, but I thought every high school senior wanted the big cap-tossing thing and all. He just wants a quiet dinner with us after the ceremony, and then to leave the next day for the camping trip."

"Yellowstone, huh? Well, now I'm thinking that will free you up for a potential week on London's bookshop circuit. Perfect!"

"Hey, slow down. I've got a wedding to plan here!" La Costa said.

"Do you two have a date in mind?" Tess asked, shifting through a messy desk of files.

"No idea. When life slows down long enough for either one of us to catch our breath, I guess we will figure that out. I promise, you'll be the first to know."

"As long as I don't have to squeeze into a God-awful bridesmaid's dress or anything anytime soon, I'm good. Or, at least give me a thirty-day warning so that I can shed a few pounds."

"I'll keep that in mind." La Costa laughed.

"*Mazel tov*, my friend. I just couldn't be happier for you," Tess said, signing off.

Panther pulled up to the address for the social welfare center that was scrawled on the torn piece of paper taped to her dashboard. The neighborhood was sketchy at best, so she reached over to the glove box and popped it open. A can of pepper spray rolled out onto the floorboard with a thud. She quickly snatched it up and tossed it into her tote bag. Then, she hesitantly opened the car door and stepped into the street. A carful of hoodlums roared past in a tricked-out Bronco, nearly clipping her as they sped by, shouting, "Hey, *delicious*. Give me some of that brown sugar!" and "Yo! Why don't you put those lips around my cock!" gesturing obscenities as they leaned out of the open windows, with DMX blaring from the booming speakers.

She hurried over to the nondescript building, littered with all forms of humanity leaning on the brick walls and skulking in the doorways. She pulled on the steel door handle and into a cheerless sterile office building with a glass door on the left and an elevator on the right. The name on the door matched the one on the piece of paper that she was now squeezing in her sweaty palm. She breathed a sigh of relief.

She reached for the door handle, and just as she did so, a skinny black man in saggy pants and wearing a Clippers jersey, bounded off of the elevator and collided with her, knocking her arm and causing her to drop the tote bag. The contents, along with her keys, spilled out onto the sticky linoleum floor.

"Oh, man! My bad, Miss. Sorry!" he said, helping her to retrieve her belongings, including the pepper spray that had fallen on the floor.

"It's fine," she said, not making eye contact. She stuffed everything back into the tote bag and reached for the door handle. It was then that he noticed the distinctive tattoo—a small black panther on her left wrist.

He watched as she slipped into the cool bright lights of the social services office suite.

Then, he sauntered out into the daylight, scrolled through his contacts, and dialed his buddy AJ. What were the chances? He couldn't believe his *freaking luck*.

CHAPTER FIFTY-SEVEN

LOUIS'S GRADUATION WAS A MOMENTOUS day marked with ardent celebration, starting with a breakfast fit for a boss, in which La Costa whipped up all his favorites, including pancakes with strawberries, bananas, and whipped cream. She had his best pants pressed and his blue shirt starched, hung them on his bedroom door and laid out his cap and gown regally on his bed. A new pair of shiny dress shoes, still in the box, were placed next to the suit coat that he would wear beneath the crimson robe.

The ceremony was planned for two o'clock at the high school and was to be held on the football field in the blaring sun. La Costa was ready with her favorite wide-brimmed straw hat with the satin bow that she had called her "church hat," and she had stashed plenty of mints, gum, and several bottles of water in her enormous purse. It was predicted to be hotter than six shades of hell, as Georgia was fond of saying, and La Costa was not going to take any chances.

She and Louis met Henry at the school, near the gymnasium, where most of the students were gathering to slip into their caps and gowns and take group photos. Henry wore a suit and tie despite the blaring heat.

"You look amazingly cool, Mr. Paige," La Costa said as he walked toward them, smiling.

He planted a kiss on her powdered cheek, and then shook Louis's hand with a solid grip.

"The big day is finally here, huh?"

Louis grinned. "Did you bring the extra hiking gear?"

"The jeep is packed with provisions. This time tomorrow, we will be sleeping under the stars."

"Awesome!" Louis said, adjusting his hat.

The marching band struck up the school's fight song, and the graduates started to make their way onto the field. "Let's go, guys. It's starting!"

Following the ceremony, La Costa and Louis drove back home to take a few more photos before Louis ditched his dress clothes for his jeans and high-tops. Henry followed them back to the apartment. La Costa had planned to officially present Louis with a special gift—a Rolex with his initials engraved on the back. It was a bit extravagant, but it was her privilege to indulge him with a grownup timepiece that she'd hoped he would keep forever to remember the import of this milestone day. Although Louis was the youngest in his class, due to skipping the fifth grade the year that they moved from New York to LA, he was head and shoulders ahead of his peers in all the ways that counted. La Costa could not have been prouder.

"I am going to change," Louis said, as he headed to his room.

"Don't be long. I have something I want to give you before we leave for the restaurant," La Costa said.

Henry emerged from the kitchen with a small white cake with a sparkler in the middle, at the ready to light it when Louis returned. The gift box was set innocuously on the coffee table.

"This could take a while," La Costa said, smoothing out her skirt and lowering herself onto the sofa. "That boy takes forever to pick a decent button-down shirt."

Henry chuckled. "Is he all ready for tomorrow? We're pulling out of here at five a.m."

"Who do you think packed that boy's clothes? I did!" La Costa said, shaking her head. "I do hope that he is aware that there is no maid service in the woods."

Henry laughed.

Just then, a knock at the door caused them both to exchange a glance. "Who would be stopping by at this time? The doorman hadn't called up to announce anyone," La Costa said.

The two walked to the door.

"I got it," Henry said, stepping in front of La Costa.

A middle-aged man in a plaid shirt spoke flat and quick when Henry swung the door open.

"Ma'am, are you Mayella Jackson?"

La Costa nodded, though the words caused an immediate pang, and her breath caught in her chest. Before she could speak, the man thrust an envelope at her. "You have been served." Then he turned on his retro sneakers and headed down the hallway toward the stairwell.

Henry swung around to find La Costa tearing into the envelope with mounting distress. She pulled the stack of official papers from the envelope and frantically read the words with shock and dread—it was a court summons from one Phyllis Jean St. James and—*she wanted Louis back.*

Henry barely caught La Costa before she collapsed to the floor.

CHAPTER FIFTY-EIGHT

T HE MOMENTS FOLLOWING WERE A blur. La Costa had come to on the stretcher in the elevator on the way down to the street. Still, the paramedics insisted on checking her vitals and conducting other tests on the trip to the hospital. Henry and Louis followed, speeding down the streets behind the emergency vehicle with its sirens and flashing red lights.

Thirty minutes later she was sitting up in a hospital bed in her clothes. Her blouse had been torn in the commotion, and her skirt was wrinkled. Henry was there, at her bedside, caressing her hand as the hospital staff shuffled around with their charts and chatter, adjusting the beeping machines that tracked her temperature and heart rate.

"I'm okay, really," La Costa said. "Where's Louis?"

"He's out in the waiting area. He knows that you are okay. Is there anything that you need, sweetheart. Some more water, maybe?" Henry looked a fright. Like he had just weathered a storm, or plowed a field with his bare hands.

La Costa shook her head. "What happened?"

"The doctor will be by to fill us in on some tests they took—an EKG and some blood work, I think, from when you first arrived here. Do you remember fainting?"

She nodded. Then, the flash of memory about the envelope suddenly caused her heart rate to spike and her nerves to reel. "Henry—the envelope!"

"I put it in your office drawer," he said, reading her mind. "Louis didn't see it."

She closed her eyes and leaned her head back onto the stiff pillow. "Thank God," she whispered.

Henry stroked her forehead. "How are you feeling, babe?"

"I am fine, really."

Just then the doctor, a woman of about thirty, with long, dark hair twisted in a snaky braid down her back, appeared from behind the plastic drape and greeted them cheerfully.

"Hello, Ms. Reed! Pleased to meet you. I'm Dr. Keller. I see that you had a little incident this evening."

"I was at my son's graduation this afternoon, and I'm afraid that I might have gotten a bit too much sun," La Costa said.

"Is this your husband, Ms. Reed?" she said, gesturing toward Henry.

"My fiancé," La Costa said, giving Henry's hand a little squeeze. "You can speak freely in front of him."

"I see, well, it looks like your sugar levels were a bit low, but everything checks out concerning your heart rhythm and vitals."

"Thank God," La Costa said. "Am I cleared to go?"

"If you don't mind, I would like to keep you a bit longer for one more test, seeing as how there was a little something of note with your blood work."

La Costa's face puzzled. "Of note?"

The doctor checked the chart once again, and then asked, "Ms. Reed, your health records indicate that you are in menopause?"

"Yes, I am. I haven't had a period in over a year."

"I see," she said. Then, jotting something onto the clipboard, she exhaled sharply and smiled. "Well, I'd like to do an ultrasound just to confirm. But it does appear, Ms. Reed, that you are pregnant."

CHAPTER FIFTY-NINE

T HE RIDE HOME WAS QUIET. La Costa and
Henry had agreed not to mention the news about
the pregnancy to Louis—not yet, at least. It had been a
harrowing evening that followed a wonderful afternoon,
and they didn't need to add the news of the incredible
new development of the past hour to the mix. *What was
happening?* La Costa wondered, as Henry drove in silence
and Louis struggled to make small talk from the back seat.

"Who wants one with cheese?" he said, rifling through
a grease-stained sack of burgers and fries from the drive-
thru.

"I'll take one," Henry said. "Pass it up here."

La Costa had no appetite. The smell of the onion rings
was vile.

"I'm glad you're okay, Mom," Louis said. "Are you going
to miss me when Henry and I are out there in the wild?"

"What, sweetheart? Oh, you know I will. I'm just going
to have to find a way to keep myself busy, since I won't have
any dirty gym socks to pick up or cans of soda to clear off
of the coffee table. Yeah, I think I'll manage." She chuckled
to make light of it all, when, deep inside, she was reeling.
A mixture of dread and euphoria collided in her mind,

seemingly at the same time. How could the two emotions co-exist in one woman without killing her dead?

It was a surreal feeling that reduced her to tears once she arrived home and stood naked in the shower, stripped bare and overwhelmed. *Panther had come back—she had come back for Louis!* Panther would tear apart every bit of good that she had done these past seventeen years. Years that belonged to *them*, not her! *Why now?*

La Costa sobbed into her hands beneath the water jets until she was so exhausted, she had to call Henry to assist her into her pajamas and onto the bed.

"It's going to all be okay, babe. We will fight this thing that Panther has brought into our lives and beat it. She can't touch you—or Louis. She won't. I promise."

"How do you know that? Sweetheart, I was wrong to do all of this. To put myself out there to the world like I was bullet-proof. I swear, last I heard, Panther was locked away—I *believed* that she could never touch us. Not ever. But now—*I* did this!" She broke into another fit of sobs, letting the guilt and disbelief feed her anguished and tormented thoughts.

"Stop it. Do you hear me? I promise you. She will not touch us," Henry said, as if his very word could make it so.

La Costa looked deeply into his piercing blue eyes. The eyes that made her always feel safe and secure and invincible. For the first time ever, what she saw there, besides great and unconditional love, was fear. She knew it. He knew it.

"Just hold me," she said, curling up like a frightened child. "Just hold me, Henry. What are we going to do?"

"We've got this, babe," he whispered.

She buried her head into his chest, and then quietly said, "Henry, we are going to have a baby."

"I know," he said, smiling, letting the emotion override

the gravity of the fear and the unknown.

La Costa's face broke into a trembling smile. It was a fact, and it was an undeniable truth that God had blessed her yet again with the greatest of all blessings.

"Oh, baby!" Henry said, caressing her tummy and laughing softly at first, and then with great glee.

This sent her into a fit of giggles, tears, and then more laughter. "Lord have mercy! Henry, we are having a *baby!*"

CHAPTER SIXTY

L A COSTA CONTACTED THE BEST family law attorney that money could buy. His name was Hugo Maldonado of the firm Guzman and Maldonado. The practice had a pricey Rodeo Drive address and a track record of winning custody cases. Most importantly, the team was well versed in handling high-profile cases for celebrity clients who needed to keep things clean and out of the media spotlight.

"Gaining custody as a non-biological parent can be difficult," Hugo told La Costa and Henry at their first meeting. "But it *is* definitely possible to prove abandonment of the child from infancy due to Ms. St. James's indiscretions, and later, in light of her incarceration. Plus, seeing as how Louis will be eighteen in December, I don't see there being any trouble in doing so."

"Except for the damage that Panther can do by showing up here. Now, out of the blue." La Costa was inconsolable. "Louis mustn't find out—not this way."

Henry clasped her trembling hand and leaned forward. "What can we expect?"

"At present, it is just a petition for Determination of Child Custody. A judge will decide. We should easily be able to prove unfitness, or incapacity at the very least. The initial hearing is where it all starts. We have already requested relevant information from Ms. St. James's attorney for discovery. It's a bit of a waiting game at this point."

"What can we do?" La Costa said, clutching a shredded tissue in her palm.

"Sit tight. Wait to hear from me. We'll be contacting you to get some additional statements."

La Costa nodded. "Of course. Whatever you need."

"I will let you know the soonest we can get this before a judge. In the meantime, try to carry on with your life. I know it's difficult."

Henry stood to shake Hugo's hand. "Thank you."

La Costa and Henry headed back to the car. La Costa felt less at ease than before.

"What is all of this? Discovery? Petition for Determination? Henry, I am not sure if I am going to be able to get through this."

"That's why you have me," he said cheerily. "How does a couple of weeks in Hawaii sound? Just you, me, and Louis. Let's take a break from all of this and let Hugo do his job. You know, Louis has never surfed anywhere other than here. Let's do a little island hopping and find him some bucket-list swells to check off his list. What do you say? Florian can take care of things while you're gone."

La Costa considered the alternative. Sitting around and waiting at home, or at the beach house, would only drive her crazy. She needed a change of scenery, now more than ever. "I say, yes. It will make a great distraction. I'll have Florian run interference with Tess. As long as there's a Wi-Fi connection, I can work while you and Louis hit the waves."

"Perfect," Henry said. "Just us, the sea turtles, and the sunshine. *Aloha!*"

Five days later they were on a plane and landed at Kahului Airport, where the warm summer breezes hit their senses with a mix of fragrant floral and salt-scented air. The thirty-minute car ride to the Four Seasons resort felt like a dream as the lush green landscape and cloudless blue skies transported La Costa to a better frame of mind. She had her two favorite men by her side and the sweetest secret of all inside her. The gratitude that flowed within her felt uncontainable, like her hopes for their future.

Later that night, after they had unpacked, Henry had planned for a private dinner for just the three of them. Room service arrived and set up the feast on the terrace outside of their suite, overlooking the ocean, which was perfection. The stunning view through the palms of the sapphire-blue ocean beneath the setting sun was magical. Even Louis managed to ditch his iPod to take in the sounds of the surf that entranced the mind and senses. He shared his thoughts freely with Henry and La Costa about the move ahead, college choices, and concerns about his studies.

He barely touched his ahi tuna, talking away instead, at a mile a minute. "I'm sort of leaning toward NYU, but of course, there's a great sports management program at Duke. I wonder what it would be like to live in a dorm? Maybe Reyce and I could room together."

"That's a possibility, sweetheart," La Costa said, smiling.

He was enjoying the uninterrupted attention as he

slurped the fruity mango mock-tail with the sweetest chunks of pineapple floating at the bottom.

"This is so cool. Thanks for suggesting this trip. Just when I thought things couldn't get any better, you guys keep surprising me!"

La Costa gave Henry a glance and winked. The plan was to enjoy a delicious sunset dinner and then take a walk on the beach to find the perfect place and moment, to tell him the news about the baby.

His reaction was priceless. Louis's smile burst from ear to ear, and he actually turned three cartwheels in the sand when he heard the news. "What! I'm going to be a brother?"

"It sure looks like it," La Costa said, as he flopped down into a heap of exhaustion and giggles right at the water's edge. "In about six months—right around your birthday, too, it seems."

"So cool," Louis said, gazing out at the horizon and wedging his feet deep into the wet sand.

Henry and La Costa did the same. They all buried their feet in the macadam sludge created from the foamy waves. It was a moment, indeed. The three of them stuck to the earth and stuck with each other—soon to be four. It was a dream of dreams, and so much of a karmic interlude for La Costa.

"Can I just ask," Louis finally said, after a long soulful pause.

"What, dear-heart?"

"Can we name the baby something cool, like *Rainbow* or *Zeus*?"

"Uh, I'm not sure about that, Champ," Henry said. "Maybe we should leave the baby-naming to your mother, the writer."

"You're probably right," Louis said, and then added, "If it's a girl and you ever write her into one of your stories, Mom, be sure to make her a bad-ass, smart woman, like you."

La Costa held on to the moment and resisted the urge to cry. If love were an ocean, she was sure her portion could fill the universe to the brim.

Together, they stared out at the horizon.

CHAPTER SIXTY-ONE

L A COSTA EMERGED FROM THE hotel cabana, where she had been poring over the second edits for the trilogy. Henry and Louis had been gone since early morning "sloping waves" at Kihei Cove. She had been doing her best to ignore the string of emails from Tess that had been dinging on her phone since they had arrived. *"I know you are relaxing, but can you take a look at this proposal?"* And *"Can you do a signing at B&N in Palm Desert on the fourteenth, when you get back?"* Tess was relentless. Didn't she know that La Costa had deadlines to meet in addition to planning a wedding and a move to New York City?

When her phone vibrated from the pocket of her beach bag, La Costa figured it was Tess, once again, checking in. She answered it with a bit of curt humor. "Sorry, girl, La Costa is not here. She's thrown her phone to the sharks. Leave your message at the beep!"

"Hello?" the voice on the other end of the line was definitely not Tess's. It was Pastor Parks, from the non-denominational church that La Costa belonged to. He was her one and only choice of officiate for her and Henry's nuptials. He was a bit of a rock star in the valley, and La Costa had her fingers crossed to get on his calendar.

"Oh, Pastor Parks! Thank you for getting back to me.

Yes, it's La Costa Reed. I am hoping that the request is not too last minute. We were hoping to move up the ceremony prior to my leaving for New York." She didn't see any reason to explain about an unplanned pregnancy factoring in just a smidge. "Can you accommodate us within the next few months?"

"Ms. Reed, I would be more than happy to re-work the booking for you, but I am afraid that I have but one date available before I and the missus take off for our mission trip to Ghana."

"I see. What date is that, Pastor? I am sure that we can make it work."

"August twenty-first."

La Costa's stomach lurched. It was the day of the Global Network signing. But what could she do? It would be a small, but manageable glitch. The proverbial gods of fate had now caused the unfortunate reality of scheduling two momentous occasions on the same day. The story of her own life was turning out to be stranger than fiction, for certain.

"That will work just fine, Pastor," she said in an effort to convince herself more than him. "We will take the date."

"Very good, dear. I'll email you the paperwork."

"Oh, and Pastor?"

"Yes, dear?"

"How do you feel about doing the ceremony in New York City?"

AJ had rolled into Los Angeles in the late morning. He had sped out of Nevada early, making the four-hour drive in three and some change. He had only stopped once to piss, get gas, and to load up on pork rinds and Mountain Dew.

He pulled up to the social welfare center in the downtown district and parked by a patch of scorched grass near a quiet curb. The address matched the one that his buddy, Crank, had given him. It was an ordinary day, and the locals were out in force, claiming their spots on the street corners and park benches. A few street walkers were trolling near the park. The sun was climbing high in the sky. He turned off the engine and slouched down in the bucket seat, tipped his hat over his shades, and waited.

He had nothing but time. He would sit there forever if he had to.

CHAPTER SIXTY-TWO

(TWO WEEKS LATER)

L A COSTA ARRIVED HOME TO a stack of mail and the daunting task of doing more loads of laundry than she had ever found herself on the folding end of. Henry had returned to his townhome and the bistro in La Jolla, and Louis was busying himself with last-minute college applications and essays, which admittedly made her heart soar. If she and her brood were nothing else, they were doers, and keeping busy these days seemed to be La Costa's best defense from worrying herself sick, or drowning in a deep abyss of depression.

Much to her relief, Tess had decided to fly into LA for a few days and meet with her favorite client face-to-face. As far as Tess was concerned, all business was better when conducted over a couple of refreshing drinks on a pier at the marina or at an upscale trendy haunt in Newport Beach. La Costa was pleased to hear that Tess was planning a visit. It was time to come clean about the news of the baby that would soon be progressively harder for her to keep from her trusted agent. And more importantly, she needed to know if it would be a deal-breaker for the folks at Global Network. It would be unfair not to let Tess in on

the new development. At least, this one. The news about
Panther would be kept in the vault that was La Costa's
soul. No one would need to know her most guarded
secret. Not even Tess.

La Costa was already seated at the table when Tess
arrived, all smiles and loaded down with shopping bags
from boutiques and shops from the local mall. "I see that
you did a little retail therapy," La Costa said, giving Tess an
earnest hug. It felt good to feel the embrace of the woman
she owed so much of her livelihood to.

"Can I just say, that you look amazing, *Bubbi*. I think
that trip to the islands did you a world of good!"

"It did. I was able to finish all of the edits for the trilogy,
and I'm ready to start discussions about the new series," La
Costa said brightly.

"That's just what I wanted to hear. Oh, by the way,
I think I found someone to take a hard look at Henry's
debut thriller. Well, he's more of a mentor than an agent,
but I think he can definitely help him get the manuscript
ready to shop around, or to self-publish, if he chooses to
go that route. I hear it's a viable alternative, but don't *you*
get any ideas."

La Costa smiled. "That's a deal."

The waiter arrived, and Tess was quick to order. "I'll
have a Mojito, please." Then, turning to La Costa. "I'm
feeling a little 'Miami vibes' today, what do you say?"

"Just an iced tea for me, please."

The waiter headed to the bar.

Tess eyed La Costa suspiciously. The silence said it all.
"Wait a minute. You're not drinking? Your skin is glowing,
you've been weepy—and dare I say—an emotional *mess*,
for weeks. Wait! You're *not*—?"

La Costa nodded, letting a tear slip from her eye onto her mahogany cheek. "Yep. Just about four months now."

"What!" Tess nearly made a scene. She quickly lowered her voice, leaned forward across the table, and took La Costa's hand. "*Mazel tov!* Girlfriend, this is amazing. Oh my God, what do Henry and Louis think? I mean, it is great news, right?"

"Yes, they are over the moon. And so am I, frankly. But I just want to be sure that this is not going to throw a wrench in the deal with Global and the talk show. How are they going to feel about hiring on a co-host who is nearly six months pregnant?"

"Honestly, I don't know. But I can tell you that this is some of the best news I have heard in a very long time. I will speak with Bumpy Friedman's people right after lunch, and we'll exercise full disclosure. If they are on board with it, we can have our lawyer draw something up that will put in some additional provisions for you once the baby is born. I can't believe this is happening!"

"Thank you, Tess. I don't know what I'd do without you. It's all still so much of a shock. We're not telling anyone else right now. Not even my personal assistant knows. I've gotten quite adept at keeping the doctor's appointments off of my digital calendar. I only just recently told Florian about the show deal in New York and he's lobbying to be my *virtual* assistant bi-coastally. I'm just so worried that news of the baby might change their minds."

"Don't you worry. I am certain that it will not change a thing with Global. I understand completely that you want to keep this news under wraps, though, for now."

La Costa looked relieved.

"As far as your public appearances go," Tess said, "everything can remain relatively the same, as long as you feel up to it, of course. Do you think that you can continue with your tour schedule?"

"Yes, I would like to," La Costa said.

"Great, then." Tess's eyes sparkled. "Here's to the future—and rapidly growing—Paige and Jackson family!"

La Costa raised her glass of tea and smiled. She hated that she wasn't being fully honest with Tess about Panther and the truth about Louis, but playing her cards close to her chest was sort of her go-to move.

And right now, it felt in many ways, that she was definitely in survival mode.

CHAPTER SIXTY-THREE

BY MID-SUMMER, AND AT FIVE months pregnant, La Costa was feeling more agitated and exhausted than ever. This caused her to eat incessantly in order to assuage the anxiety. She was certain that the added pounds to her already curvaceous frame and the wondrous emergence of the distinctive baby bump front and center was beginning to be apparent. None of her clothes fit, and her chronic swollen ankles often caused her to trade her stilettos for low mules whenever she made a public appearance.

In Henry's eyes, however, she could not have been more beautiful. All the pieces were falling into place, and he would not allow any outside force to rip the happiness from their lives. He worked at the beach house on weekends, flying out to Hilton Head to secure the remaining details, while continuing to work remotely to keep things running smoothly at the bistro. The bright new venue at Splendor Bay would soon be ready for its first booking—an educational kids' camp residency with a deadline looming just weeks away. He had interviewed and hired the entire staff, secured the permits, and arranged all the marketing. It was a joyful distraction for him too. He was committed at all costs, to keep fires out and the wolves at bay; to keep La Costa as far away from the stress and chaos of planning the all-consuming launch venture.

"Everything is on track," he assured La Costa, across a crackling cell line, even as the national news back in California was squawking about the potential for hurricane-strength gale winds heading toward the coastline that could "go either way."

"Are you sure we are going to be ready? What if the storm hits and causes damage?" La Costa was relentless with the questions.

"Babe, we've got everything tightened down, and nothing bad is going to happen. I promise. This storm will be long gone by the camp opening. Splendor Bay is stronger than any of these tinderbox hotels on the island. She's a fortress, just like you."

This caused La Costa to laugh. Leave it to Henry to downplay a hurricane. "When are you coming back?" she asked.

"I will be home on Monday. In the meantime, kiss your tummy for me."

"Yeah, like that is even *possible.*" La Costa chuckled.

The call-waiting tone sounded, and La Costa could see that it was Hugo Maldonado. "Listen, sweetie. I have to jump off. I will call you back."

She clicked off the line and left Henry standing on the balcony of the second floor, overlooking the agitated ocean waves beginning to lap in long, taunting strikes against the jagged rocks. The sky was growing dark, and ominous clouds were descending. He had spent a good part of the morning and afternoon boarding up the back bay windows, checking the generators, and storing away loose items in the shed. He hoped that he was right about the old house's mettle. Why not? It had been through a thousand storms, and much like life, one never knows whether the rafters are going to give or to hold. There were no guarantees, but if he knew anything, he knew this: *Nothing was going to come in the way of La Costa and Louis's happiness.* He wasn't quite sure how or why he knew this. He just did.

Off in the distance, a tumultuous thunder was rolling toward him overhead, and the waves were beginning to crest close to the shore. He checked his phone and could see that he did not have a cell signal. He stood a moment more in the wind, and then went back inside, poured himself a drink, and braced for the worst.

By morning, the storm was over. The tempest had passed overnight, and Splendor Bay was still intact. A quick examination of the property revealed that they lost a few shingles, but nothing that could not be patched.

Henry smiled widely when he saw La Costa's little boat at the end of the dock, gleaming in the sunlight, unscathed. "Yeah." He chuckled. "It takes more than a hurricane to knock us down."

CHAPTER SIXTY-FOUR

AUGUST 19TH
LOS ANGELES, CA

THE COURTROOM OF THE HONORABLE Percival Rutherford was quiet and nearly empty. A contrast to the throngs of people outside the double wooden doors in the lobby, who were bustling about with leather briefcases, stacks of files, and stern faces. Well-suited men and women, all checking their wristwatches, cell phones, and resolve, disappearing into cloistered rooms at the top of the hour.

La Costa and Henry stared ahead at the judge's bench, which was empty. Someone cleared their throat, and La Costa swung her head around to look for Panther to walk through the door for the twentieth time. She was not there—yet.

Panther's attorney, a plain a woman with large hips, sat across from La Costa, Henry, and their lawyer, Hugo Maldonado. She was shuffling through some paperwork, and more than once, checked her phone. A younger woman was with her, looking fidgety. The hearing was scheduled to begin at precisely nine a.m.

La Costa leaned into Hugo's ear. "Isn't it time?"

He merely patted her hand and motioned for her to relax. He was prepared, was he not? He had a stack of files of his own, and hours of La Costa's deposed statements, proving in more ways than one that on all accounts, she was singularly Louis's one and only loving mother.

From where she and Henry sat, the room looked cavernous and cold. A large clock above the bench ticked soundlessly, marking the top of the hour, and a second clock, a digital version, was positioned near the witness stand.

"All rise." The bailiff announced Judge Rutherford, and everyone stood, and then folded into their seats. It was stunningly obvious that Panther was not present. This made La Costa thrill with mounting hope. Every few minutes she checked the door for the inevitable entrance of the stunning and elusive Panther St. James, who had come to reclaim her son, whereby ripping him from La Costa's life, and with the single act—destroying her very soul.

Panther's lawyer was at the ready for battle. La Costa could see it in her cold, unfeeling eyes. The woman continued to watch the door at every moment's turn for any sign of her tardy client. "We ask, Your Honor, for a few minutes more for Ms. St. James to appear. Perhaps the elevators—"

The judge looked irritated, seated atop the towering pulpit, staring through tiny, horn-rimmed spectacles chopped off at the tops, forming two perfect half-moons, resting on either side of the largest nose La Costa ever seen before. Judge Rutherford sighed heavily, finally removing his glasses in order to reveal compassionate yet weary eyes that had little tolerance for plaintiffs who wasted the court's time.

"Fifteen minutes," he growled.

La Costa's attorneys from the firm of Guzman and

Maldonado had brought along with them a cadre of stern-faced paralegals heaving heavy files of depositions and witness testimonies, painstakingly collected from medical, church, and school district personnel to further plea the case for La Costa's competence and compliance. But now, with Panther's blatant absence in the courtroom, Hugo contended with rising aplomb that little else needed to be done, but to wait.

Henry squeezed La Costa's hand. They watched as the clock ticked toward the quarter hour mark, ever closer. Soon it would be over, and they would all be able to reclaim their lives.

At the quarter hour mark, the gavel put an end to La Costa's suffering and angst. The case was dismissed. Louis was still, and would always be, hers.

Halfway across town, Panther had awoken that morning feeling more fully alive than she had in several years—maybe ever. She did some light yoga on a mat that she had rolled out in the middle of the living room floor, pushing aside the tiny thrift shop coffee table up against the well-worn couch. Then, she prepared herself a poached egg, wheat toast, and black coffee. She retrieved a small journal from her tote bag and turned it to the next blank page. She wrote the date at the top, and then began to pour her thoughts and feelings into words, as she had been doing faithfully for many months now. She wanted to record all of her hopes and dreams for Louis to see. To hear her side of the story. He would, she hoped, be able to forgive her.

The day was finally here. She had made it. Seventeen years and thousands of miles to find her way back. She smiled when she had finished the lengthy entry that had taken twenty minutes to write. Then, she signed it with a

"P" and closed the cover.

She placed the journal on the counter and took a deep breath. Who would ever think that change like hers was possible? She would prove to them all that it was—and that she deserved to make amends for her mistakes.

She was ready.

Grabbing her keys, she opened the door and stepped out onto the balcony. A force greater than one hundred demons pushed her forcefully back into the apartment. A violent slap rendered her stunned, and then a punishing thrust slammed her hard against the wall. A violent heave pulled her to her feet, and then dragged her by the hair into the bathroom. There, she was kicked, punched, and beaten, until all she could see thorough the blood and the tears was AJ, towering above her, grinning, with a gun pointed at her face.

She tried to speak, cry, scream. Nothing came from her throat but a garbled moan.

She could hear his heavy breaths and taste the tinny blood as he lifted her into the tub and jammed the drain shut. Finding her voice, she shrieked, "No! Please!"

A single blow to the head instantly silenced her.

Everything went black.

He turned the water jets on full-force and stood still and silent. He smiled perversely as the bloody water spilled over the edges, onto the tile, as the water enveloped her, taking her light.

CHAPTER SIXTY-FIVE

AUGUST 21ST
NEW YORK CITY

L A COSTA AWOKE WELL BEFORE dawn, unable to sleep. As she lay there, next to Henry, she closed her eyes and counted her blessings, about to embrace the second happiest day of her life, next to two days prior, when the nightmare was put behind her. She checked her phone and had a number of texts from her lawyer, Maldonado, but whatever he had to tell her could wait. It was about to be the first day of the rest of their lives.

The day was going to be a breeze compared to the trials that La Costa had weathered over most of her forty-four years. She had long given up the belief that she would ever find a life partner, let alone be giving birth to her own child, although Louis was as much a part of her as her arms and legs. He was her soul.

Among the many congratulatory emails, letters, and reviews that had flooded in on the jubilant days and months preceding the release of her memoir, *No Secrets*, La Costa had received, above all things—a new love and a new life. She didn't know who was more excited, she or

Henry? Louis? Tess? It was all happening so fast. But one thing was for certain—it was happening *today*.

Sure, it all mattered. The talk show offer, the signing, the dream job of a lifetime, but only half as much as the pleasure of marrying her soon-to-be loving husband, who was lying there next to her. Rolling over and yawning contentedly, La Costa greeted the dawn, smiling happily at Henry, now peering over at her from beneath the hotel covers.

"Good morning, Ms. Reed," he said with a smile that promised every tomorrow to come. "Got any big plans for today?"

The ceremony was scheduled at the unholy hour of seven a.m., at a cathedral in downtown Manhattan, side altar, due to the simultaneous near-miss bookings of both the wedding and La Costa's eminent show signing with Global Network. Immediately following, La Costa would take a car across town to attend the early-morning network signing at Global Studios, and then head for a celebratory reception in honor of her and her new husband, at The Palm with Tess and her family, Henry's sons, and Louis. Then, it would be off to New England for a quiet, restful honeymoon in an undisclosed location, sans computers, cell phones, and galleys.

Hours later, when she entered the conference room at the offices of Global Network to join the others, in the company of producers, the show director, and television corporate executives, she could scarcely believe the dream that she was living.

Bumpy Friedman greeted her with a wide grin and a

handshake. "Welcome to the team, La Costa."

"It's a big day, indeed, Mr. Friedman."

CHAPTER SIXTY-SIX

TWO WEEKS LATER
NEW YORK CITY

THE PHOTO SHOOT WAS SEAMLESS. The new set, flawless. It was a blend of high-tech stage and studio lighting, contrasted with a highly stylistic feminine touches; elegant, creamy soft pastels and sweeping chiffon backdrops swagged throughout the contemporary studio set with plush theater seating designed to bring the live audience close into the action.

The new cast would be showcased in the "chat corner," a sort of informal living room set featuring several exquisitely upholstered couches and imperial striped chairs, festooned with a generous array of colorful pillows. La Costa thrilled in the moment as she took her place alongside two larger-than-life stunning media celebrities, Hannah Courtland Murphy, of radio talk show fame, as well as fashion maven Kathryn Delacorte, who was taking some preliminary photos in the first chair. A large video screen bordered with a colossal gilded Victorian frame was suspended above them. A myriad of dissolving images of women, children, nature, celebrities, cuisine—all manner of topics and teasers, were displayed in stunning graphics, featuring the show's eclectic themes, scrolling in complement to the high-energy music pulsing from the speakers. Thin cables held the large fiberglass lighted signboard featuring the show's signature logo looped across the lighted scrim in gilded script, welcoming viewers to *The Gab.*

The photographer, Ellie Logan, leaned into the lens to check the framing for the money shot, just as the youngest cast member, Casey Singer, bounded into the room, all buck wild and fired up, "Let's DO this thing!" she shouted as she joined the others on the set.

The theme music blared as the foursome gathered together beneath the bright lights, for the first time all together, posing and smiling for the camera. It was perfection. Bumpy could see it in one brilliant sweep from the producer's booth.

The flashes burst in rapid fire as Ellie Logan clicked away. "Beautiful! Ladies—just beautiful! A few more to go. That's it!" She rallied the group as she captured it all, frame by beautiful frame.

La Costa dazzled from the far right. Her sleek, dark hair and crimson blouse were striking in the studio lights. But not as electrifying as the skyrockets that lit up her eyes; a look placed there by the covert and loving knowledge of the little secret that burned within her that would have to wait just a few weeks more, until when she would share the news with the entire world. For now, she just wanted to keep word of the baby to herself, and a few choice others, a little bit longer. The shocking report about Panther had been horrific, but left La Costa's resolve unshattered. Her self-redemption, her joy, and her purpose was clear. And the vivacious Queen of Contemporary Romance never looked better!

"Okay, everyone. Give me one last shot," Ellie prodded.

"C'mon, a great big hello from the ladies of *The Gab*. Let's give America something to talk about!"

La Costa took a deep breath and delivered a billion-dollar smile, as the flash exploded.

ABOUT THE AUTHOR

Jamie Collins, author of the Secrets and Stilettos women's fiction series, writes larger than life fiction about the fact-track world of media and entertainment.

As a former model/actress, she infuses her stories with Hollywood grit, sizzle and heat reminiscent of the great women's fiction writers (Jackie Collins, Sidney Sheldon, and Olivia Goldsmith) of decades past on which she cut her writing chops reading and emulating their iconic styles.

Collins brings a fresh, modern-day take on the throwback pocket novel tomes that defined an era of extravagance and excess in exchange for a world where women are more powerful, smart, and driven than ever.

Collins's stilettos have been everywhere from nightclubs in Japan, to the Playboy mansion, to dinner with a Sinatra. Her aim is to delight and entertain readers of women's fiction everywhere. Visit Jamie Collins's website where you can join her reader list if you haven't already and get started with a **free** copy of the prequel to the series, *Sign On!*

Follow Jamie Collins on Twitter. Check out Jamie on Facebook and Instagram

Head over to Jamie's website for contact and other information about all of her books at: *www.jamiecollinsauthor. com*

ALSO FROM JAMIE COLLINS

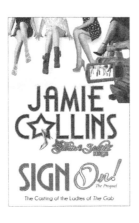

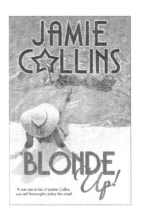

Made in the USA
Las Vegas, NV
22 April 2024

89011732R10184